Praise for
A DRINK BEFORE THE WAR

"Harsh and chilling...An absolutely terrific story."
—*The Boston Sunday Globe*

"[Dennis Lehane is one of] the very best young mystery writers." —*Esquire*

"Smart, hip, and moving. Dennis Lehane has the savvy and heads-up irony of Robert Crais combined with the lyricism and insight of a young James Lee Burke. Buy two copies. One to read and savor, one to collect."
—James W. Hall, author of
Under Cover of Daylight and *Hard Aground*

"Reading *A Drink Before the War* is like watching Robert B. Parker and John Updike duke it out phrase by phrase on some steamy night in Boston's Combat Zone. Christ, Lehane writes beautiful sentences! His gritty and disturbing first novel is the rare thing— a tale of frenzied and relentless violence told with grace and intelligence....With a single stroke, Dennis Lehane has established himself as a player to watch in the business of crime literature."
—John Dufresne, author of *Louisiana Power & Light*

A
DRINK
BEFORE
THE
WAR

DENNIS LEHANE

A DRINK BEFORE THE WAR

A Harvest Book • Harcourt, Inc.
ORLANDO AUSTIN NEW YORK
SAN DIEGO TORONTO LONDON

Requests for permission to make copies of any part of the work
should be mailed to the following address: Permissions Department,
Harcourt, Inc., 6277 Sea Harbor Drive, Orlando, Florida 32887-6777.

www.HarcourtBooks.com

Library of Congress Cataloging-in-Publication Data
Lehane, Dennis.
A drink before the war/Dennis Lehane.
p. cm.
ISBN 0-15-100093-x
ISBN 0-15-602902-2 (pbk.)
I.Title.
PS3562.E426D75 1994
813'.54—dc20 94-12274

The text was set in Minion
Designed by Scott Piehl
Printed in the United States of America
First Harvest Edition 2003
KJ

This novel is dedicated to my parents,
Michael *and* Ann Lehane,
and to Lawrence Corcoran, S.J.

Acknowledgments

During the writing of this novel, the following people provided advice, criticism, encouragement, and enthusiasm for which I'll always be more grateful than they could possibly know:

John Dempsey, Mal Ellenburg, Ruth Greenstein, Tupi Konstan, Gerard Lehane, Chris Mullen, Courtnay Pelech, Ann Riley, Ann Rittenberg, Claire Wachtel, and Sterling Watson.

Author's Note

Most of the action in the novel takes place in Boston, but certain liberties have been taken in portraying the city itself and its institutions. This is wholly intentional. The world presented here is a fictitious one, as are its characters and events. Any resemblance to actual incidents, or to actual persons living or dead, is entirely coincidental.

A
DRINK
BEFORE
THE
WAR

My earliest memories involve fire.

I watched Watts, Detroit, and Atlanta burn on the evening news, I saw oceans of mangroves and palm fronds smolder in napalm as Cronkite spoke of unilateral disarmament and a war that had lost its reason.

My father, a fireman, often woke me at night so I could watch the latest news footage of fires he'd fought. I could smell the smoke and soot on him, the clogging odors of gasoline and grease, and they were pleasant smells to me as I sat on his lap in the old armchair. He'd point himself out as he ran past the camera, a hazy shadow backlit by raging reds and shimmering yellows.

As I grew, so did the fires, it seemed, until recently L.A. burned, and the child in me wondered what would happen to the fallout, if the ashes and smoke would drift northeast, settle here in Boston, contaminate the air.

Last summer, it seemed to. Hate came in a maelstrom, and we called it several things—racism, pedophilia, justice, righteousness—but all those words were just ribbons and wrapping paper on a soiled gift that no one wanted to open.

People died last summer. Most of them innocent. Some more guilty than others.

And people killed last summer. None of them innocent. I

know. I was one of them. I stared down the slim barrel of a gun, looked into eyes rabid with fear and hatred, and saw my reflection. Pulled the trigger to make it go away.

I heard the echoes of my gunshots, smelled the cordite, and in the smoke, I still saw my reflection and knew I always would.

ONE

THE BAR AT THE RITZ-CARLTON LOOKS OUT ON THE PUBLIC Garden and requires a tie. I've looked out on the Public Garden from other vantage points before, without a tie, and never felt at a loss, but maybe the Ritz knows something I don't.

My usual taste in clothes runs to jeans and diver's shirts, but this was a job, so it was their time, not mine. Besides, I'd been a little behind on the laundry recently, and my jeans probably would've hopped the subway and met me there before I got a chance to put them on. I picked a dark blue, double-breasted Armani from my closet—one of several I received from a client in lieu of cash—found the appropriate shoes, tie, and shirt, and before you could say, "*GQ*," I was looking good enough to eat.

I appraised myself in the smoked-glass bar window as I crossed Arlington Street. There was a bounce to my step, a bright twinkle in my eyes, and nary a hair out of place. All was right with the world.

A young doorman, with cheeks so smooth he must have skipped puberty altogether, opened the heavy brass door and said, "Welcome to the Ritz-Carlton, sir." He meant it, too—his voice trembling with pride that I'd chosen his quaint little hotel. He held his arm out in front of him with a flourish, showing me the way in case I hadn't figured it out by myself, and before I could thank him, the door had closed behind me and he was hailing the best cab in the world for some other lucky soul.

My shoes clacked with military crispness on the marble floor, and the sharp creases of my pants reflected in the brass ashtrays. I always expect to see George Reeves as Clark Kent in the lobby of the Ritz, maybe Bogey and Raymond Massey sharing a smoke. The Ritz is one of those hotels that is resilient in its staid opulence: the carpeting is deep, rich oriental; the reception and concierge desks are made of a lustrous oak; the foyer is a bustling way station of lounging power brokers toting futures in soft leather attaché cases, Brahmin duchesses in fur coats with impatient airs and daily manicure appointments, and a legion of navy blue-uniformed manservants pulling sturdy brass luggage carts across the thick carpeting with the softest whoosh accompaniment as the wheels find their purchase. No matter what is going on outside, you could stand in this lobby, look at the people, and think there was still a blitz going on in London.

I sidestepped the bellman by the bar and opened the door myself. If he was amused he didn't show it. If he was alive, he didn't show it. I stood on the plush carpet as the heavy door closed softly behind me, and spotted them at a rear table, facing the Garden. Three men with enough political pull to filibuster us into the twenty-first century.

The youngest, Jim Vurnan, stood and smiled when he saw me. Jim's my local rep; that's his job. He crossed the carpet in three long strides, his Jack Kennedy smile extended just behind his hand. I took the hand. "Hi, Jim."

"Patrick," he said, as if he'd been standing on a tarmac all day waiting for my return from a POW camp. "Patrick," he repeated, "glad you could make it." He touched my shoulder, appraised me as if he hadn't seen me just yesterday. "You look good."

"You asking for a date?"

Jim got a hearty laugh out of that one, a lot heartier than it deserved. He led me to the table. "Patrick Kenzie, Senator Sterling Mulkern and Senator Brian Paulson." Jim said "Senator" like some men say "Hugh Hefner"—with uncomprehending awe.

Sterling Mulkern was a florid, beefy man, the kind who carried weight like a weapon, not a liability. He had a shock of stiff white hair you could land a DC-10 on and a handshake that stopped just short of inducing paralysis. He'd been state senate majority leader since the end of the Civil War or so, and he had no plans for retirement. He said, "Pat, lad, nice to see you again." He also had an affected Irish brogue that he'd somehow acquired growing up in South Boston.

Brian Paulson was rake thin, with smooth hair the color of tin and a wet, fleshy handshake. He waited until Mulkern sat back down before he did, and I wondered if he'd asked permission before he sweated all over my palm too. His greeting was a nod and a blink, befitting someone who'd stepped out of the shadows only momentarily. They said he had a mind though, honed by years as Mulkern's step-and-fetch-it.

Mulkern raised his eyebrows slightly and looked at Paulson. Paulson raised his and looked at Jim. Jim raised his at me. I waited a heartbeat and raised mine at everyone. "Am I in the club?"

Paulson looked confused. Jim smiled. Slightly. Mulkern said, "How should we start?"

I looked behind me at the bar. "With a drink?"

Mulkern let out a hearty laugh, and Jim and Paulson fell in line. Now I knew where Jim got it. At least they didn't all slap their knees in unison.

"Of course," Mulkern said. "Of course."

He raised his hand, and an impossibly sweet young woman, whose gold name tag identified her as Rachel, appeared by my elbow. "Senator! What can I get you?"

"You could get this young man a drink." It came out somewhere between a bark and a laugh.

Rachel's smile only brightened. She swiveled slightly and looked down at me. "Of course. What would you like, sir?"

"A beer. Do you have those here?"

She laughed. The pols laughed. I pinched myself and remained serious. God, this was a happy place.

"Yes, sir," she announced. "We have Heineken, Beck's, Molson, Sam Adams, St. Pauli Girl, Corona, Löwenbräu, Dos Equis—"

I cut in before dusk fell. "Molson would be fine."

"Patrick," Jim said, folding his hands and leaning toward me. Time to get serious. "We have a slight…"

"Conundrum," Mulkern said. "A slight conundrum on our hands. One we'd like cleared up discreetly and forgotten."

No one spoke for a few moments. I think we were all too impressed by the realization that we knew someone who used "conundrum" in casual conversation.

I shook off my awe first. "What is this conundrum, exactly?"

Mulkern leaned back in his chair, watching me. Rachel appeared and placed a frosted glass in front of me, poured two-thirds of the Molson into it. I could see Mulkern's black eyes holding steady with my own. Rachel said, "Enjoy," and left.

Mulkern's gaze never wavered. Probably took an explosion to make him blink. He said, "I knew your father well, lad. A finer man...well, I've never known one. A true hero."

"He always spoke fondly of you, Senator."

Mulkern nodded, that being a matter of course. "Shame, him going early like he did. Seemed fit as Jack LaLanne, but"—he tapped his chest with his knuckles—"one never knows with the old ticker."

My father had lost a six-month battle with lung cancer, but if Mulkern wanted to think it was a coronary, who'd complain?

"And now, here's his boy," Mulkern said. "Almost all grown."

"Almost," I said. "Last month, I even shaved."

Jim looked like he'd swallowed a frog. Paulson squinted.

Mulkern beamed. "All right, lad. All right. You have a point." He sighed. "I'll tell you, Pat, you get to be my age, and everything but yesterday seems young."

I nodded sagely, completely clueless.

Mulkern stirred his drink, removed the stirrer, and placed it gently on a cocktail napkin. "We understand that when it comes to finding people, no one's better." He spread his hand, palm up, in my direction.

I nodded.

"Ah. No false modesty?"

I shrugged. "It's my job. Might as well be good at it." I sipped the Molson, the bittersweet tang spreading across my tongue. Not for the first time, I wished I still smoked.

"Well, lad, our problem is this: we have a rather important bill coming to floor next week. Our ammunition is heavy, but certain methods and services we employed to garner that ammunition could be...misconstrued."

"As?"

Mulkern nodded and smiled as if I'd said, "Atta boy."
"Misconstrued," he repeated.

I decided to play along. "And there is documentation—
records of these methods and services?"

"He's quick," he said to Jim and Paulson. "Yes sir.
Quick." He looked at me. "Documentation," he said, "exactly, Pat."

I wondered if I should tell him how much I hated being
called Pat. Maybe I should start calling him Sterl, see if he
minded. I sipped my beer. "Senator, I find people, not
things."

"If I may interject," Jim interjected, "the documents are
with a person who has recently turned up missing. A—"

"—Formerly trusted employee at the State House,"
Mulkern said. Mulkern had the "iron hand in the velvet
glove" routine down to an art. There was nothing in his
manner, his enunciation, his bearing to suggest reproach,
but Jim looked like he'd been caught kicking the cat. He
took a long pull on his scotch, rattling the ice cubes against
the rim. I doubted that he'd interject again.

Mulkern looked at Paulson, and Paulson reached into
his attaché case. He pulled a thin sheaf of papers out and
handed them to me.

The top page was a photograph, a rather grainy one. A
blowup of a Statehouse personnel ID. It was of a black
woman, middle-aged, worn eyes, a tired expression on her
face. Her lips were parted slightly, and skewed, as if she were
about to voice her impatience with the photographer.
I flipped the page and saw a Xerox of her driver's license
centered on a white page. Her name was Jenna Angeline.
She was forty-one, but looked fifty. She had a class three
Massachusetts driver's license, unrestricted. Her eyes were
brown, her height—five feet six inches. Her address was 412

Kenneth Street in Dorchester. Her social security number was 042-51-6543.

I looked at the three pols and found my eyes pulled toward the middle, into Mulkern's black stare. "And?" I said.

"Jenna was the cleaning woman for my office. Brian's too." He shrugged. "As jigs go, I had no complaints."

Mulkern was the kind of guy who said, "jigs," when he wasn't sure enough of the company to say, "niggers."

"Until...," I said.

"Until she disappeared nine days ago."

"Unannounced vacation?"

Mulkern looked at me as if I'd just suggested college basketball wasn't fixed. "When she took this 'vacation,' Pat, she also took those documents with her."

"Some light reading for the beach?" I suggested.

Paulson slapped the table in front of me. Hard. Paulson. "This is no joke, Kenzie. Understand?"

I looked at his hand, sleepy eyed.

Mulkern said, "Brian."

Paulson removed the hand to check the whip marks on his back.

I stared at him, still sleepy eyed—dead eyes, Angie calls them—and spoke to Mulkern. "How do you know she took the...documents?"

Paulson dropped his eyes from mine, considered his martini. It was still untouched, and he didn't take a drink. Probably waiting for permission.

Mulkern said, "We checked. Believe me. No one else is a logical suspect."

"Why is she?"

"What?"

"A logical suspect?"

Mulkern smiled. A thin one. "Because she disappeared

the same day the documents did. Who knows with these people?"

"Mmm," I said.

"Will you find her for us, Pat?"

I looked out the window. Perky the Doorman was hustling someone into a cab. In the Garden, a middle-aged couple with matching *Cheers* T-shirts snapped picture after picture of the George Washington statue. Sure to wow them back in Boise. A wino on the sidewalk supported himself with one hand on a bottle; the other he held out, steady as a rock, waiting for change. Beautiful women walked by. In droves.

"I'm expensive," I said.

"I know that," Mulkern said. "So why do you still live in the old neighborhood?" He said it like he wanted me to believe his heart still resided there too, as if it meant any more to him now than an alternative route when the expressway got backed up.

I tried to think of a response. Something to do with roots, and knowing where you belong. In the end, I told the truth: "My apartment's rent-controlled."

He seemed to like that.

TWO

THE OLD NEIGHBORHOOD IS THE EDWARD EVERETT SQUARE section of Dorchester. It's a little less than five miles from the center of Boston proper, which means, on a good day, it takes only half an hour to reach by car.

My office is the bell tower of St. Bartholomew's Church. I've never found out what happened to the bell that used to be there, and the nuns who teach at the parochial school next door won't tell me. The older ones plain don't answer me, and the younger ones seem to find my curiosity amusing. Sister Helen told me once it had been "miracled away." Her words. Sister Joyce, who grew up with me, always says it was "misplaced," and gives me the sort of wicked smile that nuns aren't supposed to be capable of giving. I'm a detective, but nuns could stonewall Sam Spade into an asylum.

The day after I got my investigator's license, the church pastor, Father Drummond, asked me if I'd mind providing some security for the place. Some unfaithfuls were breaking in to steal chalices and candlesticks again, and in Pastor Drummond's words: "This shit better stop." He offered me three meals a day in the rectory, my very first case, and the thanks of God if I set up in the belfry and waited for the next break-in. I told him I didn't come that cheap. I demanded use of the belfry until I found office space of my own. For a priest, he gave in pretty easy. When I saw the state of the room—unused for nine years—I knew why.

Angie and I managed to fit two desks in there. Two chairs too. When we realized there was no room for a file cabinet, I hauled all the old files back to my place. We splurged on a personal computer, put as much as we could on diskettes, and stowed a few current files in our desks. Impresses the clients almost enough to make them ignore the room. Almost.

Angie was sitting behind her desk when I reached the top step. She was busy investigating the latest Ann Landers column, so I stepped in quietly. She didn't notice me at first—Ann must have been dealing with a real headcase—so I took the opportunity to watch her in a rare moment of repose.

She had her feet propped up on the desk, a pair of black suede Peter Pan boots covering them, the cuffs of her charcoal jeans tucked into the boots. I followed her long legs up to a loose white cotton T-shirt. The rest of her was hidden behind the newspaper except for a partial view of rich, thick hair, the color of rainswept tar, that fell to her olive arms. Behind that newsprint was a slim neck that trembled when she pretended not to be laughing at one of my jokes, an unyielding jaw with a near-microscopic brown beauty mark on the left side, an aristocratic nose that didn't fit her personality at all, and eyes the color of melting caramel. Eyes you'd dive into without a look back.

I didn't get a chance to see them, though. She put the paper down and looked at me through a pair of black Wayfarers. I doubted she'd be taking them off any time soon.

"Hey, Skid," she said, reaching for a cigarette from the pack on her desk.

Angie is the only person who calls me "Skid." Probably because she's the only person who was in my father's car with me the night I wrapped it around a light pole in Lower Mills thirteen years ago.

"Hey, gorgeous," I said and slid into my chair. I don't think I'm the only one who calls her gorgeous, but it's force of habit. Or statement of fact. Take your pick. I nodded at the sunglasses. "Fun time last night?"

She shrugged and looked out the window. "Phil was drinking."

Phil is Angie's husband. Phil is an asshole.

I said as much.

"Yeah, well..." She lifted a corner of the curtain, flapped it back and forth in her hand. "What're you gonna do, right?"

"What I did before," I said. "Be only too happy to."

She bent her head so the sunglasses slipped down to the slight bump at the bridge of her nose, revealing a dark discoloration that ran from the corner of her left eye to her temple. "And after you're finished," she said, "he'll come home again, make this look like a love tap." She pushed the sunglasses back up over her eyes. "Tell me I'm wrong." Her voice was bright, but hard like winter sunlight. I hate that voice.

"Have it your way," I said.

"Will do."

Angie and Phil and I grew up together. Angie and I, best friends. Angie and Phil, best lovers. It goes that way sometimes. Not often in my experience, thank God, but sometimes. A few years ago, Angie came to the office with the sunglasses and two eight balls where her eyes should have been. She also had a nice collection of bruises on her arms and neck and an inch-tall bump on the back of her head. My face must have betrayed my intentions, because

the first words out of her mouth were, "Patrick, be sensible."
Not like it was the first time, and it wasn't. It was the worst
time though, so when I found Phil in Jimmy's Pub in Up-
hams Corner, we had a few sensible drinks, played a sensible
game of pool or two, and shortly after I'd broached the sub-
ject and he responded with a "Whyn't you fucking mind
your own business, Patrick?" I beat him to within an inch of
his life with a sensible pool stick.

I felt pretty pleased with myself for a few days there. It's
possible, though I don't remember, that I engaged in a few
fantasies of Angie and myself in some state of domestic
bliss. Then Phil got out of the hospital and Angie didn't
come to work for a week. When she did, she moved very
precisely and gasped every time she sat down or stood up.
He'd left the face alone, but her body was black.

She didn't talk to me for two weeks. A long time, two
weeks.

I looked at her now as she stared out the window. Not
for the first time, I wondered why a woman like this—a
woman who took shit from absolutely nobody, a woman
who'd pumped two rounds into a hard case named Bobby
Royce when he resisted our kind efforts to return him to his
bail bondsman—allowed her husband to treat her like an
Everlast bag. Bobby Royce never got up, and I'd often wondered when Phil's time would come. But so far it hadn't.

And I could hear the answer to my question in the soft,
tired voice she adopted when she talked about him. She
loved him, plain and simple. Some part of him that I
certainly can't see anymore must still show itself to her in
their private moments, some goodness he possesses that
shines like the grail in her eyes. That has to be it, because
nothing else about their relationship makes any sense to me
or anyone else who knows her.

She opened the window and flicked her cigarette out. City girl to the core. I waited for a summer schooler to scream or a nun to come hauling ass up the staircase, the wrath of God in her eyes, a burning cigarette butt in her hand. Neither happened. Angie turned from the open window, and the cool summer breeze creased the room with the smell of exhaust fumes and freedom and the lilac petals which littered the schoolyard.

"So," she said, leaning back in the chair, "we employed again?"

"We're employed again."

"Ya-hoo," she said. "Nice suit, by the way."

"Makes you want to jump my bones on the spot, doesn't it?"

She shook her head slowly. "Uh, no."

"Don't know where I've been. That it?"

She shook her head again. "I know exactly where you've been, Skid, which is most of the problem."

"Bitch," I said.

"Slut." She stuck her tongue out at me. "What's the case?"

I pulled the information about Jenna Angeline from my inside breast pocket and tossed it on her desk. "Simple find-and-a-phone-call."

She perused the pages. "Why's anyone care if a middle-aged cleaning lady disappears?"

"Seems some documents disappeared with her. State-house documents."

"Pertaining to?"

I shrugged. "You know these politicians. Everything is as secret as Los Alamos until it hits the floor."

"How do they know she took them?"

"Look at the picture."

"Ah," she said, nodding, "she's black."

"Evidence enough to most people."

"Even the resident senate liberal?"

"The resident senate liberal is just another racist from Southie when he ain't residing in the House."

I told her about the meeting, about Mulkern and his lapdog, Paulson, about the Stepford wife employees at the Ritz.

"And Representative James Vurnan—what was he like in the company of such Masters of State?"

"You ever see that cartoon with the big dog and the little dog, where the little dog keeps panting away, jumping up and down, asking the big dog, 'Where we going, Butch? Where we going, Butch?'"

"Yes."

"Like that," I said.

She chewed on a pencil, then began tapping it against her front teeth. "So, you gave me the fly-on-the-wall account. What really happened?"

"That's about it."

"You trust them?"

"Hell no."

"So there's more to this than meets the eye, Detective?"

I shrugged. "They're elected officials. The day they tell the whole truth is the day hookers put out for free."

She smiled. "As always, your analogies are splendid. You're just a product of good breeding, you are." Her smile widened as she watched me, the pencil tapping against her left front tooth, the slightly chipped one. "So, what's the rest of the story?"

I loosened my tie enough to pull it over my head. "You got me."

"Some detective," she said.

THREE

JENNA ANGELINE, LIKE ME, WAS BORN AND RAISED IN Dorchester. The casual visitor to the city might think this would serve as a nice common denominator between Jenna and myself, a bond—however minimal—forged by location: two people who started out of their separate chutes at identical hash marks. But the casual visitor would be wrong. Jenna Angeline's Dorchester and my Dorchester have about as much in common as Atlanta, Georgia, and Russian Georgia.

The Dorchester I grew up in was working class traditional, the neighborhoods, more often than not, delineated by the Catholic churches they surrounded. The men were foremen, crew chiefs, probation officers, telephone repairmen, or, like my father, firemen. The women were housewives who sometimes had part-time jobs themselves, sometimes even had education degrees from state colleges. We were all Irish, Polish, or close enough to pass. We were all white. And when the federal desegregation of public schools began in 1974, most of the men worked overtime and most of the women went to full time and most of the kids went to private Catholic high schools.

This Dorchester has changed, of course. Divorce—

practically unheard of in my parents' generation—is com-
monplace in mine, and I know a lot fewer of my neighbors
than I used to. But we still have access to the union jobs, we
usually know a state rep who can get us into civil service. To
some extent, we're connected.

Jenna Angeline's Dorchester is poor. The neighborhoods, more often than not, are delineated by the public
parks and community centers they surround. The men are
dockworkers and hospital orderlies, in some cases postal
clerks, a few firemen. The women are the orderlies, the
cashiers, the cleaning women, the department store clerks.
They are nurses, too, and cops, and civil service clerks, but
chances are, if they've reached that kind of pinnacle, they
don't live in Dorchester anymore. They've moved to Dedham or Framingham or Brockton.

In my Dorchester, you stay because of community and
tradition, because you've built a comfortable, if somewhat
poor, existence where little ever changes. A hamlet.

In Jenna Angeline's Dorchester, you stay because you
don't have any choice.

Nowhere is it harder to try and explain the differences
between these two Dorchesters—White Dorchester and
Black Dorchester—than in White Dorchester. This is particularly true in my neighborhood, because we're one of the
boundary neighborhoods. The moment you pass through
Edward Everett Square heading south, east, or west, you're
in Black Dorchester. So, people around here have a lot of
trouble accepting the differences as anything other than
black and white. A guy I grew up with once put it about as
plainly as you'll ever hear it: "Hey, Patrick," he said, "enough
of this bullshit. I grew up in Dorchester. I grew up poor.
No one ever gave me nothing. My old man left when I was a
kid just like a lotta the niggers in the 'Bury. No one *begged*

me to learn how to read or get a job or be something. Nobody gave me affirmative action to help me out either, that's
for damn sure. And I didn't pick up an Uzi, join a gang, and
start doing drivebys. So spare me this shit. They got no excuse."

People from White Dorchester always call Black Dorchester "the 'Bury." Short for Roxbury, the section of Boston
that begins where Black Dorchester ends, where they load
dead young black kids into meat wagons on the average of
eight a weekend sometimes. Black Dorchester gives up its
young on a pretty regular basis too, and those in White
Dorchester refuse to call it anything but the 'Bury. Somebody just forgot to change it on the maps.

There's truth to what my friend said, however narrow it
is, and the truth scares me. When I drive through my neighborhood, I see poor, but I don't see poverty.

Driving into Jenna's neighborhood, I saw a lot of
poverty. I saw a big, ugly scar of a neighborhood with several boarded-up storefronts. I saw one that hadn't been
boarded up yet, but was just as closed. The front window
was blown out and bullet holes pocked the walls in jagged
patterns of lethal acne. The inside was scorched and gutted
and the fiberglass sign overhead that once said delicatessen
in Vietnamese was shattered. The deli business wasn't what
it once was in this neighborhood, but the crack business
seemed to be doing just fine.

I turned off Blue Hill Avenue up a rutted hill that
looked like it hadn't been paved since the Kennedy adminis-
tration. The sun was setting, blood red, behind an overgrown yard of rotting weeds at the top of the hill. A group of
laconic black kids crossed the street in front of me, taking
their time, staring into my car. There were four of them, and
one had a broomstick in his hand. He turned his head to

look at me and whacked the stick off the street with a harsh snap. One of his buddies, bouncing a tennis ball in front of him, laughed and pointed an admonishing finger at my windshield. They passed over the sidewalk and cut through a rotted brown pathway between two three-deckers. I continued on up the hill, and something primal reassured me that my gun was hanging heavily from the holster on my left shoulder.

My gun is, as Angie would say, "not a fuck-around thing." It's a .44 magnum automatic—an "automag," they call it gleefully in *Soldier of Fortune* and like publications—and I didn't purchase it out of penis envy or Eastwood envy or because I wanted to own the goddamned biggest gun on the block. I bought it for one simple reason: I'm a lousy shot. I need to know that if I ever have to use it, I hit what I'm aiming at and I hit it hard enough to knock it down and keep it there. Shoot some people in the arm with a .32 and they just get angry. Shoot them in the same place with the automag and they ask for a priest.

I've fired it twice. Once when a brain-dead sociopath who was only slightly bigger than Rhode Island wanted me to prove how tough I was. He'd jumped out of his car and was six feet away from me and coming on fast, when I fired a round that went straight through his engine block. He stared at his Cordoba like I'd just shot his dog and almost wept. But the steam pouring out of the torn metal on his hood convinced him that there were things out there that were tougher than the two of us.

The other time was Bobby Royce. He had his hands on Angie's neck at the time, and I blew a chunk out of his leg. Tell you something about Bobby Royce: he got back up. He raised his gun toward me and still had it pointed that way even after Angie's two rounds had picked him up and drilled him against a hydrant and the light had left his eyes. Bobby Royce, going into rigor with his gun pointed at me, flat dead eyes not much different than they'd been when he was breathing.

I was wearing a pearl gray, unstructured linen jacket when I stepped out of my car in front of Jenna's last-known address. It was oversized and concealed the gun entirely. The group of teenagers sitting on the cars in front of Jenna's house was definitely fooled. As I crossed the street toward them, one of them said, "Hey, Five-O, where's your backup?"

The girl beside him giggled. "Under his coat, Jerome."

There were nine of them. Half of them sat on the trunk of a faded blue Chevy Malibu with a bright yellow Denver boot strapped to the front tire because the owner hadn't paid his parking tickets. The rest of them sat on the hood of the car behind the Malibu, a puke green Granada. Two kids slipped off the cars and walked quickly up the street, heads down, hands rubbing their foreheads.

I stopped by the cars. "Jenna around?"

Jerome laughed. He was lean and hard, but held himself loosely in his purple tank top, white shorts, and black Air Jordans. He said, " 'Jenna around?' " in a high-pitched falsetto. "Like he and Jenna old friends." The rest of them laughed. "No, man, Jenna's gone for the day." He looked at me and rubbed his chin. "I'm, like, her service, though. Why don't you leave your message with me?"

The other kids cracked up at "service."

I liked it too, but I was supposed to act like I was in control. I said, "Like have my agent call her agent?"

Jerome looked at me, deadpan. "Yeah, man, like that. Whatever you say."

More laughter. Lots more.

That's me, Patrick Kenzie, got a real way with youth. I walked between the two cars, hard to do when no one moves to the side for you, but I managed. "Thanks for your help, Jerome."

"Hey, man, don't mention it. Just part of the wonderfulness of me."

I started up the front steps of Jenna's three-decker. "I'll put in a good word for you with Jenna when I see her."

"Damn white of you too," Jerome said as I opened the door into the hallway.

Jenna lived on the third floor. I trudged up the steps, smelling the familiar smells of all inner-city three-deckers—chipped, sun-baked wood, old paint, kitty litter, wood and linoleum that had soaked up decades of melting snow and dirt from wet boots, spilled beers and sodas, the ashes of a thousand discarded cigarettes. I was careful not to touch the railing; it looked like it could easily crumble away from the banisters.

I turned into the top hallway and reached Jenna's door, or what was left of it. Something had imploded the wood by the knob, and the knob itself lay in a pile of splinters on the floor. A quick glance at the corridor in front of me revealed a thin stretch of dark green linoleum littered with broken chair legs, a shattered drawer, some shredded clothing, pillow stuffing, pieces of a small transistor radio.

I pulled my gun, inched inside, checking each doorway with my eyes and gun in tandem. The house had that certain stillness that only comes when nothing living remains inside, but I'd been fooled by that stillness before, and I have a rewired jaw to prove it.

It took me ten minutes of laborious, stiff-necked searching to decide the place actually was empty. By this time, my skin was covered in sweat, my back ached, and the muscles in my hands and arms felt about as pliable as Sheetrock.

I let the gun hang loosely from my hand as I went more casually through the apartment, rechecking the rooms, looking at things in more detail. Nothing jumped from the bedroom and danced in front of me with a neon sign overhead that said CLUE!!! Not in the bathroom either. Kitchen and living room were equally uncooperative. All I knew was that someone had been looking for something and delicacy had not been a primary concern. Nothing that was breakable was unbroken, nothing slitable unslit.

I stepped into the corridor and heard a sound to my right. I spun and stared down the fat barrel at Jerome. He crouched, hands in front of his face. "Ho! Ho! Ho, ho, ho, ho! Don't fucking shoot!"

"Jesus," I said, a hard wave of exhausted relief curling over my razor-blade adrenaline.

"God damn!" Jerome straightened up, brushed at his tank top for some reason, smoothed the cuffs of his shorts. "The fuck you carrying that thing for? I ain't seen no elephants 'round here since I don't know when."

I shrugged. "What're you doing up here?"

"Hey, I *live* in this neighborhood, white bread. Seems to me, you the one needs the excuse. And put that fucking thing *away*."

I slid the gun back into my holster. "What happened here, Jerome?"

"You got me," Jerome said, walking inside, looking at the mess like he'd seen it a hundred times before. "Old Jenna ain't been around in over a week. This was done over the weekend." He guessed my next question. "And no, man, no one saw anything."

"I'm not surprised," I said.

"Oh, like people in your neighborhood, they just up and volunteer information to the police all the time too, I bet."

I smiled. "Not on their best days."

"Uh-huh." He looked at the mess again. "This got to be about Roland. Got to be."

"Who's Roland?"

He chuckled at that one, looked at me. "Yeah, right."

"No, I'm serious. Who's Roland?"

He turned and walked out. "Go home, white bread."

I followed him down the stairs. "Who's Roland, Jerome?"

He shook his head the whole way down to the bottom floor. When he reached the porch, where his friends had re-assembled on the steps, he jerked his thumb behind him at me as I came through the doorway. "He asking who Roland is."

His friends laughed. I had to be the funniest white man they'd seen in days.

Most of them stood up as I came out on the porch. The girl said, "You want to know who Roland is?"

I walked halfway down the steps. "I want to know who Roland is."

One of the bigger guys stabbed my shoulder with his index finger. "Roland your worst fucking nightmare."

The girl said, "Worse than your wife."

They all laughed and I walked down the steps and cut between the blue Malibu and the green Granada.

"Stay away from Roland," Jerome said. "What kill elephants, don't so much as faze Roland. Cause he ain't human."

I stopped, turned back, my hand resting on the Malibu. "Then what is he?"

Jerome shrugged, folded his arms across his chest. "He just plain bad. Bad as it gets."

FOUR

SHORTLY AFTER I GOT BACK TO THE OFFICE, WE ORDERED
out for some Chinese and went over the day.

Angie had done the paper trail while I followed the
physical one. I told her what my trail had brought us, added
the names "Jerome" and "Roland" to the first page of our
file, entered it into the computer. I also wrote "Break-in" and
"Motive?" and underlined the latter.

The Chinese food arrived and we went to work clogging
our arteries and forcing our hearts to work double time.
Angie told me the results of the paper trail between mouth-
fuls of pork fried rice and chow mein. The day after Jenna
disappeared, Jim Vurnan had gone to the restaurants and
shops around Beacon Street and the State House to see if
she'd been in recently. He didn't find her, but in a deli on
Somerset he got a copy of one of her credit-card receipts
from the owner. Jenna had paid for a ham on rye and a Coke
with a Visa. Angie had taken the receipt and using the tried-
and-true "Hi, I'm (Insert target's name) and I seem to have
misplaced my credit card" method, she found that Jenna
carried the Visa only, had a spotty credit history (one run-in
with a collection agency back in '81), and had last used her
card on June 19, the first day she didn't show up to work, at

the Bank of Boston on the corner of Clarendon and St. James for a cash advance of two hundred dollars. Angie had then called the Bank of Boston claiming to be a representative of American Express. Mrs. Angeline had applied for a credit card and would they mind verifying her account?

What account?

She got the same response at every bank she tried. Jenna Angeline had no bank account. Which is fine, as far as I'm concerned, but it makes a person harder to find.

I started to ask Angie if she'd missed any banks, but she held up her hand, managed a "Not finished yet," around some spare rib. She wiped her mouth with a napkin and swallowed. Then she downed a gulp of beer and said, "'Member Billy Hawkins?"

"Of course." Billy would be doing a dime in Walpole Penitentiary if we hadn't found his alibi.

"Well, Billy works for Western Union now, out of one of those Check Cashing Express places." She sat back, pleased.

"Well?"

"Well what?" She was enjoying herself.

I picked up a greasy spare rib and cocked my arm.

She held up her hands. "OK, OK. Billy's going to run a check for us, find out if she's used any of their offices. She can't have survived on two hundred dollars since the nineteenth. Not in this city anyway."

"And when's Billy going to get back to us?"

"He couldn't do anything today. He said his boss would be suspicious if he hung around for too long after the end of his shift, and his shift ended five minutes after I called. He'll have to do it tomorrow. Said he'll call us by noon."

I nodded. Behind Angie the dark sky was streaked with four fingers of scarlet and the slight breeze blew the thinnest wisps of her hair from behind her ear onto her cheekbone.

Van Morrison was singing about "crazy love" on the boom box behind me, and we sat in the cramped office, staring at each other in the afterglow of the heavy Chinese food and the humid day and the satisfaction of knowing where our next paycheck was coming from. She smiled, a slightly embarrassed one, but didn't look away, and began tapping that pencil lightly against the chipped tooth again.

I let the stillness settle between us for a good five minutes before I said, "Come home with me."

She shook her head, still smiling, and swiveled the chair slightly.

"Come on. We'll watch a little TV, chat about old times—"

"There's a bed in this story somewhere. I know it."

"Only as a place to sleep. We'll lie down and...talk."

She laughed. "Uh-huh. And what about all those lovely young things who tend to camp out on your doorstep and tie up your phone?"

"Who?" I asked innocently.

"Who," she said. "Donna, Beth, Kelly, that *chick with the ass*, Lauren—"

"That *chick with the ass*, excuse me?"

"You know the one. The Italian girl. The one who goes"—her voice rose about two octaves—"'Oooooh, Patrick, can we take a bubble bath now? Hee!' That one."

"Gina."

She nodded. "Gi-na. That's the one."

"I'll give them all up for one night with—"

"I know that, Patrick. I hope you don't think that's something to be proud of."

"Well, gee, Mom..."

She smiled. "Patrick, the major reason you think you're in love with me is because you've never seen me naked—"

"In—"

"In thirteen years," she said hurriedly, "and we both agreed that was forgotten. Besides, thirteen years is a lifetime to you where a woman is concerned."

"You say it like it's a bad thing."

She rolled her eyes at me. "So," she said, "what's on tomorrow's agenda?"

I shrugged, drank some beer from the can. Summer was definitely here; it tasted like tea. Van had finished singing about "crazy love," and was heading "into the mystic." I said, "I guess we wait for Billy to call, call him at noon if he doesn't."

"Sounds almost like a plan." She drained her beer, made a face at the can. "Any more cold ones?" I reached into my wastebasket, which was doubling as a cooler, tossed a can to her. She cracked it, took a sip. "What do we do when we find Mrs. Angeline?"

"Haven't a clue. Play it by ear."

"You're such a professional at this."

I nodded. "That's why they let me carry a gun."

She saw him before I did. His shadow fell across the floor, crept up the right side of her face. Phil. The Asshole.

I hadn't seen him since I hospitalized him three years ago. He looked better than he had then—lying on the floor holding his ribs, coughing blood onto a sawdust floor—but he still looked like an asshole. He had a hell of a scar beside his left eye, compliments of that sensible pool stick. I'm not sure, but I think I beamed when I noticed.

He wouldn't look at me. He looked at her. "I've been downstairs honking for the last ten minutes, hon'. You didn't hear me?"

"It was pretty noisy outside, and…" She pointed at the boom box, but Phil chose not to look at it because that would have meant looking at me.

He said, "Ready to go?"

She nodded and stood. She drained the beer in one long swallow. That didn't seem to make Phil's day. Probably made it worse when she flipped the can airborne in my direction and I tapped it into the wastebasket.

"Two points," she said, coming around the desk. "See you tomorrow, Skid."

"See you," I said, as she took Phil's hand and started walking out the door.

Just before they reached the door, Phil turned, her hand in his, and looked at me. He smiled.

I blew him a kiss.

I heard them work their way down the narrow, winding steps. Van had stopped singing and the quiet that replaced him felt thick and decayed. I sat in Angie's chair, saw them below me. Phil was getting in the car, Angie standing at the passenger door, holding the handle. Her head was down and I got the feeling she was making a conscious effort not to look back up at the window. Phil opened her door from the inside, and a moment after she got in, they pulled out into traffic.

I looked at my boom box, at the cassettes scattered around it. I considered taking Van out and putting in some Dire Straits. Or maybe some Stones. No. Jane's Addiction perhaps. Springsteen? Something really different, then. Ladysmith-Black-Mambazo or The Chieftains. I considered them all. I considered what would best fit my mood. I considered picking up the boom box and hurling it across the room at the exact spot where Phil had turned, Angie's hand in his, and smiled.

But I didn't. It'd pass.

Everything did. Sooner or later.

FIVE

I LEFT THE CHURCH A FEW MINUTES LATER. NOTHING LEFT to keep me. I walked through the empty schoolyard, kicked a can in front of me as I went. I passed through the opening in the short wrought-iron fence that lined the yard and crossed the avenue to my apartment. I live directly across from the church in a blue-and-white three-decker that somehow missed the scourge of aluminum siding that overtook all its neighbors. My landlord is an old Hungarian farmer whose last name I couldn't pronounce with a year of practice. He spends all day fussing about in the yard, and he's said maybe a total of two hundred and fifty words to me in the five years I've lived there. The words are usually the same and there are three of them: "Where's my rent?" He's a mean old bastard, but he's unfriendly.

I let myself into my second-floor apartment and tossed the bills that awaited me on a pile on the coffee table with their relatives. There were no women camped by my door, inside or out, but there were seven messages on my answering machine.

Three were from Gina of the Bubble Bath. Each of her messages was backed by the grunts and moans emanating from the aerobics studio where she worked. Nothing like a little summer sweat to get the wheels of passion turning.

One was from my sister, Erin, long distance from Seattle. "Staying out of trouble, kid?" My sister. I'll have my teeth in a glass and a face like a prune, and she'll still be calling me "kid." Another was from Bubba Rogowski, wondering if I wanted to have a beer, shoot some pool. Bubba sounded drunk, which meant someone would bleed tonight. I nixed the invitation as a matter of course. Someone, I think it was Lauren, called to make nasty promises concerning a pair of rusty scissors and my genitalia. I was trying to recall our last date to decide if my behavior warranted such extreme measures, when Mulkern's voice drifted into the room and I forgot all about Lauren.

"Pat, lad, it's Sterling Mulkern. I assume you're out earning your money, which is grand, but I wonder if you had the time to read today's *Trib*? That dear boy, Colgan, was at my throat again. Ah, the boy would have accused your own father of setting fires just so he could put them out. A real Peck's bad boy, that Richie Colgan. I wonder, Pat, if you might have a word with him, ask him to lighten up a bit on an old man for a time? Just a thought. We've a table for lunch at the Copley, Saturday at one. Don't forget." The recording ended with a dial tone, then the cassette began rewinding.

I stared at the small machine. He wondered if I might have a word with Richie Colgan. Just a thought. Toss in the memory of my father for good measure. The hero fireman. The beloved city councilor. My father.

Everyone knows Richie Colgan and I are friends. It's half the reason people are a little more suspicious of me than used to be the case. We met when we were both majoring in Space Invaders with a Pub Etiquette minor at the Happy Harbor Campus of UMass/Boston. Now Richie's the *Trib*'s top columnist, a vicious bastard if he thinks you're one of the three great evils—an elitist, a bigot, or a hypocrite. Since Sterling Mulkern is an embodiment of all three, Richie orders him for lunch once or twice a week.

Everyone loved Richie Colgan—until they ran his picture over his byline. A good Irish name. A good Irish boy. Going after the corrupt, fat party bosses in city hall and the Statehouse. Then they ran his picture and everyone saw that his skin was blacker than Kurtz's heart, and suddenly he was a "troublemaker." But he sells papers, and his favorite target has always been Sterling Mulkern. Among the monikers he's given the Senator there's "Santa's Evil Twin," "Siphoner Sterling," "Three-Lunch Mulkern," and "Hypo the Hippo." Boston's not a town for the sensitive pol.

And now, Mulkern wanted me to "have a word with him." In for a penny, in for a pound. Next time I saw Mulkern, I decided, I'd give him the "Your money rents, it doesn't buy" speech and tell him to leave my hero father out of it while I was at it.

My father, Edgar Kenzie, had his fifteen minutes of local fame almost twenty years ago. He'd made the front page of both dailies; the photo even hit the wires and ended up on the back pages of the *New York Times* and the *Washington Post*. The photographer damn near won a Pulitzer.

It was a hell of a photograph. My father, swathed in the black and yellow of the BFD, an oxygen tank strapped to his back, climbing *up* a ten story building on a rope of sheets. A woman had come down those sheets a few minutes earlier. Well, halfway down. She'd lost her grip and died on impact. The building was an old nineteenth-century factory that someone had converted into tenements, made of red brick and cheap wood that could have been tissue and gasoline as far as the fire was concerned.

The woman had left her kids inside, telling them, in a moment of panic, to follow her down, instead of the other way around. The kids saw what happened to her and stopped moving, just stood in the black window and looked at their broken doll mother as smoke poured out of the room behind them. The window faced a parking lot and firemen were waiting for a tow truck to get the cars out so they could back a ladder in. My father grabbed an oxygen tank without a word, walked up to the sheets and started climbing. A window on the fifth floor blew out into his chest, and there's another photo, slightly out of focus, of him flapping in the air as shards of glass explode off his heavy black coat. He reached the tenth floor eventually and grabbed the kids—a four-year-old boy, a six-year-old girl— and went back down again. No big deal, he'd say with a shrug.

When he retired five years later, people still remembered him, and I don't think he ever paid for another drink in his life. He ran for city council on Sterling Mulkern's suggestion and lived a good life of graft and large homes until cancer settled into his lungs like smoke in a closet and ate him and the money away.

At home, the Hero was a different story. He made sure his dinner was waiting with a slap. Made sure the homework got done with a slap. Made sure everything went like clockwork with a slap. And if that didn't work, a belt, or a punch or two, or once, an old washboard. Whatever it took to keep Edgar Kenzie's world in order.

I never knew, probably never will, if it was the job that did this to him—if he was just reacting in the only way he knew how to all those blackened bodies he'd found, scorched into final fetal positions in hot closets or under smoking beds—or if he was simply born mean. My sister claims she doesn't remember what he was like before I came along, but she's also claimed, on occasion, that there were never days when he beat us so badly we had to miss school again. My mother followed the Hero to the grave by six months, so I never got to ask her either. But I doubt she would have told me. Irish parents have never been known for speaking ill of their spouses to their children.

I sat back on the couch in my apartment, thinking about the Hero once again, telling myself this was the last time. That ghost was gone. But I was lying and I knew it. The Hero woke me up at night. The Hero hid in waiting—in shadows, in alleys, in the antiseptic hallways of my dreams, in the chamber of my gun. Just as in life, he'd do whatever he damn well pleased.

I stood and walked past the window to the phone. Outside, something sudden moved in the schoolyard across the street. The local punks had shown up to lurk in the shadows, sit in the deep stone window seats and smoke a little reefer, drink a few beers. Why not. When I was a local punk, I'd done the same thing. Me, Phil, Bubba, Angie, Waldo, Hale, everybody.

I dialed Richie's direct line at the *Trib*, hoping to catch him working late as usual. His voice came across the line midway through the first ring. "City desk. Hold." A Muzak version of *The Magnificent Seven* theme syruped its way over the line.

Then I got one of those what's-wrong-with-this-picture answers without ever consciously having asked myself the question. There was no music coming from the schoolyard. No matter how much it announces their position, young punks don't go anywhere without their boom boxes. It's bad form.

I looked past the slit in the curtains down into the

schoolyard. No more sudden movement. No movement at all. No glowing cigarette butts or clinking glass bottles. I looked hard at the area where I'd seen it. The school was shaped like an E without the middle dash. The two end dashes jutted out a good six feet farther than the middle section. In those corners, deep shadows formed in the ninety-degree pockets. The movement had come from the pocket on my right.

I kept hoping for a match. In the movies, when someone's following the detective, the idiot always lights a match so the hero can make him. Then I realized how ridiculously cloak-and-dagger this shit was. For all I knew, I'd seen a cat.

I kept watching anyway.

"City desk," Richie said.

"You said that already."

"Meestah Kenzie," Richie said. "How goes it?"

"It goes well," I said. "Hear you pissed off Mulkern again today."

"Reason to go on living," Richie said. "Hippos who masquerade as whales will be harpooned."

I was willing to bet he had that written on a three-by-five card, taped above his desk. "What's the most important bill coming to floor this session?"

"The most important bill—" he repeated, thinking about it. "No question—the street terrorism bill."

In the schoolyard, something moved. "The street terrorism bill?"

"Yeah. It labels all gang members 'street terrorists,' means you can throw them in jail simply because they're gang members. In simplest terms—"

"Use small words so I'll be sure to understand."

"Of course. In simplest terms, gangs would be considered paramilitary groups with interests that are in direct conflict with those of the state. Treat them like an invading army. Anyone caught wearing colors, wearing Raiders baseball caps even, is committing treason. Goes straight to jail, no passing Go."

"Will it pass?"

"Possibly. Good possibility, actually, when you consider how desperate everyone is to get rid of the gangs."

"And?"

"And, it'll get struck down within six months in a courtroom. It's one thing to say, 'We should declare martial law and get these fuckers off the streets, civil rights be damned.' It's another to actually do it, get that much closer to fascism, turn Roxbury and Dorchester into another South Central, helicopters and shit flying overhead day and night. Why the interest?"

I tried to put Mulkern or Paulson or Vurnan with this and it didn't fit. Mulkern, the house liberal, would never publicly stand behind something like this. But Mulkern, the pragmatist, would never take a public stand in favor of the gangs either. He'd simply take a vacation the week the bill came to floor.

"When's it coming to floor?" I asked.

"Next Monday, the third of July."

"There's nothing else coming up you can think of?"

"Not really, no. They got a mandatory seven bill for child molesters will probably sail through."

I knew about that one. Seven years mandatory prison time for anyone convicted of child molestation. No parole possibility. The only problem I had with it was that it wasn't called the mandatory life bill, and that there wasn't a provision that ensured that those convicted would be forced to enter mainstream population, and get back a little of what they gave.

Again Richie said, "Why the interest, Patrick?"

I considered Sterling Mulkern's message: Talk to Richie Colgan. Sell out. For the briefest moment, I considered telling Richie about it. Teach Mulkern to ask me to help him soothe his ruffled feathers. But I knew Richie would have no choice but to put it in his next column, in bold print, and professionally speaking, crossing Mulkern like that would be the same as cutting my wrists in a bathtub.

"Working on a case," I told Richie. "Very hush-hush at the moment."

"Tell me about it sometime," he said.

"Sometime."

"Good enough." Richie doesn't press me and I don't press him. We accept the word no from each other, which is one reason for the friendship. He said, "How's your partner?"

"Still mouthwatering."

"Still not coming across for you?" He chuckled.

"She's married," I said.

"Don't matter. You've had married before. Must drive you nuts, Patrick, a beautiful woman like that around you every day, and nary a single desire to touch your dick in her whole luscious being. Damn, but that's got to hurt." He laughed.

Richie's under the impression that he's a real hoot sometimes.

I said, "Yeah, well, I got to run." Something moved again in the black pocket of the schoolyard. "How about a couple of beers soon?"

"Bring Angie?" I thought I could hear him panting.

"I'll see if she's in the mood."

"Deal. I'll send over a few file reports on those bills."

"*Gracias.*"

He hung up and I sat back and looked through the slit in the curtains. I was familiar with the shadows now, and I could see a large shape sitting within them. Animal, vegetable, or mineral, I couldn't tell, but something was there. I thought about calling Bubba; he was good for times like these when you weren't sure what you were walking into. But he'd called me from a bar. Not a good sign. Even if I could track him down, he'd just want to kill the trouble, not investigate it. Bubba has to be used sparingly, with great care. Like nitro.

I decided to press Harold into service.

Harold is a six-foot stuffed panda bear that I won at the Marshfield Fair a few years back. I tried to give him to Angie at the time; I'd won him for her, after all. But she gave me that look she'd give me if I lit up a cigarette during sex, the withering one. Why she didn't want a six-foot stuffed panda in bright yellow rubber shorts adorning her apartment is beyond me, but since I couldn't find a trash barrel big enough to take him, I welcomed him into my home.

I dragged Harold from the bedroom into the dark kitchen and sat him in the chair by the window. The shade was drawn, and on my way out, I flicked on the light. If someone was watching me from the shadows, Harold should pass as me. Although my ears are smaller.

I crept through the back of the house, took my Ithaca from behind the door, and went down the back stairs. The only thing better than an automag for the total firearms incompetent is an Ithaca .12 gauge shotgun with a pistol grip. If you can't hit your target with that, you're legally blind.

I stepped out into my backyard, wondering if possibly there were two of them. One for the front, one for the back. But that seemed as unlikely as there being one of them in the first place. Paranoia had to be checked.

I hopped a few fences until I got to the avenue, slipped the Ithaca under my blue trench coat. I crossed the intersection and walked past the church on the south side. A road runs behind the church and the school, and I took that north. I passed a few people I knew along the way, gave curt nods, keeping my coat closed with one hand; have gun, will offend the neighbors.

I slipped into the back of the schoolyard, soundless in my Avia high-tops, and pressed close against the wall until I reached the first corner. I was at the edge of the E and he was ten feet away, around another corner, in the shadows. I considered how to approach it. I thought of just walking up on him, fast, but people tend to die that way. I thought of crawling along the ground like they used to on *Rat Patrol*, but I wasn't even positive anyone was there, and if I crawled up on a cat or two kids in a lip lock, I wouldn't be able to show my face for a month.

My decision was made for me.

It wasn't a cat and it wasn't teen lovers. It was a man and he was holding an Uzi. He stepped out from the corner in front of me with the ugly weapon pointed at my sternum, and I forgot how to breathe.

He was standing in darkness and wearing a dark blue baseball cap like they wear in the navy, with gold leafs embroidered on the brim, and gold writing of some sort on the front. I couldn't make out what it said, or maybe I was just too scared to concentrate.

He wore black wraparound sunglasses. Not the best thing to see properly when you wanted to shoot someone in the dark, but with that gun at this range, Ray Charles could put me in the grave.

He wore black clothes over black skin and that's about all I could tell about him.

I started to mention that this neighborhood wasn't known for its courtesy toward its darker neighbors after sunset when something fast and hard hit my mouth, and something else, equally hard, hit my temple, and just before I lost consciousness, I remember thinking: Harold the Panda doesn't fool 'em like he used to.

SIX

WHILE I SLEPT THE SLEEP OF IDIOTS, THE HERO CAME TO visit. He was dressed in his uniform, carrying a child under each arm. His face was covered with soot, and smoke rolled off his shoulders. The two children were crying, but the Hero was laughing. He looked at me and laughed. And laughed. The laugh turned into a howl just before brown smoke began pouring from his mouth, and I woke up.

I was on a rug. That much I knew. There was a guy dressed in white kneeling over me. I'd either been committed or he was a paramedic. He had a bag beside him and a stethoscope around his neck. A paramedic. Or a very authentic impersonator. He said, "You gonna be sick?"

I shook my head and threw up on the rug.

Someone started screaming at me in high-pitched gibberish-speak. Then I recognized it. Gaelic. She remembered what country she was in and switched to English with a heavy brogue. It didn't make much difference, but at least I knew where I was now.

The rectory. The screaming banshee was Delia, Pastor Drummond's housekeeper. In a moment, she'd begin hitting me with something. The paramedic said, "Father?" and I could hear the pastor hustling Delia out of the room. The paramedic said, "You finished?" He sounded like he had things to do. A real angel of mercy. I nodded and rolled over onto my back. I sat up. Sort of. I hooked my arms around my knees and sat there, holding on, my head swimming. The walls were doing a psychedelic dance in front of me and my mouth felt like it was full of bloody pennies. I said, "Ouch."

"You got a way with words," the paramedic said. "You also got a mild concussion, some loose teeth, a busted lip, and a hell of a shiner growing by your left eye."

Great. Angie and I would have something to talk about in the morning. The Ray-Ban twins. "That it?"

"That's it," he said, dropping the stethoscope into the bag. "I'd tell you to come down to the hospital with me, but you're from Dorchester, so I figure you're into all that macho bullshit and won't come."

"Mmm," I said. "How'd I get here?"

Pastor Drummond, behind me, said, "I found you." He stepped in front of me, holding my shotgun and the magnum. He placed them gently on the couch across from me.

"Sorry about the rug," I said.

He pointed at the vomit. "Father Gabriel, when he was in his cups, used to do that quite often. If I remember right, that's why we picked that color pattern." He smiled. "Delia's making up a bed for you now."

"Thanks, Father," I said, "but I think if I can walk to the bedroom, I can walk across the street to my own place."

"That mugger might still be out there."

The paramedic picked up his bag from beside me and said, "Have a good one."

"It's been swell for me too," I managed.

The paramedic grimaced and gave us a little wave before letting himself out the side door.

I reached out my hand and Pastor Drummond took it, pulling me up. I said, "I wasn't mugged, Father."

He raised his eyebrows. "Angry husband?"

I looked at him. "Father," I said. "Please. You have to stop getting illicit thrills from my lifestyle. It has to do with a case I'm on. I think." I wasn't even sure. "It was a warning."

He supported me as far as the couch. The room was still about as stable as quarters on the *Titanic*. He said, "This is some warning."

I nodded. Bad move. The *Titanic* overturned and the room slid sideways. Pastor Drummond's hand pushed me back against the couch. I said, "Yes. Some warning. Did you call the police?"

He looked surprised. "You know, I didn't think of it."

"Good. I don't want to spend all night filling out reports."

"Angela might have, though."

"You called Angie?"

"Of course he called me." She was standing in the doorway. Her hair was a wreck, messy strands hanging over her forehead; it made her look sexier, like she'd just woken up. She was wearing a black leather jacket over a burgundy polo shirt that hung untucked over gray sweatpants and white aerobic sneakers. She had a purse you could hide Peru in, which she dropped on the floor as she crossed to the couch.

She sat beside me. "Don't we look beautiful," she said, her hand under my chin, tilting it upward. "Jesus, Patrick, who'd you run into—an angry husband?"

Father Drummond giggled. A sixty-year-old priest, giggling into his fist. Not my day.

"I think it was a relative of Mike Tyson," I said.

She looked at me. "What, you don't have hands?"

I pushed her hand away. "He had an Uzi, Ange. Probably what he hit me with."

"Sorry," she said. "I'm a little anxious. I didn't mean to snap." She looked at my lips. "This wasn't done with the Uzi. Your temple, maybe. But not the lips. Looks like a speed glove to me, the way it tore the skin."

Angie, the expert on physical abrasions.

She leaned in close, whispered. "You know the guy?"

I whispered back. "No."

"Never saw him before?"

"Nope."

"You're sure?"

"Angie, I wanted this, I would've called the cops."

She leaned back, hands up. "OK. OK." She looked at Drummond. "OK if I take him back to his place, Father?"

"It would make Delia's day," Drummond said.

"Thanks, Father," I said.

He folded his arms. "Some security you are," he said, and winked.

He's a priest, but I could've kicked him.

Angie picked up the guns and then lifted me to my feet with her free hand.

I looked at Father Drummond. "G'night," I managed.

"God bless," he said at the door.

As we went down the steps into the schoolyard, Angie said, "You know why this happened, don't you."

"No, why?"

"You don't go to church anymore."

"Ha," I said.

•

She got me across the street and up the stairs, the queasiness steadily evaporating as the warmth of her skin and the feel of the blood rushing through her body reawakened my senses.

We sat down in the kitchen. I kicked Harold the Panda

out of my chair, and Angie poured us each a glass of orange juice. She sniffed hers before she drank. "What'd you tell the Asshole?" I asked.

"After I told him what happened, he seemed so pleased someone finally kicked your ass, he would've let me fly to Atlantic City with the savings account."

"Glad to know some good came out of this."

She put her hand on mine. "What happened?"

I gave her the rundown from the time she left the office to ten minutes ago.

"Would you recognize him again?"

I shrugged. "Maybe. Maybe not."

She sat back, one leg raised and propped beside her on the chair, the other tucked under her. She looked at me for a long time. "Patrick," she said.

"Yeah?"

She smiled sadly and shook her head. "You're going to have a hard time getting a date for a while."

SEVEN

WE WERE JUST ABOUT TO CALL BILLY HAWKINS THE NEXT day at noon when he walked into the office. Billy, like a lot of people who work in Western Union offices, looks like he just got out of detox. He's extremely skinny and his skin has that slightly yellowish texture of someone who spends all his time indoors in smoke-filled rooms. He accentuates his lack of weight by wearing tight jeans and shirts, and rolls his half-sleeves up to his shoulders as if he has biceps. His black hair looks like he combs it with a clawhammer, and he has one of those drooping Mexican bandit mustaches that nobody, not even your average Mexican bandit, wears anymore. In 1979, the rest of the world went on, but Billy didn't notice.

He plopped himself lazily into the chair in front of my desk and said, "So, like, when you guys going to get a bigger office?"

"The day I find the bell," I said.

Billy squinted. Slowly, he said, "Oh, right. Yeah."

Angie said, "How you doing, Billy?" and actually looked like she cared.

Billy looked at her and blushed. "I'm doing...I'm doing all right. All right, Angie."

Angie said, "Good. I'm glad." What a tease.

Billy looked at my face. "What happened to you?"

"Had a fight with a nun," I said.

Billy said, "You look like you had a fight with a truck," and looked at Angie.

Angie gave it a small giggle, and I didn't know who I wanted to pitch out the window more.

"You run that check for us, Billy?"

"'Course, man. 'Course. You owe me big time on this one too, I'll tell ya."

I raised my eyebrows. "Billy, remember who you're talking to."

Billy thought about it. Thought about the ten years he'd be doing in Walpole, fetching cigarettes for his boyfriend, Rolf the Animal, if we hadn't saved him. His yellow skin whitened considerably, and he said, "Sorry, man. You're right. When you're right, you're right." He reached into the back pocket of his jeans and tossed a somewhat greasy, very wrinkled piece of paper on my desk.

"What am I looking at here, Billy?"

"Jenna Angeline's reference check," he said. "Copped from our Jamaica Plain office. She cashed a check there on Tuesday."

It was greasy, it was wrinkled, but it was gold. Jenna had listed four references, all personal. Under the Job heading, she'd written, "Self-employed," in a small, birdlike scrawl. In the personal references she'd listed four sisters. Three lived in Alabama, in or around Mobile. One lived in Wickham, Massachusetts. Simone Angeline of 1254 Merrimack Avenue.

Billy handed me another piece of paper—a Xerox of the check Jenna had cashed. The check was signed by Simone Angeline. If Billy hadn't been such a slimy-looking dude, I would have kissed him.

•

After Billy left, I finally got up the nerve to take a look in the mirror. I'd avoided it all last night and this morning. My hair's short enough to make do with a finger comb, so after my shower this morning, that's exactly what I did. I'd skipped shaving too, and if I had a little stubble, I told myself it was hip, very *GQ*.

I crossed the office and entered the tiny cubicle that someone had once referred to as "the bathroom." It's got a toilet all right, but even that's in miniature, and I always feel like an adult locked in a preschool whenever I sit on it and my knees hit my chin. I shut the door behind me and raised my head from the munchkin sink and looked in the mirror.

If I hadn't been me, I wouldn't have recognized my face. My lips were blown up to twice their size and looked like they'd French-kissed a weed whacker. My left eye was fringed by a thick rope of dark brown and the cornea was streaked with bright red threads of blood. The skin along my temple had split when Blue Cap hit me with the butt of the Uzi, and while I slept, the blood had clotted in some hair. The right side of my forehead where I assume I'd hit the school wall was raw and scraped. If I wasn't the manly detective type, I might have wept.

Vanity is a weakness. I know this. It's a shallow dependence on the exterior self, on how one looks instead of what one is. I know this well. But I have a scar the size and texture of a jellyfish on my abdomen already, and you'd be surprised how your sense of self changes when you can't take your shirt off at the beach. In my more private moments, I pull up my shirt and look at it, tell myself it doesn't matter, but every time a woman has felt it under her palm late at night, propped herself up on a pillow and asked me about it, I've made my explanation as quick as possible, closed the doors to my past as soon as they've opened, and not once, even when Angie's asked, have I told the truth. Vanity and dishonesty may be vices, but they're also the first forms of protection I ever knew.

The Hero always gave me a dope slap upside the head whenever he caught me looking in the mirror. "Men built those things so women would have something to do," he'd say. Hero. Philosopher. My father, the Renaissance man.

When I was sixteen, I had deep blue eyes and a nice smile, and little else to take confidence in, hanging around the Hero. And if I was still sixteen, staring into the mirror, working up some nerve, telling myself *tonight* I'd finally do something about the Hero, I'd definitely be at a loss.

But now, damnit, I had a genuine case to solve, a Jenna Angeline to locate, an impatient partner on the other side of the door, a gun in my holster, detective's license in my wallet, and...a face that looked like it belonged to a Flannery O'Connor character. Ah, vanity.

•

When I opened the door, Angie was rifling through her purse, probably looking for a misplaced microwave or an old car. She looked up. "You ready?"

"I'm ready."

She pulled a stun gun from the purse. "What's this guy look like again?"

I said, "Last night he was wearing a blue cap and wrap-arounds. But I don't know if it's like his regular uniform or anything." I opened the door. "Ange, you won't need the stun gun. If you spot him, lay back. We just want to verify that he's still around."

Angie looked at the stun gun. "It's not for him, it's for me. Case I need something to keep me awake in cow country."

Wickham is sixty miles from Boston, so Angie thinks they don't have telephones yet.

I said, "You can take the girl out of the city…"

"But you'll have to shoot her first," she said and headed down the stairs.

She stayed in the church, giving me a minute head start and watching the street through the lower opening of a stained-glass window.

I crossed the street to what I call my "company car." It's a dark green 1979 Volaré. The Vobeast. It looks like shit, sounds like shit, drives like shit, and generally fits in well in most of the places where I have to work. I opened the door, half expecting to hear a rush of feet on the street behind me, followed by the snap of a weapon hitting the back of my skull. That's the thing about being a victim; you start to think it'll happen to you on a regular basis. Suddenly everything looks suspect and any brightness you may have noticed the day before has dissipated into the shadows. And the shadows are everywhere. It's living with the reality of your own vulnerability, and it sucks.

But nothing happened this time. I didn't see Blue Cap in my rearview as I pulled a U-turn and headed for the expressway. But then, unless he'd really enjoyed last night's encounter, I didn't think I would see him again; I'd just have to assume he was there. I pushed the Vobeast down the avenue, then turned onto the northern on-ramp for I-93 and drove downtown.

Twenty minutes later I was on Storrow Drive, the Charles River running by in copper flashes on my right. A couple of Mass. General nurses lunched on the lawn; a man ran over one of the footbridges with a mammoth chocolate Chow beside him. For a moment, I thought of picking one up for myself. Probably do a hell of a lot better job protecting me than Harold the Panda ever would. But then, I didn't really need an attack dog; I had Bubba. By the boathouse, I saw a group of BU or Emerson students, stuck in the city for the summer, passing around a bottle of wine. Wild kids. Probably had some brie and crackers in their backpacks, too.

I got off at Beacon Street, U-turned again onto the service road, and banged a quick right onto Revere Street, following its cobblestones across Charles Street and up Beacon Hill. No one behind me.

I turned again onto Myrtle Street, the whole street no wider than a piece of dental floss, the tall colonial buildings squeezing in on me. It's impossible to follow someone in Beacon Hill without being spotted. The streets were built before cars, and I presume, before fat or tall people.

Back when Boston was this wonderful mythic world of midget aerobics instructors, Beacon Hill must have seemed roomy. But now, it's cramped and narrow and shares more than a little in common with an old French provincial town—very pleasing to the eye, but functionally a disaster. A truck stopped for a delivery on the Hill can back up traffic for a mile. The streets are apt to be one-way in a northern direction for two or three blocks, then arbitrarily turn one-way to the south. This usually captures the average driver unaware and forces him to turn onto yet another narrow street with much the same problem, and before he knows it, he's back on Cambridge or Charles or Beacon Street, looking up at the Hill, wondering how the hell he ever ended up down here again, but getting the distinct, if irrational, impression that the Hill itself threw him off.

It's a wonderful place to be a snob. The homes are gorgeous red brick. The parking spaces are guarded by the Boston Police. The small cafés and shops are manned by imperious owners who close their doors whenever someone they don't recognize looks as if he may want to enter. And no one can find your address unless you, personally, draw them a map.

I looked in my rearview as I crested the Hill, the gold dome of the State House peeking out through the wrought-iron fence of a roof garden ahead of me. Two blocks behind me, I saw a car driving slowly, the driver's head turning left and right as if looking for an unfamiliar address.

I took a left on Joy Street and coasted the four blocks down to Cambridge Street. As the light turned green and I crossed the intersection, I saw the same car coasting down the hill behind me. At the very top of Joy Street, another car appeared—a station wagon with a broken luggage rack on the roof. I couldn't see the driver, but I knew it was Angie. She'd busted the luggage rack with a hammer one morning, pretending the flimsy metal was Phil.

I turned left on Cambridge Street and drove a few blocks to the Charles Plaza. I pulled into the parking lot, took the ticket at the gate—only three dollars per half hour; what a bargain—and pulled across the lot until I was in front of the Holiday Inn. I walked inside the hotel like I had business there, turned right past the front desk and hopped the elevator to the third floor. I walked down the corridor until I found a window and stared down into the parking lot.

Blue Cap wasn't wearing a blue cap today. He had on a white bicycler's cap, the brim pushed back flat against his forehead. He still wore the wraparounds, though, and a white Nike T-shirt and black sweatpants. He stood just out-side of his car—a white Nissan Pulsar with black racing stripes—and leaned on the open door while he decided if he should follow me in or not. I couldn't see his license plate numbers from this angle, and from this height, I could only guess at his age, but I put him at twenty to twenty-five. He was big—six two or so—and he looked like he knew his way around a Nautilus machine.

Out on Cambridge Street, Angie's car idled, double-parked.

I looked back at Blue Cap. No point sticking around. He'd follow me into the hotel or he wouldn't. Either way, it didn't make any difference.

I took the stairs down to the basement, opened a door onto a service driveway that smelled of exhaust fumes, and jumped off the loading dock. I walked past a dumpster that reeked of slowly stewing fruit and worked my way down onto Blossom Street. I took my time, but before you could say slick-as-a-wet-goose, I was back on Cambridge Street.

All over Boston, in places you'd never notice, there are garages. It doesn't compensate for a city as short on parking space as Moscow is on toilet paper, but at least the rental fees are exorbitant. I stepped into one between a hair salon and a florist, strolled along the garage until I came to space number eighteen, and removed the slipcover from my baby.

Every boy needs a toy. Mine is a 1959 Porsche Roadster convertible. It's royal blue, with a wood finish steering wheel and a twin cowl cockpit. True, "cockpit" is a term usually reserved for jets, but when I've taken this thing up to a hundred and forty or so, I've gotten the distinct impression that liftoff's only a few more blurred road signs away. The interior is a rich white leather. The stick shift gleams like polished pewter. The horn has a keen horse emblem on it. I work on it more than I drive it, pampering it on weekends, polishing it, bringing it new parts. I'm proud to say I've never gone so far as to give it a name, but Angie says that's only because I lack the imagination.

It started with the growl of a jungle cat on the first turn of the key. I took a baseball cap from under the seat, slipped off my jacket, adjusted my sunglasses, and left the garage.

Angie was still double-parked in front of the Plaza, which meant Blue Cap was present and accounted for. I waved and pulled out onto Cambridge, heading toward the river. She was still behind me when I reached Storrow Drive, but by the time I got to I-93, I'd left her in the dust, simply because I could. Or maybe, simply because I'm so immature. One of the two.

EIGHT

THE DRIVE TO WICKHAM IS NOT A FUN ONE. YOU HAVE TO switch interchanges every third mile or so, and one wrong turn dumps you in New Hampshire, trying to talk directions with eastern rednecks who don't speak the language. To top it off, there's nothing to look at but the occasional industrial park, or as you get closer to the belt of towns that lie along the Merrimack River, the Merrimack River. Not a pleasant sight. Usually you have to look down a sewer grate to find water as brown and sluggish as the Merrimack's—a casualty of the textile business that built a lot of New Hampshire and Massachusetts. The next thing you see as you drive through this region are the mills themselves, and the sky turns to soot.

I had *Exile on Main St.* pumping through my speakers the whole way so I didn't mind it that much, and by the time I found Merrimack Avenue, the only thing I was worried about was leaving the car unattended.

Wickham is not an upwardly mobile community. It's dingy and gray as only a mill town can be. The streets are the color of a shoe bottom, and the only way to tell the difference between the bars and the homes is to look for the neon signs in the windows. The roads and sidewalks are uneven, the tar cracked and pale. Many of the people, especially the workers as they trudge home from the mills in the dying light, have the look of those who've long ago gotten used to the fact that no one remembers them. It's a place where the people are grateful for the seasons, because at least they confirm that time is actually moving on.

Merrimack Avenue is the main strip. Simone Angeline's address was a good ways past the center of town—the bars, gas stations, mills, and clothing factories were five miles behind me before I reached the twelve hundred block. Angie was back in my rearview mirror by then, and she passed me when I pulled onto a side street and parked the car. I set the Chapman lock and disengaged the radio, taking it with me as I got out. I took one last look back at the car and hoped that we would find Jenna soon. Real soon.

I didn't win my car in a card game or have it bequeathed to me by an overly generous client. I banked my money and waited, banked some more money and waited. Finally I saw it advertised and I went to the bank for a loan. I sat through an excruciating interview with a condescending loan officer who reminded me of every bitter, high-school geek who sees his adult life as a mission to avenge adolescence by being a total prick to anyone he assumes would have treated him badly in homeroom. Luckily, my practice grew and my fees rose and I soon had that monkey off my back. But I still pay the price of being constantly anxious about the only material possession I've ever given a damn about.

I slid into the passenger seat of Angie's car and she took my hand. "Don't wowwy, baby, nothing will happen to your pride and joy. I promise."

She's funny enough to shoot sometimes.

I said, "Well, least in this neighborhood, nobody will be suspicious of this thing."

She said, "Oh, good one. You ever think of going into stand-up?"

It went like that. We sat in the car and passed around a can of Pepsi and waited for our meal ticket to make a guest appearance.

By six o'clock we were cramped and sick of each other and even sicker of looking at 1254 Merrimack Avenue. It was a faded A-frame that might have been pink once. A Puerto Rican family had entered it an hour ago, and we'd watched a light go on in the second-floor apartment a minute or so later. Short of our second can of Pepsi exploding all over the dashboard when I opened it, that was the closest we'd come to excitement in four hours.

I was looking through the tape collection on Angie's floor, trying to find a group I'd heard of, when she said, "Heads up."

A black woman—rope thin, with a stiff, almost regal bearing—was stepping from an '81 Honda Civic, her right arm around a bag of groceries, resting them on her hip. She looked like the picture of Jenna, but younger by a good seven or eight years. She also seemed to have too much energy for the tired woman in the photograph. She slammed the car door with her free hip, a hard, swift move that would have left Gretzky on the ice with a wet ass. She marched to the front door of the house, slid her key into the lock, and disappeared inside. A few minutes later, she appeared in silhouette by the window, a telephone receiver to her ear.

Angie said, "How do you want to play it?"

"Wait," I said.

She shifted in her seat. "I was afraid you were going to say that." She held her chin with her fingers, moved it around in a semicircle for a moment. "You don't think Jenna's in there?"

"No. Since she disappeared, she's played it relatively careful. She has to know her apartment's been trashed. And the beating the guy in the schoolyard gave me tells me she's probably into more than the petty theft we're after her for. With people like that after her—maybe this Roland guy too—I don't think she's going to set herself up in her sister's place."

Angie half shrugged, half nodded in that way she has, and lit a cigarette. She hung her arm out the window and the gray smoke pooled by the rearview mirror, then separated into equal strands and floated out the windows. She said, "If we're smart enough to figure out where she is, wouldn't someone else be? We can't be the only ones who know about the sister."

I thought about it. It made sense. If whoever "they" were had put a tail on me in the hopes of following me to Jenna, then they must have put a tail on Simone. "Shit."

"Now, what do you want to do?"

"Wait," I repeated, and she groaned. I said, "We follow Simone when she goes somewhere—"

"*If* she goes somewhere."

"Positive energy, please. When she goes somewhere, we follow, but we hang back first, see if we have company."

"And if our company is already on to us? If they're watching us right now as we speak, thinking the same thing? What then?"

I resisted the urge to turn around and look for other cars with two immobile occupants, staring in our direction. "We deal with it," I said.

She frowned. "You always say that when you don't have a clue."

"Do not," I said.

At seven-fifteen, things started happening.

Simone, wearing a navy blue sweatshirt over a white T-shirt, faded jeans, and generic sneakers the color of an oyster, walked out of the house with determination and opened her car the same way. I wondered if she did everything the same way—with that set look on her face, that the-hell-with-you-if-you-can't-keep-up air about her. Could people *sleep* that way?

She went straight up Merrimack, so we gave her a few blocks, waiting to see if we were the only interested party. It seemed to be the case, and if not, I wasn't about to lose my only lead. We pulled out, and with one last look at my thirty-seven thousand dollars worth of automobile—insurance company estimate, mind you—we tailed her through Wickham. She went straight through the center of town and hopped on I-495. I was tired of being in the car and hoped like hell she didn t have Jenna stowed away in Canada. Thankfully, that didn't seem to be the case, because she got off the expressway a few miles later, turning off into Lansington.

If possible, Lansington is uglier than Wickham, but in imperceptible ways. In most respects, they're identical. Lansington just feels dingier.

We were waiting at a traffic light near the center of town, but when the light turned green, Simone didn't move. I felt two cold spades press together around my heart and Angie said, "Shit. Think she's on to us?"

I said, "Use the horn."

She did and Simone's hand went up in apology as she realized the light had changed. It was the first undetermined thing she'd done since I'd seen her, and it felt like a jump start: we were close.

All around us were squat two-story clapboard buildings, circa the late 1800s. Trees were sparse and gnarled in hideous ways where we saw them. The traffic lights were old, still round, no Walk/Don't Walk signals or neon pictures for those who couldn't understand the Walk/Don't Walk parts. The lights made clicking sounds when they changed, and as we drifted along the two-lane road, I felt that we could just as easily have been in rural Georgia or West Virginia.

Ahead of us, Simone's left blinker went on, and a fraction of a second later, she pulled off the road into a small dirt parking lot filled with pickup trucks, a Winnebago, a couple of dusty American sports cars, and those wretched testaments to Detroit's bad taste—El Caminos. Two of them. A car that couldn't decide whether it wanted to be a truck; a truck that couldn't decide whether it wanted to be a car—obscene, hybrid results.

Angie kept going and a half mile down the road, we U-turned and went back. The parking lot belonged to a bar. Just like Wickham, you wouldn't have known what it was without the small neon Miller High Life signs in the windows. It was a low two-story building, a little deeper than most of the houses, stretching back an extra ten yards or so. From inside I could hear glasses clinking, a smattering of laughter, the babble of voices, and a Bon Jovi song coming off the jukebox. I amended that last thought; maybe it was just a stereo tuned to a radio station and no one inside had actually paid money to listen to Bon Jovi. Then I looked at the pickups and the bar again, and I wasn't hopeful.

Angie said, "We going to wait here too?"

"Nope. Going in."

"Goody." She looked at the building. "Thank God I'm licensed to carry a firearm." She checked the load in her .38.

"Damn straight," I said, climbing out of the car. "First thing you do when we get inside, shoot the stereo."

•

Simone was nowhere in sight when we entered. This was pretty easy to ascertain, because the moment we stepped through the door, everyone stopped moving.

I was wearing jeans, a denim shirt, and a baseball cap. My face looked like I'd had a disagreement with a pit bull, and the jacket that covered my gun was a raggy, faded army thing. I fit right in.

Angie was wearing a dark blue football jacket with white leather sleeves over a loose white cotton shirt that hung untucked over a pair of black leggings.

Guess which one of us they were looking at.

I looked at Angie. New Bedford isn't terribly far from here. Big Dan's Bar is in New Bedford. That's where a bunch of guys threw a girl down on a pool table and had their version of fun at her expense while the rest of the bar cheered them on. I looked at the patrons of this bar—a Heinz 57 mix of eastern rednecks, white trash, mill workers only recently immigrated from the Third World, Portuguese, a couple of black guys—all poor and hostile and gearing up to let off some steam. Probably came here because Big Dan's was closed. I looked at Angie again. I wasn't worried about her; I was considering what would happen to my business if my partner shot the dicks off a barful of people in Langsington. I wasn't sure, but I didn't think we'd be able to keep that office in the church.

The barroom was larger than it looked from the outside. To my left, just before the bar itself, was a narrow staircase of unfinished wood. The bar ran halfway down the floor on the left side. Across from it were a few tables for two against a dark plywood wall. Past the bar, the place opened up and I could see pinball and video machines on the left and the corner of a pool table on the right. A pool table. Terrific.

The place was medium to crowded. Just about everyone wore a baseball cap, even those who I assume were women. A few people had mixed drinks, but for the most part, this was Budweiser country.

We walked up to the bar and folks went back to what they were doing, or pretending to.

The bartender was a young guy, good-looking and bleached blond, but a townie if he was working this place. He gave me a slight smile. Then he gave one to Angie that, in comparison, looked as if his lips exploded. "Hi. What can I get you?" He leaned on the bar and looked into her eyes.

Angie said, "Two Buds."

"My pleasure," Blondie said.

"I'll bet," she said and smiled.

She does this all the time. Flirts her ass off with everyone but me. If I wasn't such a rock of self-confidence, it would annoy me.

My luck was good tonight, though. I felt it the moment the Bon Jovi song ended. While Blondie went for the beers, I looked at the stairs. In what passes for a moment of stillness in a bar, I could hear people moving around overhead.

When Blondie placed both beers in front of Angie, I said, "Is there a back door to this place?"

He turned his head slowly in my direction, looking at me as if I'd just bumped his knee stepping onto the bus. "Yeah," he said with extreme slowness and nodded in the direction of the pool table. Through the smoke that hung over the back I saw the door. He was looking at Angie again, but out of the corner of his mouth, he said, "Why, you planning on sticking the place up?"

"No," I said. I flipped through all the cards in my wallet until I found the right one. "I'm planning on citing you for building code violations. Lots of them, asshole." I flipped the card on the bar. It said, "Lewis Prine, State Building Inspector." Lewis made the mistake of leaving me unattended in his office once.

Blondie stopped looking at Angie, though I could see it hurt. He stepped back a bit and looked at the card. "Don't you guys have badges or something?"

I had one of those too. Good thing about badges, most of them look pretty much the same to the untrained eye, so I don't have to carry fifty of them around with me. I flipped it at him, then put it back in my pocket. "All you got's that one back door?" I said.

"Yeah," he said. Nervous. "Why?"

"Why? *Why*? Where's the owner?"

"Huh?"

"The owner. The owner."

"Bob? He's gone home for the night."

My luck was still holding. I said, "Son, how many floors you got here?"

He looked at me as if I'd just asked what the atmospheric density of Pluto was. "Floors? Uh, two. We got two. Rooming house's upstairs."

"Two," I repeated with an air of moral revulsion. "Two floors and the only exits are on the first."

"Yeah," he said.

"'Yeah'? How people on the second floor supposed to get out if there's a fire?"

"A window?" he suggested.

"A window." I shook my head. "How about I take you up there right now, see how well you land jumping out a fucking window? A window. Jesus."

Angie crossed her legs, sipping her beer, enjoying this.

Blondie said, "Well..."

I said, "Well *what*?" I gave Angie the get-ready look. She

raised her eyebrows and downed her beer happily. "Boy," I said, "you're gonna learn some shit tonight," and I crossed the floor to the plywood wall and pulled the fire alarm.

No one in the barroom ran for an exit. No one really moved at all. They just turned their heads and looked at me. They seemed a bit pissed off.

But on the second floor, no one could tell if there was a fire or not. Bars always smell like smoke.

A rather large woman with a rather small sheet over her nude body and a skinny guy with a lot less coverage came down first. They barely glanced at the bar before they hopped out the door like rabbits during hunting season.

Two kids were next. Sixteen or so, both with a little acne. Probably registered as Mr. and Mrs. Smith. They flattened against the wall as soon as they cleared the last step, staring at all of us, chests heaving.

Then suddenly, Simone was there, looking very put out, looking to find someone responsible, her eyes working their way from Blondie, around the crowd of hicks, and finally settling on *moi*. I glanced at her but passed by, my eyes slowing and holding at a point just over her shoulder.

On Jenna Angeline.

Angie left my shoulder and disappeared around the corner, on the other side of the plywood wall. I waited, my eyes fixed on Jenna Angeline, hers finally meeting mine. They were eyes that screamed resignation. Old, old eyes. Brown and numb and too beaten to show fear. Or joy. Or life. Something passed through them, briefly, and I knew that she recognized me. Not who I was. What I represented. I was just another form of cop or collection agent or landlord or boss. I was authority, and I was coming to decide something about her life whether she liked it or not. She recognized me all right.

Angie had found the main cables and the clarion blast bleated away to nothing in one wheezing second.

I was the center of attention now, and I knew I was about to face resistance, at the very least from the Angeline sisters. Everyone except them, the bartender, and a big, going-to-fat, ex-football player type to my right faded slightly behind a haze of gauze. The football player was leaning forward on his toes and Blondie had his hand under the bar. Neither of the Angeline sisters looked like they had any intention of moving without help from a crane.

My voice seemed loud and hoarse when I said, "Jenna, I need to talk to you."

Simone grabbed her sister's arm and said, "Come on, Jenna, let's go," and started leading her toward the door.

I shook my head and stepped in front of the door, my hand already in my jacket as the football player made his move. Another hero. Probably a member of the auxiliary fire department. His right hand was heading toward my shoulder and his mouth was open, a gruff voice saying, "Hey, asshole, leave the women alone." Before he reached my shoulder, my hand cleared my jacket and whacked his arm away and brushed my gun against his lips.

I said, "Excuse me?" and dug the muzzle of the gun hard against his upper lip.

He looked at the gun. He didn't say anything.

I didn't move my head, just kept my eyes on the barroom, looked everyone in the eye who'd meet mine. I felt Angie beside me, her gun steady, her breathing shallow. She said, "Jenna, Simone, I want you to get in your car and drive to the house in Wickham. We'll be right behind you and if you try to take off, believe me, our car's a lot faster than yours and we'll end up talking in a ditch somewhere."

I looked at Simone. "If I wanted to hurt you, you'd be dead now."

Simone gave off some sort of body language that only a sister would recognize, because Jenna put a hand on her arm. "We do what they say, Simone."

Angie opened the door behind me. Jenna and Simone passed by and walked out. I looked at Football Player, then pushed his face back with the gun. I felt the weight of it in my arm, the muscles beginning to ache, my hand stiffening and sweat popping out of the glands all over my body.

Football Player met my eyes and I could see he was thinking about being a hero again.

I waited. I leveled the gun and said, "Come on."

Angie said, "Not here. Let's go." She took my elbow, and we backed out of the bar into the night.

NINE

"SIT DOWN, SIMONE. PLEASE." EVERYTHING JENNA SAID came out as a weary plea.

We'd been back at the house for ten minutes and had spent all our time dealing with Simone's ego. So far, she'd tried to push past me twice, and now she was walking toward the phone.

"Man don't come into my house, tell me how to act," she told Jenna, then looked at Angie. "And the man ain't going to shoot me with the neighbors awake upstairs." She'd started to believe that by the time she reached the phone.

I said, "Simone, who're you going to call? The police? Fine."

Jenna said, "Put the phone down, Simone. Please."

Angie looked bored and antsy. Patience is not one of her prime virtues. She walked over and pulled the phone cord out of the wall.

I closed my eyes, then opened them. "Jenna, I'm a private investigator, and before any of us decides to do anything else, I have to talk to you."

Simone looked at the phone, then at Angie and me, finally at her sister. She said, "Your bed, girl, lie in it," and sat down on the couch.

Angie sat beside her. "You have a very nice place here."

This was true. It was small, and the outside was nothing to look at, and it wasn't like there was a baby grand by the window, but Simone definitely had an eye. The floor had been stripped, the blonde wood underneath polished to a high gloss. The couch where Simone and Angie sat was a light cream color with an oversize throw pillow that Angie was itching to hug to her chest. Jenna sat in a mahogany shell chair to the right of the couch and I leaned on its twin across from her. Four feet from the windows the floor rose eight inches and a small alcove had been created around the two windows facing the street, cushions on the window seats, a small wooden magazine rack, a hanging plant overhead, and the wooden telephone desk. A bookcase ran the length of the half wall behind Jenna and I saw poetry by Nikki Giovanni, Maya Angelou, Alice Walker, and Amiri Baraka, plus novels by Baldwin and Wright as well as Gabriel García Márquez, Toni Morrison, Pete Dexter, Walker Percy, and Charles Johnson.

I looked at Simone. "Where'd you go to school?"

She said, "Tuskegee," a little surprised.

"Good school." A friend of mine played ball there for a year before he found out he wasn't good enough. I said, "Nice book collection."

"You just surprised the nigger knows how to read."

I sighed. "Right. That's it, Simone." I said to Jenna, "Why'd you quit your job?"

Jenna said, "People quit their jobs every day."

"This is true," I said, "but why'd you quit yours?"

She said, "I didn't want to work for them no more. Plain and simple."

"And when you raided their files, how plain and simple was that?"

Jenna looked confused. So did Simone. It's possible they actually were, but then, if she had stolen the files, looking completely aware of what I was talking about probably wasn't the best idea. Simone said, "What the hell are you talking about?"

Jenna was watching me steadily, her hands kneading the fabric of her skirt. She was considering something and, for a moment, the intelligence that entered her eyes swamped all that weariness like a wave over a rowboat. Then it was gone again and the eyes dulled. She said, "Simone, I'd like to talk to this man alone for a few minutes."

Simone didn't like it, but after a minute or so, she and Angie went into the kitchen. Simone's voice was loud and unhappy, but Angie has a way with loud and unhappy. You don't live in a marriage of arbitrary rages, unfounded jealousies, and sudden accusations without growing adept at dealing with another's hostility in a small room. When dealing with whiners or ragers of any sort—those who always see themselves as victims of life's vast conspiracy to ruin their day or are unreasonable or choking on some predictable, paltry anger—Angie's gaze grows flat and level, her head and body become as still as a statue, and the whiner or the rager vents until that gaze forces them to sputter, to weaken, to exhaust themselves. You either wither under the calm logic of it, blanch in the face of its daunting maturity, or you lash out against it, like Phil, and negate yourself. I know; I've been the focus of that gaze a time or two myself.

In the living room, Jenna's eyes were fastened firmly on the floor and if she kneaded that skirt any harder the thread would begin pooling at her feet. She said, "Whyn't you tell me why you've come up here for me."

I thought about it. I've been wrong about people before. Several times. I go on the presumption that everyone's full of shit until proven otherwise, and this usually serves me in good stead. But every now and then, I think a person has proven himself otherwise, only to discover the shit later, usually in painful ways. Jenna didn't strike me as a liar. She didn't look like she knew how, but often it's people just like that who wouldn't know the truth if it was wearing an ID card on its lapel.

I said, "You have certain documents. I was hired to retrieve them." I spread my hands, palms up. "Simple as that."

"Documents?" she said, spitting it. "Documents. Damn." She stood and began pacing and suddenly she looked a lot stronger than her sister, a lot more determined.

She had no trouble meeting my eyes now. Hers were red and hard, and I realized, once again, that people aren't born weary and beaten, they get that way.

She said, "Let me tell *you*, Mr. Kenzie"—and pointed a stiff finger at me—"that's one hell of a funny word. 'Documents.'" Her head was down again and she was pacing in a tight circle with borders only she could see. "Documents," she said again. "Well, OK, call them what you will. Yes, sir. Call them what you will."

"What would you call them, Mrs. Angeline?"

"I ain't no missus."

"OK. What would you call them, Ms. Angeline?"

She looked at me, her whole body beginning to quiver with rage. The red of her eyes had darkened and her chin was pointed out straight and unyielding. She said, "All my life, nobody ever need me. Know what I mean?"

I shrugged.

"Need," she said. "Nobody ever need me. People *want* me, sure. For a few hours or so, a week maybe, they say, 'Jenna clean room one-oh-five,' or 'Jenna, run down the store for me,' or real sweet they say, 'Jenna, honey, come on over here and lie down a spell.' But then, when they done, I'm just a piece of furniture again. Don't care if I'm around; don't care if I ain't. People can always find someone to clean for 'em, or run to the store for 'em, or lie down with 'em."

She walked back to her chair and rummaged through her purse until she found a pack of cigarettes. "Hadn't smoked in ten years—until a few days ago." She lit one, blew the smoke out in a rush that clouded the small room. "Ain't no documents, Mr. Kenzie. You understand? Ain't no documents."

"Then what—"

"There are things. There *are* things." She nodded to herself, stabbed her cigarette downward into the air, kept pacing.

I leaned forward in my chair a bit, my head following her like I was at Wimbledon. I said, "What things, Ms. Angeline?"

"You know, Mr. Kenzie," she said, as if she hadn't heard me, "all of a sudden, everyone looking for me, hiring people like yourself, hiring worse people probably, trying to find Jenna, to talk to Jenna, to get what Jenna got. All of a sudden, everyone *need* Jenna." She crossed the floor quickly to me, her cigarette poised over me like a butcher knife, her jaw clenched. She said, "Nobody getting what I got, Mr. Kenzie. You hear me? No one. 'Cept who I decide to give it to. I make the decision. I get what I want. I do a little using myself. Send someone to the store for *me*, maybe. See people work for *me* for a change. See them fade into furniture when I don't have no use for them anymore." She stabbed the glowing cigarette in toward my eye. "I *decide*. Jenna Angeline." She leaned back a bit, took a drag on the cigarette. "And what I got ain't for sale."

"Then what's it for?"

"Justice," she said through a stream of smoke. "And lots of it. People going to be in pain, Mr. Kenzie."

I looked at her hand, shaking so badly the cigarette quivered up and down like a recently abandoned diving board. I heard the anguish in her voice—a torn, slightly hollow sound—and saw its ravages on her face. She was a wreck of a person, Jenna Angeline. A heart beating fast in a shell of a body. She was scared and tired and angry and howling at the world, but unlike most people in the same situation, she was dangerous because she had something that, at least as far as she was concerned, would give her something back in this world. But the world usually doesn't work that way, and people like Jenna are time bombs; they might take a few people down with them, but they'll go up in the inferno too.

I didn't want anything bad to happen to Jenna, but I was even more certain that I wasn't going to get hit with any shrapnel if she self-destructed. I said, "Jenna, here's my problem: we call this sort of case a 'find-and-a-phone-call' because that's pretty much all I'm paid to do—find you and call the client and then go on my merry way. Once I make the phone call, I'm out of it. The client usually brings in the law or deals with it personally or whatever. But I don't stick around to find out. I'm—"

"A dog," she said. "You run around with your nose on the ground, sniffing through bushes and piles of warm shit until you find the fox. Then you step back and let the hunters shoot it dead." She stabbed out her cigarette.

It wasn't the analogy I would have chosen, but it wasn't entirely false no matter what I wanted to think. Jenna sat back down and looked at me and I held her dark eyes. They had the odd mixture of terror and resilient bravery of a cat backed into a corner; the look of someone who isn't sure she's up to the task, but has decided there's no other way out but straight ahead. It's the look of the crumbling soul trying to pull it all together for one last worthwhile breath. It's not a look I've ever seen in the eyes of people like Sterling Mulkern or Jim Vurnan or Brian Paulson. I never saw it on the Hero's face or a president's or a captain of industry's. But I've seen it in the faces of most everyone else.

"Jenna, you tell me what you think I should do."

"Who hired you?"

I shook my head.

"Well, it was either Senator Mulkern or Socia, and Socia'd just have you shoot me where I sit, so it got to be Senator Mulkern."

Socia? "Is Socia any relation to Roland?" I asked.

I could have broadsided her with a wrecking ball and had less impact. She closed her eyes for a moment and rocked in place. "What you know about Roland?"

"I know he's bad news."

"You stay away from Roland," she said. "You hear? Away from him."

"That's what people keep telling me."

"Well," she said, "you listen."

"Who's Roland?" I asked.

She shook her head.

"OK. Who's Socia?"

Another head shake.

"I can't help you, Jenna, if—"

"Ain't asking for your help," she said.

"Fine," I said. I stood up and walked over to the phone. I reconnected it, began to dial.

She said, "What're you doing?"

I said, "Calling my client. You can talk to him. My job's done."

She said, "Wait."

I shook my head. "Sterling Mulkern, please."

An electronic voice was telling me the time when Jenna pulled the phone cord out of the wall again. I turned and looked at her.

She said, "You got to trust me."

"No, I don't. I can leave you here and walk down to the nearest phone booth and make my call there."

"But what if—?"

"What if what?" I said. "Lady, I got better things to do than fuck around with you. You got a card to play? Play it."

She said, "What sort of documents you supposed to be looking for?"

No point in lying. I said, "They pertain to an upcoming bill."

"Oh, they do?" she said. "Well, Mr. Kenzie, someone been lying to you. What I got don't have nothing to do with bills and politics or the State House."

Everything has to do with politics in this town, but I let it go. "What do they pertain—No, fuck it. What do you got, Ms. Angeline?"

"I got some things in a safety-deposit box in Boston. Now, you want to find out what those things are, you come with me tomorrow when the banks open, and we'll see what you're made of."

"Why should I?" I said. "Why shouldn't I call my client right now?"

She said, "I think I know people pretty well, Mr. Kenzie. Ain't much of a talent for a poor black woman to have, but it's the only one I got. And you, well, maybe you don't mind being someone's dog every now and again, but you sure ain't nobody's bag boy."

TEN

Angie said, "Are you out of your fucking mind?" It came out in a harsh whisper. We were sitting in the alcove, looking out at the street. Jenna and Simone were in the kitchen, probably having a similar conversation.

I said, "You don't like it?"

"No," she said, "I don't like it."

"Twelve hours more or less won't make much difference."

"Bullshit. Patrick, this is retarded. We were hired to find her and call Mulkern. OK. We found her. Now, we should be making the call and going home."

"I don't think so."

"*You* don't think so?" she hissed. "How nice. Except you're not the only component in this equation. This is a partnership."

"I know it's—"

"Do you? I have a license too. Remember? You may have started the agency, but I've put my time in now too. I get shot at and beat up and sit on forty-eight-hour stakeouts too. I'm the one who had to sweat out the DA's decision whether to indict on Bobby Royce. I have a say, here. Fifty percent of one."

"And you say?"

"I say this is bullshit. I say we do what we were hired to do and go home."

"And I say…" I checked myself. "And I *ask* that you trust me on this and give me till morning. Hell, Ange, we'd end up sitting on her till then anyway. Mulkern's not going to get out of bed and drive up to Wickham at this time of night anyway."

She considered that. Her olive skin was darkened to the shade of coffee in the ill-lit alcove and her full lips were pursed tightly. She said, "Maybe. Maybe."

"Then what's the problem?" I said and started to get up.

She grabbed my wrist. "Not so fast, boy."

"What?"

"Your logic is good, Skid; it's your motives I have a problem with."

"What motives?"

"You tell me."

I sat back down, sighed. I looked at her, gave it my best "Who me?" look. "I don't see that it hurts to learn everything we can while we have the chance. That's my only motive."

She shook her head slowly, watching me steadily and with some sadness. She ran a hand through her hair, let the loose bangs fall back down on her forehead. "She's not a cat somebody left out in the rain, Patrick. She's a grown woman who committed a crime."

"I'm not so sure," I said.

"Either way it's irrelevant. We're not social workers."

"What's your point, Ange?" I said, suddenly tired.

"You're not being honest with yourself. Or me." She stood up. "We'll play it your way if you want. I can't say it'll make all that much difference. But, remember something."

"What?"

"When Jim Vurnan asked us if we'd take the job, I was willing to refuse it. You're the one who said working for Mulkern and his kind wouldn't be a problem."

I held out my hands. "And my position hasn't changed."

"I hope it hasn't, Patrick, because we're not so goddamn successful that we can afford to botch a job like this."

She walked out of the alcove, into the kitchen.

I looked at my reflection in the glass. It didn't seem too pleased with me either.

•

I pulled my car in front of the house where I could keep an eye on it from the alcove. Nothing was stolen or broken or keyed and I thanked the great auto god in the sky.

Angie came back out of the kitchen and called Phil to tell him she'd be staying overnight and it turned into an ordeal, his voice plainly audible through the receiver as he ranted on about *his* fucking needs, damnit. Angie got a blank, faraway look on her face, and she held the receiver in her lap and closed her eyes for a moment. She turned her head and opened her eyes. "You need me?"

I shook my head. "I'll see you at the office tomorrow around ten or so."

She spoke back into the phone in a voice so soft and placating that it made me nauseous, and shortly after she hung up, she was gone.

I'd checked to see that it was the only phone and bolted the back door so no one could open it without making noise. I sat in the window seat and listened to the house. Through the bedroom wall, I could hear Jenna still trying to explain our deal to Simone.

Earlier, Simone had made some squawking noises about kidnapping and federal offenses, quoting me a whole

shit-load of legal references that she learned from *L.A. Law*.
She was on something of a tear, babbling at the top of her
voice about "enforced incarceration" or some such non-
sense, when I assured her that the alternative to my handling
of the situation would be a swift legal execution of her sister's affairs by Sterling Mulkern and company. She shut up.

The voices in the bedroom died out and a few minutes
later I heard the door open and Jenna's reflection rose up
over my shoulder in the window. She was wearing an oversize T-shirt over a pair of old, gray sweatpants, and her face
was scrubbed clean of makeup. She held two cans of beer in
her hand and when I turned, she put one in my hand. She
said, "My sister made me promise to replace these."

"I'll bet."

She smiled and sat on the window seat across from
mine. "She told me to tell you to stay out of her fridge. She
don't want you touching her food."

"Understandable," I said and cracked the beer. "Maybe
I'll go in after you guys fall asleep, move things around just
to piss her off."

She took a sip of the beer. "She's a good girl, Simone.
Just really angry."

"At?"

"Who you got? The world in general, I s'pose. The white
man in particular."

"I don't suppose I'm doing much to change her impression."

"No, you're not."

She seemed almost serene, sitting there in the window,
head resting against the pane, beer in her lap. Without any
makeup, she looked younger somehow, less exhausted.
Once, she might have even been pretty, someone men com-
mented on as she walked down the street. I tried to picture

her that way—a young Jenna Angeline with a glow of confidence flushing her face because she was young and under the illusion that her youth and her beauty gave her options—but I couldn't. Time had laid too heavy a hand on her.

She said, "Your partner, she didn't seem all that pleased, either."

"She wasn't. It was all up to her, we'd have made the phone call and gone home by now."

She nodded and took another sip of the beer. She shook her head slightly. "Simone," she said, "sometimes I don't understand that girl."

"What's to understand?" I said.

"All that hate," she said. "You know?"

"There's a lot to hate out there," I said.

"I know," she said. "Believe me, I know. Seems there's so much, you got to kind of pick and choose. Earn what you hate, I guess. Simone, now, she just hate everything. And sometimes..."

"What?"

"Sometimes, I think she hate cause she don't know what else to do with herself. I mean, me, I got good reason to hate what I hate, believe me. But her, I'm not so sure she's..."

"Earned it?"

She nodded. "Exactly."

I thought about that. I couldn't see much to argue with. I've learned more about the capacity to hate than anything else since I started doing this work.

She drank some more beer. "Seems to me, the world going to give you plenty to be angry about, either way. Getting a chip on your shoulder before you've even seen how bad it can be, what the world can do to you when it really sets its mind to it...seems to me, that's just foolish thinking."

"Damn straight," I said and held up my can. She smiled, a small one, and glanced her can off mine, and I realized what part of me had known since I'd first seen her photograph: I liked her.

She finished her beer a minute or so later and went to bed with a small wave behind her as she entered the bedroom.

The night passed slowly and I shifted in my seat a lot, paced a bit back and forth, stared at my car. Angie was home now, taking another few steps in that grotesque dance of pain she called a marriage. A harsh word, a slap or two, a few screamed accusations, and on to bed until the next day. Love. I wondered again why she was with him, what possessed a person of her quality and judgment to put up with such shit, but before I slipped completely into the realms of the self-righteous, my palm rested on my abdomen, on the patch of scar tissue, which always reminded me of the price of love in its least idealized form.

Thank you, father.

Sitting in the quiet of the dark living room, I also remembered my own marriage, which had lasted about a minute and a half. Angie and Phil at least had a sense of dedication to the love between them, however twisted that love might be, which Renee and I never had. The only thing our marriage had taught me about love was that it ends. And looking out at the empty street from Simone Angeline's window seat, it occurred to me that one of the reasons I'm successful at the work I do is that come three o'clock in the morning, when most of the world is asleep, I'm still up doing my job because I don't have any place better to be.

I played some solitaire and told my stomach it wasn't

hungry. I considered raiding Simone's fridge but figured she might have booby-trapped it; I'd grab the mustard and trip a wire, take an arrow in the head.

Dawn came in a faded line of pale gold that pushed up the black cover of night, then an alarm clock went off in the next room, and soon I heard the shower running. I stretched until I heard the satisfactory crack of bones and muscles, then did my morning regimen of fifty sit-ups and fifty push-ups. By the time I'd finished, the second turn in the shower had been taken, and the two sisters were standing by the door, ready to go.

Simone said, "You take anything from my fridge?"

"No," I said, "but I think I may have mistaken it for the toilet last night. I was really tired. Do you keep vegetables in the toilet?"

She brushed past me into the kitchen. Jenna looked at me and shook her head. She said, "Bet you were real popular in the second grade."

"Good humor has no age limit," I said, and she rolled her eyes.

Simone had a job, and I'd debated all night whether I should let her go to it. In the end I figured Simone hadn't shown any homicidal tendencies toward her sister that I'd noticed, so I was pretty sure she'd keep her mouth shut.

As we stood on the porch watching her drive off, I said, "Does this Socia guy know about Simone?"

Jenna was working her way into a light cardigan even though the temperature was already on a steady cruise toward the seventies at eight in the morning. She said, "He met her. Long time ago. In Alabama."

"How long since she moved up north?"

She shrugged. "Two months."

"And Socia definitely doesn't know she's here?"

She looked at me like I was drugged. "We both be dead now, Socia knew that."

We walked to my car and Jenna looked at it as I opened the door. "Never grew up totally, did you, Kenzie?"

And I'd once thought the car would impress people.

•

The drive back was as boring as the one up. I had Pearl Jam's *Ten* playing, and if Jenna minded, she didn't say anything. She didn't talk much, period, just stared out at the road and kneaded the bottom of her cardigan with her thin fingers when they weren't occupied with a cigarette.

As we neared the city, the Hancock and Prudential buildings rising up in pale blue to greet us, she said, "Kenzie."

"Yeah."

"You ever feel needed?"

I thought about it. "Sometimes," I said.

"Who by?"

"My partner. Angie."

"You need her?"

I nodded. "Sometimes, yeah. Hell, yeah."

She looked out the window. "You best hold on to her then."

•

Rush hour was in full swing by the time we got off 93 near Haymarket, and it took us close to half an hour to move the mile up onto Tremont Street.

Jenna's safety-deposit box was in the Bank of Boston on Tremont, across from the Boston Common at the Park Street corner. The Common runs back in a mall of cement here, past two squat buildings that serve as the Park Street T-station entrances, past a gaggle of vendors and street musicians and newspaper hawkers and winos. Crowds of businessmen and women and politicians walk briskly up the walkways where the Common turns green again and rises in a slope to the steep steps that climb to Beacon Street, the State House towering overhead, its gold dome looking down on the minions.

It's impossible to park on Tremont or even idle there for more than thirty seconds. A platoon of meter maids, imported from the female Hitler Youth shortly after the fall of Berlin, roam the street, at least two to a block, pit bull faces on top of fire hydrant bodies, just waiting for someone stupid enough to stall traffic on their street. Say, "Have a nice day," to one of them and she'll have your car towed for being a smart-ass. I turned onto Hamilton Place, behind the Orpheum Theater, and parked in a loading zone. We walked the two blocks to the bank. I started to walk in with her, but she stopped me. "An old black lady going into a bank with a big young white boy. What they going to think?"

"I'm your gigolo?"

She shook her head. "They going to think you're the law, escorting the nigger who got caught doing something. Again."

I nodded. "All right."

She said, "I didn't go through all this just so I could run on you now, Kenzie. I could have climbed out a window last night, that was the case. So, whyn't you wait across the street?"

Sometimes you got to trust people.

She went in alone, and I crossed Tremont and stood near Park Street Station, in the middle of the mall, the shadow of Park Street Church's white spire falling on my face.

She wasn't in there long.

She came out, saw me, and waved. She waited for a

break in the traffic then came across the street. Her stride was full, her purse held tightly in her hand as she came across the mall. Her eyes had brightened, brown marble with flames glowing in the center, and she looked much younger than the picture I'd been given.

She came up close to me and said, "What I got here is a little part of it."

I said, "Jenna—"

"No, no," she said. "It's something, believe me. You'll see." She glanced up at the State House, then looked back at me. "You prove you're ready to help me on this, show what side you're on, and I give you the rest. I give you…" Her eyes lost their fire and filled; her voice stuck like a worn clutch. "I give you…the rest," she managed. I hadn't known her for more than twelve hours, but I had the feeling that whatever "the rest" was, it was bad. Tearing her apart from the inside out.

She smiled then, a nice soft one, and touched her hand to my face. She said, "I think we're going to turn out all right, Kenzie. Maybe the two of us get some justice while we're at it." The word "justice" came off her tongue as if she were trying to taste it.

I said, "We'll see, Jenna."

She reached into her purse and handed me a manila envelope. I opened it and extracted an eight-by-eleven black-and-white photograph. It was slightly grainy, as if it had been transferred from another type of film, but it was clear. There were two men in the photograph, standing by a cheap chest and mirror, drinks in their hands. One of them was black, the other, white. The black guy I didn't know. The white guy was wearing a pair of boxer shorts and black socks. His hair was brown, the gray that would consume it in a tin sheath, still a few years off. He was smiling tiredly, and the picture seemed old enough that possibly he'd only been Congressman Paulson at that point.

I said, "Who's the black guy?"

She looked at me and I could tell she was sizing me up. The wet ass hour, as it were, deciding if she could trust me. I felt like we were in a pocket—the crowds of people hurrying past us, not really there but existing on a matte screen behind us, like in an old movie.

Jenna said, "What're you in this for?"

I was considering my answer when something familiar moved out of the screen to our right, heading for our pocket, and I recognized it as if I was underwater—a blue baseball cap with yellow stitching.

I said, "Get down," and had my hand on Jenna's shoulder when Blue Cap set himself into his stance and a hammering metallic chatter drilled the morning air. The first burst of bullets slammed through the front of Jenna's chest as if it wasn't there, and I ducked as they blew past my head, still trying to pull her down as her chest jerked forward at all sorts of angles. Blue Cap had his finger pulled back on the trigger and the gun at full auto, the metal stitching slicing from Jenna's body to the cement, coming around in an arc for me. The crowd in the mall had turned into a stampede, and as I cleared my gun from its holster, someone trampled my ankle. Jenna's body crashed down on top of mine, and cement chips shot off the ground into my face. He was firing more methodically now, trying to get around Jenna's body to hit mine. In a moment, he'd just begin firing into her body again, and the bullets would pass through it as if it were paper and punch their way into mine.

Through the blood in my eyes, I could see him raising the Uzi up over his head, then bending it in at an angle, the muzzle a white flame. The line of bullets jackhammered toward my forehead and stopped suddenly in a white cloud of cement dust. The slim clip dropped from the gun toward the pavement and he had another one slammed home before it hit the ground. He pulled back on the bolt and I leaned out from under Jenna's body and fired.

The magnum went off with a harsh *whoomp* and he flipped into the air sideways as if he'd been broadsided by a truck. He came back down onto the pavement and bounced, the gun skittering out of his hand. I rolled Jenna off me, wiped her blood from my eyes, and watched him try to crawl to his Uzi. It was eight feet away and he was having a hard time covering the distance because his left ankle was almost completely obliterated.

I walked over and kicked him in the face. Hard. He groaned and I kicked him again, and he went out.

I crossed back to Jenna and sat on the cement in a growing puddle of her blood. I lifted her off the pavement and held her in my arms. Her chest was gone and so was she. No last words, just death, splayed out like a broken doll at the edge of the Boston Common at the beginning of a new day. Her legs were askew, and the curious vultures were coming back for a second look now that the shooting was over.

I pulled her legs together and tucked them under her. I looked at her face. It told me nothing. Another death. The more I see, the less I know.

No one needed Jenna Angeline anymore.

ELEVEN

LIKE THE HERO, I MADE THE FRONT PAGE OF BOTH newspapers. Some rookie photographer was in the crowd when the shooting started, and once he'd cleaned the mess out of his underpants, he came back.

I'd walked back to Blue Cap by this time and picked up his Uzi by the sling. I slid it over my shoulder and squatted down beside him, my head down, magnum in my hand. That's when the photographer took his shots. I never noticed him. One shot showed me squatting by Blue Cap, a strip of green and the State House beyond us. In the extreme right foreground, almost out of focus, was Jenna's corpse. You could barely notice her.

The *Trib* carried it in the bottom left corner of page one, but the *News* plastered it completely over the front page with a hysterical black headline across the Statehouse— HERO P.I. IN MORNING GUNFIGHT!!! How they could print "hero" with Jenna's corpse lying in plain view was just beyond me. I guess LOSER P.I. IN MORNING GUNFIGHT didn't have the same ring.

The police showed up around that time and hustled the photographer behind a hastily set up sawhorse. They took my gun and the Uzi and gave me a cup of coffee and we went over it. And over it.

An hour later I was at headquarters on Berkeley Street and they were deciding whether to book me or not. They read me my rights in English and Spanish while they figured out what to do.

I know quite a few cops, but none I recognized seemed to be taking part in this investigation. The two guys who had been assigned to me looked like Simon and Garfunkel on a bad day. Simon's name was Detective Geilston, and he was short, neatly dressed in dark burgundy pleated trousers, a light blue oxford with a roll in the collar and cream criss-cross stripes. He wore a burgundy tie with a subtle blue diamond pattern. He looked like he had a wife and kids and CD accounts. He was Good Cop.

Bad Cop was Garfunkel, or Detective Ferry as they called him around the station. He was tall and lanky and wore a drab brown two-piece suit that was too short in the arms and legs. Underneath he wore a wrinkled white shirt and a dark brown knit tie. Mr. Fashion. His hair was strawberry blond, but a wide bare patch ran up the middle now and the bushy remains shot out from the sides of his head like a cleaved afro.

They'd both been friendly enough at the crime scene—giving me cups of coffee and telling me to take my time, take it slow, relax—but Ferry started getting more and more pissed off the more I kept answering his questions with, "I don't know." He got downright nasty when I refused to tell him who had hired me or exactly what I was doing with the deceased. Since I hadn't been booked yet, the photograph was folded and tucked into the ankle of one of my high-tops. I had a feeling what would happen if I gave it up—a formal inquiry, maybe a few nasty details about Senator

Paulson's lifestyle, maybe nothing at all. But definitely no arrests, no justice, no public acknowledgment of a dead cleaning lady who'd only wanted to be needed.

If you're a private detective, it helps to be nice to cops. They help you out from time to time and vice versa and that's how you build contacts and keep business thriving. But I don't tolerate animosity very well, especially when my clothes are saturated with someone else's blood and I haven't eaten or slept in twenty-four hours. Ferry was standing with one foot on the chair beside me in the interrogation room, telling me what was going to happen to my license if I didn't start "playing ball."

I said, "'Playing ball'? What, do you guys have a police cliché manual or something? Which one of you says, 'Book him, Danno'?"

For the thirtieth time that morning Ferry sighed deeply through his nostrils and said, "What were you doing with Jenna Angeline?"

For the fiftieth time that morning, I said, "No comment," and turned my head as Cheswick Hartman walked through the door.

Cheswick is everything you could want in an attorney. He's staggeringly handsome, with rich chestnut hair combed straight back off his forehead. He wears eighteen-hundred-dollar custom-made suits from Louis and he rarely wears the same one twice. His voice is deep and smooth like twelve-year-old malt and he has this annoyed look that he gets just before he buries an opponent with a barrage of Latin phrases and flawless elocution. Plus, he has a really nifty name.

Under normal circumstances, I'd have to have won the lottery to afford Cheswick's retainer, but a few years ago, just when he was being considered for partnership in his firm, his sister, Elise—a sophomore at Yale—developed a cocaine problem. Cheswick controlled her trust fund, and by the time Elise's addiction had blossomed into an eight-ball-a-day habit, she'd depleted her yearly allowance and still owed several thousand more to some men in Connecticut. Rather than tell Cheswick and risk his disappointment, she made an arrangement with the men in Connecticut, and some pictures were taken.

One day Cheswick got a phone call. The caller described the photos and promised they'd be on the desk of the firm's senior partner by the following Monday if Cheswick didn't come up with a high five-figure sum by the end of the week. Cheswick was livid. It wasn't the money that bothered him—his family fortune was huge—it was the advantage they'd taken of both his sister's problem and his love for her. So concerned was he for his sister that not once during our first meeting did I get the feeling it was the jeopardy to his job that angered him, and I admired that.

Cheswick got my name from a guy he knew in legal aid, and gave me the money to deliver with the express demand that I bring back all photos and negatives, and an absolute assurance that this would stop here and now. Elise's debt, I was to tell these men, was paid in full.

For reasons I can't even remember anymore, I brought Bubba along for the ride when I went down to Connecticut. After finding out that the blackmailers were a rogue group with no connections, no real muscle, and absolutely no juice with any politicians, we met two of them in a Hartford high-rise. Bubba held one guy by his ankles out a twelfth floor window while I negotiated with the guy's partner. By the time Bubba's victim had voided himself, his partner had decided that yes, one dollar was a very fair settlement price. I paid him in pennies.

Cheswick has been returning the favor to me by representing me gratis ever since.

He raised his eyebrows at the blood on my clothes. Very quietly he said, "I'd like a moment alone with my client, please."

Ferry crossed his arms and leaned in toward me. "So fucking what," he said.

Cheswick yanked the seat out from under Ferry's foot. "So fucking get out of the room now, *Detective*, or I'll slap this department with enough false arrest, harassment, and unlawful detainment citations to keep you in court until long after you've reached your twenty." He looked at me. "Have you been Mirandized?"

"Yes."

"Of course he's been fucking Mirandized," Ferry said.

"You're still here?" Cheswick said, reaching into his briefcase.

Geilston said, "Come on, partner."

Ferry said, "Hell no. Just because—"

Cheswick was looking at the both of them flatly, and Geilston had his hand on Ferry's arm. He said, "We don't mess with this, Ferry."

Cheswick said, "Listen to your partner, Detective."

Ferry said, "We'll meet again." Professor Moriarty to Sherlock Holmes.

Cheswick said, "At your inquest, no doubt. Start saving now, Detective. I'm expensive."

Geilston gave one last tug on Ferry's arm and they left the room.

I said, "What's up?" expecting he had something private to tell me.

"Oh, nothing," he said. "I just do that to show them who's boss. It gives me a woody."

"Swell."

He looked at my face, at the blood. "You're not having a good day, are you?"

I shook my head slowly.

His voice lost its levity. "Are you all right? Really? I've heard snippets of what happened, but not much."

"I just want to go home, Cheswick. I'm tired and I got blood all over me, and I'm hungry, and I'm not in the best of moods."

He patted my arm. "Well, I have good news from the DA then. From everything he's heard, they have nothing to charge you with. You are to consider yourself released pending further investigation, don't take any sudden trips, blah, blah, blah."

"My gun?"

"They keep that, I'm afraid. Ballistic tests, etcetera."

I nodded. "Figures. Can we leave now?"

"We're gone," he said.

•

He took me out the back entrance to avoid the press, and that's when he told me about the photographer. "I confirmed it with the captain. The man definitely took pictures of you. He strings for both papers in town."

I said, "I saw them hustling him out of there, but it didn't register."

We walked through the parking lot toward his car. His hand was on my back, as if he were ready to run interference for me or simply to hold me up. I wasn't sure which. He said, "Are you OK, Patrick? You may want to stop at Mass. General, have yourself checked out."

"I'm fine. What about the photographer?"

"You'll be on the front page of the *News* late edition, which should be coming out any minute now. I hear the *Trib* picked it up too. The papers love this sort of thing. Hero detective, a morning—"

"I'm no hero," I said. "That's my father."

•

We drove through the city in Cheswick's Lexus. It seemed strange, everyone going about their business. I'd half expected time to have stopped, everyone frozen in place, holding their breath, awaiting further news. But people ate lunch, made phone calls, canceled dentist appointments, got their hair cut, made dinner plans, worked their jobs.

Cheswick and I argued about my ability to drive in my present state, but in the end he dropped me back at Hamilton Place and told me to call him day or night on his private line if I required his services. He drove up Tremont, and I stood outside my car, ignored the ticket on the windshield, and looked at the Common.

In the four hours since it had happened, everything had gone back to normal. The barricades had been taken away, all the questions asked, all the witnesses' names written down. Blue Cap had been lifted into an ambulance and driven off. They'd rolled Jenna into a body bag and zipped it up, carted her off to the morgue.

Then someone had come along and hosed the blood off the cement until everything was clean again.

I took one last look and drove home.

TWELVE

When I got home, I called Angie across the street. "You heard?"

"Yes." Her voice was small and quiet. "I called Cheswick Hartman. Did he—?"

"Yeah. Thanks. Look, I'm going to take a shower, get into some clean clothes, eat a sandwich. Then I'll be over. Any calls?"

"A ton," she said. "But they'll keep. Patrick, are you OK?"

"No," I said, "but I'm working on it. I'll see you in an hour."

The shower was hot and I kept turning it hotter, the jet blast pounding into the top of my head, water pellets drumming against my skull. No matter how lapsed, I'm still sort of Catholic, and my reactions to pain and guilt are all tied up with words like "scalding" and "purge" and "white-hot." In some theological equation of my own making, heat = salvation.

I stepped out after twenty minutes or so and dried slowly, my nostrils still thick with the clogging scent of blood and the bitter aroma of cordite. Somewhere in all the shower steam, I told myself, was the answer, the relief, the purchase necessary to turn the next corner and get past all this. But the steam cleared, and nothing remained but me and my bathroom and the smell of something burning.

I wrapped the towel around my waist and entered the kitchen and saw Angie blackening a steak on my stove. Angie cooks about once every leap year and never with any success. If it was up to her, she'd trade in her kitchen for a take-out counter.

I instinctively hitched the towel up over my scar and came up behind her and reached around her waist to shut off the burner. She turned in my arms, her chest against mine, and I guess it's the consummate declaration of my state of mind that I stepped around her and checked the rest of the oven for damage.

She said, "What'd I do wrong?"

"I think your first mistake was turning on the stove."

She slapped the back of my head. "See the next time I cook for *you*."

"And they say Christmas comes only once a year." I turned from the stove and saw her watching me the way you watch a baby walking on the edge of a swimming pool. I said, "Thank you for the gesture. Really."

She shrugged, continued staring at me, those caramel eyes warm and slightly damp. "You need a hug, Patrick?"

I said, "God, yes."

She felt like everything good. She felt like the first warm gust of spring and Saturday afternoons when you're ten years old and early summer evenings on the beach when the sand is cool and the waves are colored scotch. Her grip was fierce, her body full and soft, and her heart beat rapidly against my bare chest. I could smell her shampoo and feel the downy nape of her neck against my chin.

I stepped back first. I said, "Well..."

She laughed. "Well…" She said, "You're all wet, Skid. My shirt's soaked now." She took a step back.

"Happens sometimes when you take a shower."

She took another step back, looked down at the floor. "Yeah, well…," she said again, "you have a pile of messages over there. And…" She stepped past me, picked up the steak, and carried it toward the garbage. "And…and I still can't cook, obviously."

I said, "Angie."

She kept her back to me. "You almost died this morning."

"Ange—"

"And I'm very sorry about Jenna, but you almost died."

"Yes."

"I wouldn't have…" Her voice cracked and I could hear her inhale until she got it under control. "And I wouldn't have handled it very fucking well, Patrick. I don't like thinking about it, and it's got me a little…off, right now."

I heard Jenna's voice in my head when I told her Angie needed me. "You best hold on to her then." I took a few steps across the floor and put my hands on her arms.

She tilted her head back so that it nestled under my chin.

The air seemed impossibly still in the kitchen and I don't think either of us took a breath. We stood there, our eyes closed, waiting for the fear to go away.

It didn't.

Angie's head left my chin and she said, "Let's get past this. Do some work. We're still employed, right?"

I let go of her arms and said, "Yeah, we're still employed. Let me change and we'll get to work."

I came back out a few minutes later in an oversize red sweatshirt and a pair of jeans.

Angie turned from the kitchen counter, a plate in her hand, a sandwich on it. "I think I'm safe around deli meat."

"Didn't try to cook it or anything, did you?"

She gave me that look.

I got the point and took the sandwich. She sat across the table from me as I ate. Ham and cheese. A little heavy on the mustard, but otherwise fine. I said, "Who called?"

"Sterling Mulkern's office. Three times. Jim Vurnan's office. Richie Colgan. Twice. Twelve or thirteen reporters. Also, Bubba called."

"What'd he have to say?"

"You really want to know?"

Usually one doesn't with Bubba, but I was feeling loose. I nodded.

"He said to call him next time you go 'a coon hunting.'"

That Bubba. Hitler might have won the war with Bubba at his side. I said, "Anyone else?"

"No. But Mulkern's office sounded pretty pissed off by the third call."

I nodded and chewed.

Angie said, "You going to tell me what we're into here, or you just going to sit there and do your village idiot impersonation?"

I shrugged, chewed some more, and she took the sandwich away from me. "I believe I've been chastised," I said.

"You'll be a lot worse than that, you don't start talking."

"Ooooh. Tough girl. Scold me some more," I panted.

She looked at me.

"All right," I said. "But we're going to need liquor for this."

I made us two scotches neat. Angie took one sip of hers and poured it down the sink without a word. She grabbed a beer from the fridge, sat back down, and raised an eyebrow.

I said, "We may be in over our heads on this one. Way over our heads."

"So I gathered. Why?"

"Jenna didn't have any documents that I saw. That was bullshit."

"Which you half-figured."

"True," I said, "but I didn't think it would be too far off the mark. I don't know what I thought she had, but I didn't think it was this." I handed her the photo of Paulson in his skivvies.

She raised her eyebrows. "OK," she said slowly, "but still, so what? This picture's, like, six or eight years old, and all it shows is Paulson, half-dressed. However unappetizing, it's not news. Not worth killing over."

"Maybe," I said. "Look at the guy with Paulson, though. He doesn't look like he runs in the same circles exactly."

She looked at the guy. He was slim, wearing a blue crew-neck shirt over a pair of white trousers. He wore a lot of gold—on his wrists, his neck—and his hair looked simulta-neously matted and flyaway. His eyes were all sullen re-proach, those of the terminally angry. He looked to be about thirty-five.

"No, he doesn't," she said. "We know him?"

I shook my head. "He could be Socia. He could be Roland. He could be neither. But he definitely doesn't look like a state rep."

"He looks like a pimp."

"That too." I pointed to the cheap chest and mirror in the photo. Reflected in the mirror was a bed, unmade. Beyond that, the corner of a door. On the door were two square pieces of paper. I couldn't make out what they said, but one looked like the rules and regulations of a motel, and the smaller one below it looked like a check-in, check-out time reminder. A Do-Not-Disturb sign hung from the door-knob. "And this looks like..."

"A motel," she said.

"Ver-ry good," I said. "You should be a detective."

"You should stop impersonating one," she said and flipped the photo back on the table. "So, what's all this mean, Sherlock?"

"You tell me, Spanky."

She lit a cigarette and sipped her beer and thought about it.

"These photos might be the tip of the iceberg. Maybe there're more of them, and they're a lot worse. Someone, either Socia or Roland or—dare I say it?—someone in the political machine had Jenna eliminated because they knew she'd blow the whistle on whatever it is. That what you're thinking?"

"That's what I'm thinking."

"Well," she said, "either they're really dumb, or you are."

"Why's that?"

"Jenna had the pictures in her safety-deposit box, cor-rect?"

I nodded.

"And when someone is murdered, standard police pro-cedure is to get a court warrant and open every can of worms the victim had in her pantry. Of which, the safety-deposit box is definitely one. I assume they've already fig-ured the bank was the last place before she..."

"Died," I said.

"Yes. So, they're probably on their way down to open it as we speak. And anyone with half a brain could have fore-seen that."

"Maybe they figured she'd taken everything out of there and given it to me."

"Maybe," she said. "But that's leaving an awful lot to chance. Don't you think? Unless, somehow, they were positive that she wasn't going to leave anything behind in there."

"How would they know?"

She shrugged. "You're a detective. Detect."

"I'm trying."

"Something else," she said, putting her beer down, sitting up.

"Pray tell."

"How'd they know you were going to be there this morning?"

I hadn't given it much thought. "Blue Cap," I said.

She shook her head. "We lost Blue Cap yesterday. I mean, I don't know about you, but I don't think he was hanging around on the interstate this morning, waiting to spot you driving by in a car he doesn't even know you own. *Then* he tailed you to the Common? Uh-uh. I don't buy it."

"Only two people knew where Jenna and I were going this morning."

"Damn right," she said. "And I'm one of them."

THIRTEEN

SIMONE ANGELINE'S EYES WERE RINGED WITH RED ON THE other side of the chain, and fresh tears welled in her sockets. Her hair was matted to one side of her face and she looked like she'd skipped a few decades and turned seventy when no one was looking. Her teeth gritted when she saw us. "You get the fuck off my porch."

I said, "OK," and kicked the door in.

Angie came in behind me as Simone made a scramble for the small telephone desk in the alcove. She wasn't going for the phone. She was going for the drawer underneath, and as she opened it, I put my hand behind the desk and brought the whole thing toppling down on top of her. The contents of the drawer—a small red phone book, some pens, and a .22 target pistol—bounced off her head on their way to the floor. I kicked the gun under the bookcase and grabbed Simone by the front of her shirt and dragged her over to the couch.

Angie closed the door behind her.

Simone spat in my face. "You killed my sister."

I slammed her back against the couch and wiped the spittle off my chin. Very slowly I said, "I failed to protect your sister. There's a difference. Someone else pulled the trigger, and you put the gun in his hand. Didn't you?"

She bucked against my hand and clawed at my face. "No! You killed her."

I pushed her back again and knelt on her hands. I whispered in her ear, "The bullets came through Jenna's chest like it wasn't there, Simone. Like it wasn't fucking there. She had so much blood coming out of her body that just the small percentage that got on me was enough to make the cops think I'd been shot. She died screaming in the middle of the morning with her legs spread out in front of her while a crowd of people watched, and the motherfucker who pulled the trigger used a whole clip on her and didn't so much as blink."

She was trying to head-butt me now, rocking forward on the couch as much as she could manage with my 180 pounds on top of her. "You goddamned bastard."

"That's right," I said, my mouth still a half inch from her ear. "That's right. I'm a bastard, Simone. I held your sister in my lap while she died and there wasn't a damn thing I could do about it, and I earned the right to be a bastard. But, you, you don't have any excuse. You picked her execution spot and stayed out here, sixty miles away, while she screamed her final breath. You told them where she was going and you let them kill her. Didn't you, Simone?"

She blinked.

I screamed, "Didn't you?"

Her eyes rolled back in her head for a moment and then her head dropped, the sobs tearing out of her as if someone was reaching in there and pulling them out. I stepped back because there was nothing left of her now. The sobs grew louder, gasping wracks from her heaving chest. She balled into a fetal position and banged her fists against the arm of the couch, and every time the sobs seemed to have subsided they picked up again, only louder, as if each breath pierced her like something heavy and sharp.

Angie touched my elbow, but I shrugged it off. Patrick Kenzie, great detective, able to terrorize a near-catatonic woman into hysterics. What a guy. For an encore, maybe I'd go back home and mug a nun.

Simone turned on her side, her eyes closed, speaking with half her mouth still buried in the couch. "You were working for *them*. I told Jenna she was a fool, trusting you and those fat white politicians. Ain't one of them ever gave a damn for a nigger, ain't one of them ever will. I figured as…as soon as you got what you wanted from her, you'd…"

"Kill her," I said.

Her head stretched out onto the arm and gagging sounds emanated from her throat. After a few minutes, she said, "I called him, because I figured no man could…"

"Who'd you call?" Angie said. "Socia? Was it Socia?"

She shook her head a few times, then nodded. "He…he said he'd take care of it, talk some sense into her fool head. That's all. I figured no man could do…that to his wife."

His wife?

She looked at me. "She never could have won. Not against all them. Not her. She…couldn't."

I sat on the floor beside the couch and held up the photograph. "Is this Socia?"

She looked at it long enough to nod, then buried her head back in the couch.

Angie said, "Simone, where's the rest of it? Is it in the safety-deposit box?"

Simone shook her head.

"Then where is it?" I said.

"She wouldn't tell me. She just said, 'In a safe place.' She said she put just the one picture in the safety-deposit box to throw them off the scent, case they ever follow her there."

I said, "What else is there, Simone? Do you know?"

She said, "Jenna said they were 'bad things.' That's all she'd say. She'd get all tight lipped and antsy if I asked her about it. Whatever it was, it shook her up every time she talked about it." She raised her head and looked past my shoulder as if someone stood behind me. She said, "Jenna?" and began sobbing again.

She was trembling violently and I didn't think she had much left in her. I'd done my damage, and she'd do the rest to herself in the days and years ahead. So, I let my anger go, let it flush out of my heart and body until all I saw before me was a trembling heap of humanity on a sofa. I reached out and touched her shoulder.

She screamed. "Don't you fucking touch me!"

I pulled the hand back.

"Get the hell off my floor and the hell out of my house, white man, and take your whore with you."

Angie took a step toward her on the word "whore," then stopped and closed her eyes for a second, then opened them. She looked at me and nodded.

There wasn't anything else to say, so we left.

FOURTEEN

WE WERE HALFWAY BACK TO BOSTON, AVOIDING ANY conversation about Simone Angeline or the scene in her apartment, when Angie sat up suddenly in her seat and said, "Aargghh," or a reasonable facsimile. She stabbed her index finger into the eject button of my cassette player hard enough to send *Exile on Main St.* past me like a missile. It bounced off the back of the seat and fell to the floor. Right in the middle of "Shine a Light," too. Sacrilege.

I said, "Pick it up."

She did and flipped it onto the seat beside my hip. She said, "Don't you have any New Music?" New Music, I guess, is all those bands Angie listens to. They have names like Depeche Mode and The Smiths and they all sound the same to me—like a bunch of skinny white British nerds on Thorazine. The Stones, when they started, were a bunch of skinny white British nerds too, but they never sounded like they were on Thorazine. Even if they were.

Angie was looking through my cassette case. I said, "Try the Lou Reed. More your style."

After putting in *New York*, listening for five minutes, she said, "This is all right. What, you buy it by mistake?"

Just outside the city limits, I pulled into a Store 24 and Angie went in for cigarettes. She came out with two late editions of the *News* and handed me a copy.

That's how I confirmed that I'd become the second generation of Kenzie to achieve a sort of immortality in newsprint. I'd always be there, frozen in time and black-and-white on June 30, for anyone who wished to access the file on a microfiche. And that moment, that most personal of moments—squatting by Blue Cap with Jenna's corpse behind me, my ears ringing and my brain trying to re-anchor in my skull—none of it was completely mine anymore. It had been spat out for the breakfast consumption of hundreds of thousands of people who didn't know me from Adam. Possibly the most intensely personal moment of my life and it would be rehashed and second-guessed by everyone from a barfly in Southie to two stockbrokers riding the elevator in some skyscraper downtown. The Global Village Principle at work, and I didn't like it one bit.

But I did finally learn Blue Cap's name. Curtis Moore. He was listed in critical condition at Boston City and doctors were said to be working frantically to save his foot. He was eighteen years old and a reputed member of the Raven Saints, a gang that ran out of the Raven Boulevard Projects in Roxbury and favored New Orleans Saints baseball caps and team memorabilia. His mother was pictured on page three, holding a framed photograph of him when he was ten years old. She was quoted as saying, "Curtis never ran with no gang. Never did nothing wrong." She demanded an investigation, said the whole thing was "racially motivated." She managed to compare it to the Charles Stuart case, of course, in which the DA and just about everyone else had believed Charles Stuart's story that a black guy had killed his wife. They'd arrested a black guy, and possibly would have sent him up if the insurance policy Stuart had taken out on his wife hadn't finally raised a few eyebrows. And when Chuck Stuart took a 9.5 swan dive off the Mystic River bridge, it pretty much confirmed what a lot of people had already thought was obvious in the first place. Shooting Curtis Moore had about as much in common with the Stuart case as Howard Beach has in common with Miami Beach, but there wasn't much I could do about it standing outside a Store 24.

Angie snorted loudly and I knew she was reading the same article. I said, "Lemme guess—the 'racially motivated' line."

She nodded. "The nerve of you, shoving that Uzi into that poor boy's hand and forcing him to pull the trigger."

"I don't know what comes over me sometimes."

"You should have tried to talk with him, Patrick. Told him you understood the life of deprivation that put that gun in his hand."

"I'm such a prick that way." I tossed the paper in the backseat and got behind the wheel and headed into the city. Angie kept looking at her copy in the dim light and breathing heavily through her nostrils. Eventually, she bunched it in her hand and threw it on the floor.

She said, "How can they look at themselves in the mirror?"

"Who?"

"People who say such...shit. 'Racially motivated.' Please. 'Curtis never ran with no gang.'" She looked down at the paper and spoke to the picture of Curtis's mother. "Well he wasn't out till three A.M. every night with the fucking Boy Scouts, lady."

I patted her shoulder. "Calm down."

"It's bullshit," she said.

"It's a mother," I said. "Say anything in the world to protect her child. Can't blame her."

"Oh, no?" she said. "Then, why bring race into it if all she wants to do is protect her child? What's next—Al Sharpton going to come to town, hold a vigil for Curtis's foot? Pin Jenna's death on the white man too?"

She was sounding off. Reactionary white rage. I hear more of it lately. A lot more of it. I've said similar things on occasion myself. You hear it most among the poor and working class. You hear it when brain-dead sociologists call incidents like the wilding attack in Central Park a result of "uncontrollable" impulses, and defend the actions of a group of animals with the argument that they were only reacting to years of white oppression. And if you point out that those nice, well-bred animals—who happen to be black—probably would have controlled those actions just fine if they'd thought that female jogger was protected by an army of her own, you're labeled a racist. You hear it when the media make a point out of race. You hear it when a bunch of possibly well-intentioned whites get together to sort it all out and end up saying, "I'm no racist *but...*" You hear it when judges who forcibly desegregate public schools with bussing put their own children in private schools, or when, recently, a circuit court judge said he'd never seen evidence to suggest that street gangs were any more dangerous than labor unions.

You hear it most when politicians who live in places like Hyannis Port and Beacon Hill and Wellesley make decisions that affect people who live in Dorchester and Roxbury and Jamaica Plain, and then step back and say there isn't a war going on.

There is a war going on. It's happening in playgrounds, not health clubs. It's fought on cement, not lawns. It's fought with pipes and bottles, and lately, automatic weapons. And as long as it doesn't push through the heavy oak doors where they fight with prep school educations and filibusters and two-martini lunches, it will never actually exist.

South Central L.A. could burn for a decade, and most people wouldn't smell the smoke unless the flames reached Rodeo Drive.

I wanted to sort this out. Now. To wade through it all, in the car with Angie, until our places in this war were clearly defined, until we knew exactly where we stood on every issue, until we could look into our hearts and be satisfied with what we saw there. But I feel this way a lot, and everything always ends up in circles, coming back to me with nothing solved.

I said, "What're you going to do, right?" and pulled to the curb in front of her house.

She looked at the front page of the paper, at Jenna's body. She said, "I can tell Phil we're working late."

"I'm fine," I said.

"No, you're not."

I half laughed. "No, I'm not. But you can't come into my dreams with me, protect me there. So, otherwise, I can handle it."

She was out of the car now, and she leaned back in and kissed my cheek. "Be well, Skid."

I watched her climb the stairs to her porch, fumble with her keys, then open the door. Before she got inside, a light went on in the living room and the curtain parted slightly. I waved at Phil, and the curtain fluttered closed again.

Angie entered her home and shut off the light in the hallway and I drove off.

•

The light was on in the belfry. I pulled to the curb in

front of the church and walked around to the side door, acutely aware of the fact that my gun was sitting in the police-station evidence room. There was a note on the floor as I entered: "Don't shoot. Two black men in one day will give you a bad rep."

Richie.

He was sitting behind my desk when I entered. He had his feet up and a Peter Gabriel tape going on my boom box, a bottle of Glenlivet on the desk and a glass in his hand. I said, "Is that my bottle?"

He looked at it. "I believe so, son."

"Well, help yourself," I said.

"Thank you," he said and poured another shot into his glass. "You need ice."

I found a glass in my drawer, made a double. I held up the paper. "Seen it?"

"I don't read that rag," he said. Then, "Yeah, I saw it."

Richie is not one of those Hollywood blacks with skin like coffee regular and Billy Dee Williams eyes. He's black, black as an oil slick, and he's not what one would call handsome. He's overweight, always has a five o'clock shadow, and his wife buys his clothes. A lot of times, his ensemble looks like she's experimenting again. Tonight he was wearing beige cotton trousers, a light blue shirt, and a pastel tie that looked like a poppy field had exploded on it and someone had doused the flame with rum punch. I said, "Sherilynn went shopping again?"

He looked at the tie and sighed. "Sherilynn went shopping again."

I said. "Where? Miami?"

He lifted the tie for closer inspection. "You'd think so, wouldn't you?" He sipped his scotch. "Where's your partner?"

"With her husband."

He nodded, and simultaneously, we said, "The Asshole."

"When's she going to pump a round into that boy?" he asked.

"I've got my fingers crossed."

"Well, you call me when she does. I got a bottle of Moët sitting at home for the occasion."

"To that day." I held up my glass. He met it. "Cheers." I said, "Tell me about Curtis Moore."

"Gimpy?" he said. "That's what we're calling ol' Curtis these days. Brings a tear to your eye, doesn't it?" He stretched back in the chair.

"Tragic," I said.

"It's too bad," he said. "Don't take it too lightly, though. Curtis's friends might come looking for you and they are particularly heinous motherfuckers."

"How big are the Raven Saints?"

"Not big by L.A. standards," he said, "but this ain't L.A. I'd say they got seventy-five hardcore and another sixty or so peripheral."

"So what you're saying is I got a hundred thirty-five black guys to be wary of."

He put his glass down on the desk. "Don't turn this into a 'black thing,' Kenzie."

"My friends call me Patrick."

"I'm not your friend when I hear shit like that come out of your mouth."

I was angry and damned tired, and I wanted someone to blame. My emotions were running hard along open nerve endings that stopped just short of breaking my skin, and I was feeling stubborn. I said, "Tell me about a white gang that runs around with Uzis and I'll be afraid of white people too, Richie. But until then—"

Richie banged his fist down on the desk. "The fuck you call the Mafia? Huh?" He stood up and the veins in his neck were thick, poking out as hard as I figured mine were. "The Westies in New York," he said, "those nice boys, Irish like yourself, who specialized in murder and torture and cowboy bullshit. What color were they? You going to sit there and tell me the brothers invented murder too? You going to try and pass that shit off on me, Kenzie?"

Our voices were loud in the tiny room, hoarse, slipping under the cheap walls and reverberating. I tried to talk calmly, but my voice didn't come out that way; it sounded harsh and slightly alien. I said, "Richie, one kid gets hit by a car because a bunch of retard Hitler Youth chase him into the road in Howard Beach—"

"Don't you *even* bring up Howard Beach."

"—and it gets treated like a national tragedy. Which it is. But," I said, "a white kid in Fenway gets stabbed *eighteen* times by black kids, and no one says a goddamn thing. 'Racial' never comes into it. It's off the front page the next day, and it's filed as homicide. *No* racial incident. You tell me, Richie, what the fuck is that?"

He was staring at me, holding his hand a foot in front of him, then moving it to his head where it massaged his neck, then down onto the desk, where he looked at it, not sure what to do with it. He started to speak a couple of times. Stopped. Eventually, he said quietly, but almost in a hiss, "Those three black kids killed the white boy, you think they'll do hard time?"

He had me there.

"Huh?" he said. "Come on. Tell the truth."

I said, "Of course. Unless they get a good lawyer, get—"

"No. No lawyers. No technicality bullshit. If they go to

trial and it reaches jury, will they be convicted? Will they end up doing twenty to life, maybe worse?"

"Yeah," I said. "Yeah, they will."

"And if some white guys killed a black guy and it wasn't, let's pretend, called a racial incident, if it wasn't considered a tragedy, what then?"

I nodded.

"What then?"

"There's a better chance they'd get off."

"Damn right," he said and dropped back into the chair.

"But, Richie," I said, "that sort of logic is beyond the average guy on the street, and you know it. Joe from Southie sees a black death turned into a racial incident, then sees an identical white death called a homicide, and he says, 'Hey that ain't right. That's hypocritical. That's a double standard.' He hears about Tawana Brawley, and loses his job to affirmative action, and he gets pissed off." I looked at him. "Can you blame him?"

He ran his hand through his hair and sighed. "Aww, shit, Patrick. I don't know." He sat up. "No, OK? I can't blame the guy. But what's the alternative?"

I poured myself another shot. "It ain't Louis Farrakhan."

"And it ain't David Duke," he shot back. "I mean, what—we're supposed to do away with affirmative action quotas, minority grants, racial incident cases?"

I pointed the bottle at him and he leaned forward with his glass. "No," I said, pouring his drink, "but…" I leaned back. "Damnit, I don't know."

He half smiled and leaned back in the chair again, looking out the window. The Peter Gabriel tape had ended and from the street came the sound of the occasional car scooping up air as it hummed past on the asphalt. The breeze coming through the screen had cooled and as it drifted into the room, I felt the weight of the atmosphere dissipating. Somewhat anyway.

"Know what the American way is?" Richie asked, still looking out the window, his elbow up, drink poised halfway to his mouth.

I could feel the anger in the room beginning to fuse with the slow rush of scotch in my blood, dissolving in the liquor's undertow. I said, "No, Rich. What's the American way?"

"Finding someone to blame," he said and took a drink. "It's true. You out working a construction job and you drop a hammer on your foot? Hell, sue the company. That's a ten-thousand-dollar foot. You're white and you can't get a job? Blame affirmative action. Can't get one and you're black? Blame the white man. Or the Koreans. Hell, blame the Japanese; everyone else does. Fucking whole country's filled with nasty, unhappy, confused, pissed-off people, and not one of them with the brain power to honestly *deal* with their situation. They talk about simpler times—before there was AIDS and crack and gangs and mass communications and satellites and airplanes and global warming—like it's something they could possibly get back to. And they can't figure out why they're so fucked up, so they find someone to blame. Niggers, Jews, whites, Chinks, Arabs, Russians, pro-choicers, pro-lifers—who do you got?"

I didn't say anything. Hard to argue with the truth.

He slammed his feet down on the floor and stood up, began pacing. His steps were a little uncertain, as if he expected resistance after each one. "White man blames people like me because they say quotas got me where I am. Half of 'em can't so much as read, but they think they deserve my job. Fucking pols sit in their leather chairs with their windows looking out on the Charles and make sure their stupid-fuck white constituents think the reason they're angry is because I'm stealing food from their children's mouth. Black men—brothers—they say I ain't black anymore because I live on an all-white street in a pretty much all-white neighborhood. Say I'm sneaking into the middle class. Sneaking. Like, because I'm black, I should go live in some shithole on Humboldt Avenue, with people who cash their welfare checks for crack money. Sneaking," he repeated. "Shit. Heteros hate homos, now homos are ready to 'bash back,' whatever the fuck that means. Lesbians hate men, men hate women, blacks hate whites, whites hate blacks, and...everyone is looking for someone to blame. I mean, hell, why bother looking in the mirror at your own damn self when there's so many other people out there who you *know* you're better than." He looked at me. "You know what I'm saying, or is it the booze talking?"

I shrugged. "Everyone needs someone to hate for some reason."

"Everyone's too damn stupid," he said.

I nodded. "And too damn angry."

He sat down again. "Goddamn."

I said, "So where's that leave us, Rich?"

He held up his glass. "Crying into our scotch at the end of another day."

The room was still for a while. We each poured another drink in silence, sipped them a bit more slowly. After five minutes of this, Richie said, "How do you feel about what happened today? Are you OK?"

Everyone kept asking me that. I said, "I'm all right."

"Yeah?"

"Yeah," I said. "I think." I looked at him, and for some reason I wished he'd met her. I said, "Jenna was decent. A good person. All she wanted was, once in her life, not to be pushed under the rug."

He looked at me and leaned forward, his glass extended. "You're going to make people pay for her, aren't you, Patrick?"

I leaned forward and met his glass with mine. I nodded. "In spades," I said, then held up my hand. "No offense."

FIFTEEN

RICHIE LEFT A LITTLE AFTER MIDNIGHT, AND I CARRIED THE bottle across the street to my apartment. I ignored the blinking red light on my answering machine and flicked on the TV. I dropped into the leather La-Z-Boy, drank from the bottle, watched *Letterman*, and tried not to see Jenna's death dance every time my eyelids reached half-mast. I don't usually indulge in hard liquor to excess, but I was putting one hell of a dent in the Glenlivet. I wanted to pass out, no dreams.

Richie had said Socia sounded familiar, but he couldn't quite place him. I assessed what I knew. Curtis Moore was a member of the Raven Saints. He had killed Jenna, most likely at someone else's behest, that someone probably being Socia. Socia was Jenna's husband, or had been. Socia was friendly enough with Senator Brian Paulson to have had snapshots taken with him. Paulson had slapped the table in front of me at our first meeting. "This is no joke," he'd said. No joke. Jenna was dead. Well over a hundred urban warriors who weren't afraid to die had a bone to pick with me. No joke. I was scheduled to meet Mulkern and crew for lunch tomorrow. I was drunk. Maybe it was me, but Letterman seemed to be getting stale. Jenna was dead.

Curtis Moore was missing a foot. I was drunk. A ghost in a fireman's uniform was looming up in the shadows behind the TV. The TV was getting harder to focus on. Probably the vertical hold. The bottle was empty.

•

The Hero swung his fire ax into my head and I sat bolt upright in the chair. The TV screen was snowing. I trained a blurry eye on my watch: 4:15 A.M. Molten fire surged under my sternum. All the nerves in my skull were freshly exposed by the ax, and I stood up and just made the bathroom before I yakked up the Glenlivet. I flushed the toilet and lay on the cool tile, the room smelling of scotch and fear and death. This was the second time in three nights I'd thrown up. Maybe I was getting bulimia.

I made it to my feet again and brushed my teeth for half an hour or so. I stepped into the shower, turned it on. I stepped back out, removed my clothes, and got back in. By the time I finished, it was almost dawn. Three Tylenol, and I fell on top of my bed, hoping that whatever I had up-chucked contained all those things that made me afraid to sleep.

I dozed on and off for the next three hours, and, thankfully, no one came to visit. Not Jenna, not the Hero, not Curtis Moore's foot.

Sometimes, you get a break.

•

"I hate this," Angie said. "I...hate...it."

"You look like shit too," I offered.

She gave me that look and went back to fiddling violently with the hem of her skirt in the back of the taxi.

Angie wears skirts about as often as she cooks, but I'm never disappointed. And for all her bitching, I don't think it's as painful for her as she pretends. Too much thought had gone into what she was wearing for the result to be anything less than "Wow." She wore a dark cranberry silk-crepe wrap-around blouse and a black suede skirt. Her long hair was brushed back off her forehead, pinned back over her left ear, but tumbling loosely along the right side of her face, cowling in slightly around her eye. When she raised her eyes from under her long lashes and looked at me, it hurt. The skirt was damn near painted on and she kept tugging at the hem to get comfortable, squirming in the backseat of the cab. The sight, all in all, wasn't hard to take.

I was wearing a gray herringbone double-breasted with a subtle black crisscross pattern. The jacket was tight where it hugged my hips for that cosmopolitan look, but fashion designers are usually kinder to men, and all I had to do was unbutton it.

I said, "You look fine."

"I know I look fine," she said, scowling. "I'd like to find whoever designed this skirt, because I *know* it was a man, and shove him into it. Turn his ass soprano real quick."

The cab dropped us on the corner, across from Trinity Church.

The doorman opened the door with a "Welcome to the Copley Plaza Hotel," and we went in. The Copley is somewhat similar to the Ritz: they were both standing long before I was born; they'll still be here long after I'm gone. And if the employees at the Copley don't seem as plucky as those at the Ritz, it's probably because they have less to be plucky about. The Copley's still trying to bounce back from its status as the city's most forgotten hotel. Its latest multimillion-dollar refurbishment will have to go a long way to erase its once dark corridors and staid-to-the-point-of-death atmosphere from people's minds. They started with the bar, though, and they've done a good job. Instead of George

Reeves and Bogey, I always expect to see Burt Lancaster as J. J. Hunsecker holding court at a table, a preening Tony Curtis at his foot. I mentioned this to Angie as we entered.

She said, "Burt Lancaster as who?"

I said, *"Sweet Smell of Success."*

She said, "What?"

I said, "Heathen."

Jim Vurnan didn't rise to meet me this time. He and Sterling Mulkern sat together in oaken shadows, their view protected from the trivialities of the outside world by dark brown slats. Pieces of the Westin Hotel peeked in through the window slats, but unless you were looking for it, you wouldn't notice. Which is just as well I suppose—the only hotel uglier than the Westin in this city is the Lafayette and the only hotel uglier than the Lafayette hasn't been built yet. They noticed us about the time we reached their booth. Jim started to get up, but I held up my hand and he slid over to make room for me. If only they made dogs and spouses as accommodating and loyal as they made state reps.

I said, "Jim, you know Angie. Senator Mulkern, this is my partner, Angela Gennaro."

Angie held out a hand. "Pleased to meet you, Senator."

Mulkern took the hand, kissed the knuckles, and slid along his seat, leading the hand with him. "The pleasure is completely mine, Ms. Gennaro." That smoothie. Angie sat down beside him, and he let go of her hand. He looked at me with a raised eyebrow. "Partner?" He chuckled.

Jim chuckled too.

I thought it rated a slight smile. I sat beside Jim. "Where's Senator Paulson?" I asked.

Mulkern was smiling at Angie. He said, "Couldn't get him away from his desk this afternoon, I'm afraid."

I said, "On Saturday?"

Mulkern took a sip of his drink. "So, tell me," he said to Angie, "where is it that Pat's been hiding you?"

Angie gave him a brilliant smile, all teeth. "In a drawer."

"Is that a fact?" Mulkern said. He drank some more. "Oh, I like her, Pat. I do."

"People usually do, Senator."

Our waiter came, took our drink orders, crept away silently on the deep carpet. Mulkern had said lunch, but all I saw on the table were glasses. Maybe they'd discovered a way to liquefy the menu.

Jim touched my shoulder. "You had quite a day yesterday."

Sterling Mulkern held up the morning *Trib*. "A hero like your father now, lad." He tapped the paper. "You've seen it?"

"I only read 'Calvin and Hobbes,'" I said.

He said, "Yes, well... wonderful press, really. Great for business."

"But not for Jenna Angeline."

Mulkern shrugged. "Those who live by the sword..."

"She was a cleaning woman," I said. "Closest she ever came to a sword was a letter opener, Senator."

He gave me the same shrug and I saw that his mind wasn't for the changing. People like Mulkern are used to creating the facts on their own, then letting the rest of us in.

"Patrick and I were wondering," Angie said, "if the death of Ms. Angeline means our work for you is done."

"Hardly, my dear," he said. "Hardly. I hired Pat, and you as well, to find certain documents. Unless you've brought those to the table with you, you're still working for me."

Angie smiled. "Patrick and I work for ourselves, Senator."

Jim looked at me, then down at his drink. Mulkern's face stopped moving for a moment, then he raised his eyebrows, amused. He said, "Well, exactly why did I sign that check made out to your agency?"

Angie never missed a beat. "Service charges for the loan of our expertise, Senator." She looked up as the waiter approached. "Ah, the drinks. Thank you."

I could have kissed her.

Mulkern said, "Is that the way you see it, Pat?"

"Pretty much," I said and sipped my beer.

"And, Pat," Mulkern said, leaning back, gearing up for something, "does she usually do all the talking when you're together? And all other duties, I'm assuming?"

Angie said, "She doesn't appreciate being spoken of in the third person when *she's* in the room, Senator."

I said, "How many drinks you had, Senator?"

Jim said, "Please," and held up his hand.

If this had been a saloon in the Old West, the place would have cleared about now, the loud rustling of fifty chairs pushing back from tables, wood scraping against wood. But it was a posh bar in Boston in the middle of a Saturday afternoon, and Mulkern didn't look like he'd wear a six-gun real well. Too much belly. But then, in Boston, a gun never was much of a match for a signature in the proper place, or a well-chosen slur dropped at precisely the right moment.

Mulkern's black eyes were staring at me from under heavy lids, the look of a snake whose lair has been invaded, the look of a violent drunk itching for a fight. He said, "Patrick Kenzie," and leaned across the table toward me. The bourbon on his breath could have ignited a gas station. "Patrick Kenzie," he repeated, "now you listen to me. There is absolutely no way I will be spoken to in this manner by the *son* of one of my *lackeys*. Your father, dear boy, was a dog who jumped when I told him to. And you have no other hope in this town but to carry on in his footsteps. Because"—he leaned in farther and suddenly grasped my wrist on the table, hard—"if you show disrespect to me, boyo, your business will be lonelier than an AA meeting on St. Patrick's Day. One word from me, and you'll be ruined. And as for your girlfriend here, well, she'll have a lot more to worry about than a few pops in the eye from her deadbeat husband."

Angie looked fit to decapitate him, but I put my free hand on her knee.

I took it back and reached into my breast pocket to remove the Xerox I'd made of the photograph. I held it in my hand, away from either Mulkern or Vurnan, and smiled slightly, coldly, I imagine, my eyes never leaving Mulkern's. I leaned back a little, avoiding his toxic halitosis, and said, "Senator, my father was one of your lackeys. No argument. But, dead or alive, he can piss up a rope as far as I'm concerned. I hated the bastard, so don't waste your distilled breath on appeals to my sentimentality. Angie is family. Not him. Not you." I flicked my wrist and my hand came free of his. Before he could pull his back, I closed mine around it and yanked. "And Senator," I said, "if you ever threaten my livelihood again"—I flipped the photocopy on the table in front of him—"I'll blow a fucking hole in your life."

If he noticed the photocopy, he didn't show it. His eyes never left mine, just grew smaller, pinpoints of focused hatred.

I looked at Angie and let go of Mulkern's hand. "I'm done," I said and stood up. I patted Jim's shoulder. "Always a pleasure, Jim."

Angie said, "Bye, Jim."

We walked away from the table.

If we made it to the door, I'd be on welfare come

autumn. If we made it to the door, the picture meant nothing more than guilt by association and they had nothing to hide. I'd have to move to Montana or Kansas or Iowa or one of those places where I imagine it's so boring no one would want to wield political influence. If we made it to the door, we were done in this city.

"Pat, lad."

We were eight or nine feet from the door; my faith in human nature was restored.

Angie squeezed my hand and we turned around like we had better things to do.

Jim said, "Please, come back and sit down."

We approached the table.

Mulkern held out his hand. "I'm a tad peckish this early in the day. People seem to misunderstand my sense of humor."

I took the hand. "Ain't that always the way."

He held it out to Angie. "Ms. Gennaro, please accept the apologies of an ornery old man."

"It's already forgotten, Senator."

"Please," he said, "call me Sterling." He smiled warmly and patted her hand. Everything about him screamed sincerity.

If I hadn't upchucked the night before, I think we all would have been in danger.

Jim tapped the photocopy and looked at me. "Where did you get this?"

"Jenna Angeline."

"It's a copy," he said.

"Yes, it is, Jim."

"The original?" Mulkern said.

"I have it."

"Pat," Mulkern said, his smile keeping his voice in check,

"we hired you for the purpose of retrieving documents, not their photocopies."

"I keep the original of this one until I find the rest of them."

"Why?" Jim asked.

I pointed at the front page of the newspaper. "Things have gotten messy. I don't like messy. Ange, do you like messy?"

Angie said, "I don't like messy."

I looked at Vurnan and Mulkern. "We don't like messy. Keeping the original is our way of stepping around the mess until we're sure what it is."

"Can we help you, Pat, lad?"

"Sure. Tell me about Paulson and Socia."

"A foolish indiscretion on Brian's part," Mulkern said.

"How foolish?" Angie asked.

"For the average man," Mulkern said, "not very. But for one in the public eye, extremely foolish." He nodded at Jim.

Jim folded his hands together on the table. "Senator Paulson engaged in a night of...illicit pleasure with one of Mr. Socia's prostitutes six years ago. I can hardly make light of it under the circumstances, but in the grand scheme of things, it amounts to little more than an evening of wine and women."

"None of these women being Mrs. Paulson," Angie said.

Mulkern shook his head. "That's irrelevant. She's a politician's wife; she understands what's expected of her at a time like this. No, the problem would arise if any documentation of this affair ever surfaced in the public eye. Brian is presently a very strong, silent voice advocating the street terrorism bill. Any association with people of...Mr. Socia's type could be very damaging."

I wanted to ask how anyone could be a "strong, silent

voice," but I figured it might reveal my lack of political savvy. I said, "What's Socia's first name?"

Jim said, "Marion," and Mulkern glanced at him.

"Marion," I repeated. "And how did Jenna come into play in this? How did she get ahold of these pictures?"

Jim looked at Mulkern before answering. The telepathic pols. He said, "The best we can figure it, Socia sent the photographs as an extortion attempt of some sort. Brian got very drunk that night, as you might imagine. He passed out in his chair with the photos on his desk. Then Jenna came to clean, and we assume..."

Angie said, "Wait a sec'. You're saying Jenna got so morally repulsed by photographs of Paulson with a hooker that she took them? Knowing her life wouldn't be worth a dollar if she did?" She sounded like she believed it less than I did.

Jim shrugged.

Mulkern said, "Who can tell with these people?"

I said, "So, why would Socia have her killed? Doesn't seem to me that he had all that much to lose by pictures of Paulson and some hooker going public."

Before he spoke, I knew Mulkern's answer, and I wondered why I even bothered asking in the first place.

"Who can tell with these people?" he said again.

SIXTEEN

The rest of the day was a wash.

We returned to the office and I flirted with Angie and she told me to get a life and the phone didn't ring and nobody just happened by our belfry. We ordered a pizza and drank a few beers and I kept thinking about how she'd looked in the back of the taxi, squirming in that skirt. She looked at me a couple of times, guessed what I was thinking, and called me a perv. One of those times I was actually having a purely innocent thought about my long-distance phone service, but there've been so many other times it sort of made up for it.

Angie's always had this thing about the window behind her desk. She spends half her time staring out it, chewing on her lower lip or tapping a pencil against her teeth, off in her own world. But today it was as if there was a movie out there only she could see. A lot of her responses to my comments began with a "Huh?" and I got the feeling she wasn't even in the same hemisphere. I figured it had to do with the Asshole, so I let her be.

My gun was still down at police headquarters, and I had no intention of going about town holding only my dick and an optimistic attitude with the Raven Saints looking for me. I needed one that was completely virgin, because the Commonwealth has very definite laws about unregistered handguns. Angie would need one too in case we got into something together, so I tracked down Bubba Rogowski and ordered two traceless pieces from him. He said no problem, I'd have them by five. Just like ordering the pizza.

I called Devin Amronklin next. Devin's assigned to the mayor's new Anti-Gang Task Force. He's short and powerful and people who try to cause him harm only make him angry. He has scars long enough to qualify as mile markers, but he's a pretty swell guy to have around if you're not at a cocktail party in Beacon Hill.

He said, "Love to talk, but I got shit to do. Meet me at the funeral tomorrow. You earned some points for Curtis the Gimp, no matter what that asshole Ferry told you."

I hung up and felt a slight swell of warmth in my chest, like hard liquor on a cold night before the bitter kicks in. With Bubba and Devin around, I felt safer than a condom at a eunuchs' convention. But then I realized, as I always do, that when someone wants to kill you, really kill you, nothing but caprice will save you. Not God, not an army, certainly not yourself. I had to hope my enemies were stupid, untimely, or had extremely short attention spans when it came to vengeance. Those would be the only things keeping me from the grave.

I looked over at Angie. "What's up, gorgeous?"

She said, "Huh?"

"I said, 'What's up, gorgeous.'"

The pencil went tap-tap-tap. She crossed her ankles on the windowsill, swiveled the chair partway in my direction. She said, "Hey."

I said, "What?"

"Don't do that anymore. OK?"

"Do what?"

She turned her head, met my eyes. "The gorgeous stuff. Don't do that anymore. Not now."

I said, "Well gee, Mom..."

She swiveled the chair all the way around to face me, her legs coming off the windowsill. "And don't do that shit either. That 'Well gee, Mom...' like you're being innocent. You're not being innocent." She looked out the window for a moment, then back at me. "You can be some kind of asshole sometimes, Patrick. You know that?"

I put my beer down on the corner of the desk. "Where is this coming from?"

"It's just coming," she said. "OK? It's not easy...It's not...I come here every day from my fucking...home, and I just want...Jesus. And I, I have to deal with you calling me 'gorgeous' and hitting on me like it's a goddamned reflex action and looking at me the way you do and I...just...want it to stop." She rubbed her face harshly with her hands and ran them back through her hair, groaning.

I said, "Ange—"

"Don't Ange me, Patrick. Don't." She kicked a lower drawer of her desk. "You know, between men like Sterling Mulkern the fat fuck, and Phil, and *you*, I just don't know."

It felt like there was a poodle lodged in my throat, but I managed to say, "Don't know what?"

"Anything!" She dropped her face into her hands, then looked up again. "I just don't know anymore." She stood up hard enough to spin her chair a full revolution and walked toward the door. "And I'm sick of being asked the fucking questions." She walked out.

The sound of her heels echoed off the steps like bullets, cracking upward and through the doorway. I felt a heavy ache behind my eyes, the steel spikes of a grate that had its back to a dam.

The sound of her heels stopped. I looked out the window, but she wasn't outside. The scraped beige paint of her car roof shone dully under the streetlight.

I took the stairs three at a time in the dark, the steep narrow space curving and dropping in a black rush before me. She was standing a few feet past the bottom step, leaning against a confessional. A lit cigarette stood straight out between her lips and she was placing the lighter back in her purse when I rounded the bend.

I stopped dead and waited.

She said, "Well?"

I said, "Well what?"

"This conversation sounds like it's going to be a winner."

I said, "Please, Angie, give me a break here. This sort of is coming out of the clear blue sky to me." I caught my breath as she watched me with opaque eyes, the kind that told me a challenge had been issued and I'd better figure out what it was, quick. I said, "I know what's wrong—about Mulkern, Phil, me. You got a lot of asshole men in—"

"Boys," she said.

"OK," I said. "A lot of asshole boys in your life right now. But, Ange, what's *wrong*?"

She shrugged and flicked an ash on the marble floor. "Probably burn in hell for that."

I waited.

"Everything's wrong, Patrick. Everything. When I thought about you almost dying yesterday, it made me think of a lot of other things too. And, I mean, Jesus Christ—this is my life? Phil? Dorchester?"—she swept her hand around the church—"This? I come to work, I fend you off, you have your fun, I go home, get slapped around once or twice a month, make love to the bastard sometimes the same night, and...that's all? That's who I am?"

"Nobody says it has to be."

"Oh, right, Patrick. I'll become a brain surgeon."

"I can—"

"No." She dropped her cigarette on the marble, ground it out. "It's a game to you. It's—'I wonder how *she* is in bed?' And then, once you know, you move on." She shook her head. "This is my life. No game."

I nodded.

She smiled, a rueful one, and in the little bit of light that shone through the green stained glass to my right I could see that her eyes were wet. She said, "Remember what it used to be like?"

I nodded again. She was talking about before. Before, when there weren't any limits. Before, when this place was a slightly drab, slightly bluesy romantic locale, and not a simple reality.

She said, "Who would've thought, right? Kinda funny, huh?"

"No," I said.

SEVENTEEN

BUBBA NEVER MADE IT TO MY OFFICE THAT NIGHT. Typical.

He came to my apartment the next morning while I was deciding what to wear to Jenna's funeral. He sat on my bed as I worked on my tie and said, "You look like a fag with that tie."

I said, "Didn't you know?" and blew him a kiss.

Bubba moved a foot down the bed. "Don't even fucking kid about that, Kenzie."

I considered pushing it, seeing how antsy I could make him. But pushing Bubba is a good way to find out real quick how well you fly, so I went back to working on my tie.

Bubba is an absolute anachronism in these times—he hates everything and everybody except Angie and myself, but unlike most people of similar inclination, he doesn't waste any time thinking about it. He doesn't write letters to the editor or hate mail to the president, he doesn't form groups or stage marches or consider his hate as anything other than a completely natural aspect of his world, like breathing or the shot glass. Bubba has all the self-awareness of a carburetor and takes even less notice of anyone else—unless they get in his way. He's six feet four inches,

235 pounds of raw adrenaline and disassociated anger. And he'd shoot anyone who blinked at me the wrong way.

I prefer not to consider this loyalty too closely, which is fine with Bubba. As for Angie, well, Bubba once promised to sever each of Phil's limbs and put them back on again—backward—before we talked him out of it. We promised him, swore to God in fact, that we'd take care of it some day and call him before we did. He relented. He called us losers and shitheads and every other expletive you can think of, but at least we didn't have a Murder One Conspiracy hanging over our heads.

The world according to Bubba is simple—if it aggravates you, stop it. By whatever means necessary.

He reached into his denim trench coat and tossed two guns onto my bed. "Sorry I was late."

"No problem," I said.

He said, "I got some missiles you could use."

I considered the knot in my tie, kept my breathing regular. "Missiles?" I said.

"Sure," he said. "Got a couple of stingers would fix those homeboys just right."

Very slowly I said, "But, Bubba, wouldn't they take out, like, half a neighborhood while they were at it?"

He thought about that for a second. "What's your point?" he said. He stuck his hands behind his head and leaned back on the bed. "So, you interested or what?"

"Maybe later," I said.

He nodded. "Cool." He reached into his jacket again and I waited for him to pull out an antitank gun or some claymores. He tossed four grenades on my bed. "In case," he said.

"Yeah," I said like I understood, "those could probably come in handy."

"Fucking A right," he said. He stood up. "You're good for the cost of the guns, right?"

I eyed him in the mirror and nodded. "I can pay you later this afternoon if you really need it."

"Nah. I know where you live." He smiled. Bubba's smile has been known to induce month-long periods of insomnia. He said, "You call me, day or night, you need anything." He stopped at the bedroom door. "A beer soon?"

"Oh," I said, "absolutely."

"Righteous." He waved and left.

I felt like I always felt after Bubba left—like something hadn't exploded.

I finished with the tie and crossed to the bed. In between the grenades were two guns—a .38 Smith and a nickle-plated Browning Hi-Power nine millimeter. I put on my suit jacket, slipped the Browning into my holster. I put the .38 in the pocket of the jacket and appraised myself in the mirror. The swelling on my face had gone down and my lips were semihealed. The tissue around my eye had yellowed and the scrapes on my face were starting to fade to pink. I was still no dream date, but I wasn't in the running for the Elephant Man contest, either. I could go out in public without fear of pointed fingers and muffled giggles. And if not, I was packing serious heat; anyone giggled, I'd shoot him.

I looked at the grenades. Didn't have a clue what to do with them. I had the feeling that if I left the house, they'd roll off the bed, take out the entire building. I picked them up, gingerly, and put them in the fridge. Anyone broke in to steal my beer, they'd know I meant business.

•

Angie was sitting on her steps when I pulled up. She wore a white blouse and a pair of black pants that tapered at her ankles. *She* was looking like a dream date, but I didn't mention it.

She got in the car and we drove for quite a while without a word. I'd purposely put a Screaming Jay Hawkins tape in the player, but she didn't so much as flinch. Angie likes Screaming Jay about as much as she likes being called a chick. She smoked a cigarette and stared out at the landscape of Dorchester as if she'd just emigrated here.

The tape ended as we entered Mattapan, and I said, "That Screaming Jay, he's good enough to play twice. Heck, I might just rip out the eject button, play him for eternity."

She chewed a hangnail.

I ejected Screaming Jay and replaced him with U2. The tape usually rocks Angie in her seat, but today it might as well have been Steve and Edie; she sat there like she'd had lithium with her morning coffee.

We were on the Jamaica Plain Parkway and the Dublin boys were into "Sunday Bloody Sunday," when Angie said, "I'm working some things out. Give me time."

"I can deal with that."

She turned on the seat, tucking her hair behind her ear in the wind. "Just lay off the 'gorgeous' stuff for a little while, the invitations to your shower, things like that."

"Old habits die hard," I said.

"I'm not a habit," she said.

I nodded. "Touché. You want to take some time off maybe?"

"No way." She tucked her left leg under her right. "I love the job. I just need to work through things and I need your support, Patrick, not your flirtations."

I held out my right hand. "You got it." I almost tacked a "gorgeous" to the end of that, but thankfully, I didn't. Mama Kenzie may have raised a fool, but she didn't raise no suicide.

She took my hand, shook it. "Bubba catch up with you?"

"Uh-huh. He brought you a present." I reached into my pocket, handed her the .38.

She hefted it. "He's so sentimental sometimes."

"He offered us the use of a couple of stingers, in case there's a country we want to overthrow anytime soon."

"I hear the beaches in Costa Rica are nice."

"Costa Rica it is then. You speak Spanish?"

"I thought you did."

"I *failed* it," I said. "Twice. Not the same thing."

"You speak Latin."

"OK, we'll overthrow Ancient Rome."

The cemetery was coming up on our left and Angie said, "Jesus Christ."

I looked as I made the turn onto the main road. We'd expected the sort of funeral cleaning ladies usually get—one rung higher than a pauper's—but there were cars everywhere. A bunch of beat-up street sleds, a black BMW, a silver Mercedes, a Maserati, a couple of RX-7s, then a full squadron of police cruisers, the patrolmen standing out of their units watching the grave site.

Angie said, "You sure this is the right place?"

I shrugged and pulled over onto the lawn, completely confused. We left the Porsche and crossed the lawn, pausing a couple of times when Angie's heel caught the soft soil.

The minister's baritone was calling upon the Lord our God to welcome his child, Jenna Angeline, into the Kingdom of Heaven with the love of a father for a true daughter of the spirit. His head was down as he spoke, peering at the coffin that sat on brass runners over the deep black rectangle. He was the only one looking at it, though. Everyone else was too busy looking at each other.

The group on the southern side of the coffin was

headed by Marion Socia. He was taller than he'd appeared in the photograph, his hair shorter, tight curls hugging an oversize head. He was thinner, too, the thin of adrenaline burn. His slim hands twitched constantly by his sides, as if grasping for the trigger of a gun. He was wearing a simple black suit with white shirt and black tie, but it was expensive material—silk, I guessed.

The boys behind him were dressed exactly the same, their suits of varying quality, deteriorating steadily the farther back they stood from Socia and the grave. There were at least forty of them, the whole group in a taut, structured formation behind its leader. A conspicuous air of Spartan devotion. None of them, except Socia, looked much over seventeen, and some didn't look old enough to have had an erection yet. They all started beyond the grave in the same direction as Socia, their eyes devoid of youth or movement or emotion, flat and clear and focused.

The object of their attention was on the other side of the grave, directly across from Socia. A black kid, as tall as Socia, but more solid, his body the healthy hard that a male achieves only before the age of twenty-five. He wore a black trench coat over a midnight blue shirt, buttoned at the top, no tie. His pants were pleated charcoal with light blue specks woven into the fabric. He had a single gold earring hanging from his left ear and his hair was cut in a sloping high-top fade, the sides of his head cropped extremely close, matching stripes cut into what little hair remained there. The back of his head was shorn just as close and something had been carved there too. From my vantage point, I couldn't be positive, but it looked like the shape of Africa. He held a black umbrella in his hand, pointed at the ground, even though the sky was about as cloudy as freshly blown glass. Behind him was another army: thirty of them, all young, all dressed semiformal, but not a tie among them.

The first white person we noticed was Devin Amron-klin. He was standing a good fifteen yards behind the second group, chatting with three other detectives, all four of them flashing their eyes back and forth between the two gangs and the cops on the road.

Beyond all of this, facing the foot of the coffin, I noticed a few older women, two men dressed in the clothes of State House sanitary personnel, and Simone. Simone was staring at us when we noticed her and she held the look for a solid minute before looking off at the firm elms that surrounded the cemetery. Nothing about her look suggested she'd come past me on the way out, invite me over for tea and a healing racial debate.

Angie took my hand and we walked over to Devin. He gave us each a curt nod, but didn't say anything.

The minister finished his eulogy and hung his head one last time. No one else followed suit. There was something alien about the stillness, something dangerously false and ponderous. A pigeon, gray and fat, swooped over the silence, small wings flapping fast. Then the crisp morning air cracked open with the mechanical whir of the coffin descending into the black rectangle.

The two groups moved as one, fading forward ever so slightly like slim trees in the first gust of a storm. Devin put his hand on his hip, a quarter inch from his gun, and the other three cops did the same. The air in the cemetery seemed to suck into itself and disappear in its own vortex. A current of electricity streamed into its place, and my teeth felt like they were gritted into tin foil. A gear ground somewhere in the dark hole, but the coffin continued on down. In those few moments of some of the most severe quiet I've ever felt, I think if someone had sneezed they'd have spent the rest of the day shoveling bodies off the lawn.

Then the kid in the trench coat took one step closer to the grave. Socia was a millisecond behind him, taking two steps to compensate. Trench Coat took the challenge and they reached the edge of the grave simultaneously, their bearings interchangeable, heads straight and immobile.

Devin said, "Calm. Everyone. Calm," in a whisper.

Trench Coat bent, a stiff squat, and picked up a white lily from a small pile by his feet. Socia did the same. They looked at each other as they extended their arms over the grave. The white lilies never quivered. They held their arms straight out, neither dropping his lily. A test whose limit only they knew. I didn't see which of them opened his hand first but suddenly the lilies fell toward the grave in nearly weightless surrender.

Each took two steps back from the grave.

Now it was the gangs' turn. They mimicked what Socia or Trench Coat had done, depending on their affiliation. By the time the line had dwindled to the lowest level members of each group, though, they were picking up the lilies and dropping them into the blackness in record time, barely taking a few precious moments to stare into each other's eyes and show how unafraid they were. I heard the cops behind me begin breathing again.

Socia had moved to the foot of the grave, hands folded together, staring at nothing. Trench Coat stood near the head, hand on his umbrella, eyes on Socia.

I said to Devin, "OK to talk now?"

He shrugged. "Sure."

Angie said, "The hell's going on here, Devin?"

Devin smiled. His face was only slightly colder to look at than the black hole everyone was dropping lilies into.

"What's going on," he said, "is the beginning of the biggest bloodfest this city's ever seen. It'll make the Coconut Grove fire seem like a trip to EPCOT."

A block of ice the size of a baseball nestled against the base of my spine and chilled sweat slid past my ear. I turned my head and my eyes passed over the grave and locked with Socia's. He was completely still, his eyes looking directly at me as if I weren't there. I said, "He doesn't seem too friendly."

Devin said, "You amputated the foot of his favorite lieutenant. I'd say he's downright livid."

"Enough to kill me?" It wasn't easy, but I continued to meet that sullen gaze that told me I'd already ceased to exist.

"Oh, without a doubt," Devin said.

That's Devin for you. All heart.

"What's my move?" I asked.

"A plane ticket to Tangiers would be my suggestion. He'll still get to you but at least you could say you'd seen the world." He scuffed the thick, stubby grass in front of him. "Word on the street, though, is he wants to talk with you first. Seems to think you got something he needs." He raised his foot, used his hand to brush the grass off his shoe. "Now, what could that be, Patrick?"

I shrugged. Those eyes never left me. I've seen frozen ponds with more empathy. I said, "The man's deluded."

"No argument there. Hell of a good shot though. I hear he likes to pull the trigger a lot, hit his victims in superficial places. You know, take his time. Give them the head shot about a half hour after they start begging for it. A real humanitarian, our Socia." He crossed his hands in front of him, cracked the knuckles. "So, why does he think you have something he needs, Patrick?"

Angie squeezed my hand and slipped her other hand

under my arm. It felt warm and slightly bittersweet. She said, "Who's the guy with the umbrella?"

Devin said, "I thought you two were detectives."

Trench Coat had turned now, too. He was following Socia's gaze, his eyes landing on me as well. I felt like a minnow in a shark tank.

Angie said, "No, Devin, we're still studying. So, tell us— who's the guy with the umbrella?"

He cracked his knuckles again, sighed with the ease of a man drinking a beer in a hammock. "That's Jenna's son."

I said, "Jenna's son."

"Did I stutter? Jenna's son. He runs the Angel Avengers."

Angel Avenue runs through the heart of Black Dorchester. It's not a place where you stop at red lights. Even in broad daylight.

"He got a hard-on for me, too?"

"Not as far as I know," he said.

Angie said, "Is Socia his father?"

Devin looked at the two of them, then the two of us. He nodded. "But I think it was the mother who named him Roland."

EIGHTEEN

"One angry child, our Roland," Devin was saying.

I sipped some coffee. "He didn't look much like a child to me," I said.

Devin swallowed a hunk of doughnut, reached for his coffee. "He's sixteen years old."

Angie said, "Sixteen?"

"Just *turned* sixteen," Devin said, "last month."

I thought of what I'd seen of him—a tall, muscular body, the bearing of a young general, standing on the small knoll above his mother's grave, umbrella in hand. He looked like he already knew his place in this world—at the fore-front, with his minions behind him.

When I was sixteen, I barely knew my place in the school lunch line. I said, "How's a sixteen-year-old boy run a network like the Avengers?"

"With a big gun," Devin said. He looked at me, shrugged. "He's a pretty smart boy, Roland is. He's got balls the size of truck radials, too. A good thing to have if you want to run a gang."

"And Socia?" Angie asked.

"Well, I'll tell you something about Roland and his daddy, Marion. They say the only natural force in this city that's possibly more dangerous than Roland is his daddy. And believe me, I've sat in a cold interrogation room with Marion for seven hours: the man has a cavity where his heart should be."

"And he and Roland are about to go head to head?"

"Seems to be the case," Devin said. "They ain't Ward and the Beav', that's for sure. Take my word, Roland's not walking around breathing because of any help from his old man. Socia was born without paternal instincts. The Avengers used to be a sort of brother gang to the Saints. But Roland changed all that about three months ago, broke away from his old man's organization. Socia's tried to hit Roland at least four times that we know of, but the kid doesn't die. A lot of bodies been showing up in Mattapan and the 'Bury the last few months, but none of them has been Roland."

Angie said, "But sooner or later..."

Devin nodded. "Something's got to give. Roland hates his old man something fierce. No one knows why exactly. Although now, with Jenna dead, he pretty much has all the motivation he needs, doesn't he?"

"He was close to her?" I asked.

Devin shrugged, his large palms up in front of him. "I don't know. She visited him a lot when he was in juvie lockup at Wildwood, and some say he'd drop by her place every now and then, leave her some cash. But it's really hard to say—Roland's got about as much love in him as his father."

"Great," I said. "Two machines without emotion."

"Oh, they got plenty of emotion," Devin said. "It's just all hate." He caught the waitress's eye. "More coffee."

We were sitting in the Dunkin' Donuts on Morton Street. Outside the window a few guys passed around a bottle in a brown paper bag, drinking Sunday into Monday.

Across the street, four punks prowled, eyes roving, every now and then one of them banging his fist off the top of another's—jacked up on hate and pain and ready to ignite as soon as they found a spark. Down the block, a young girl pushing a carriage veered it off the curb and began crossing to the other side of the street, head down, hoping they wouldn't notice her.

Devin said, "You know, it's too bad about Jenna. Don't seem right, a woman like that being stuck with two stone killers like Socia and Roland. Shit, the worst thing the woman ever did was rack up a lot of parking tickets. And who the hell doesn't in this city." He dipped his second doughnut into his third cup of coffee, his voice as inflectionless as a single piano key struck over and over again. "Too bad." He looked at us. "Opened her safe-deposit box last night."

Very slowly I said, "And?"

"Nothing," he said, watching me. "A government bond, some jewelry wasn't worth the rental fee on the box."

A muffled explosion went off outside, and the inside of the doughnut shop rattled. I looked toward the window and saw the group of punks. One of them was staring in, the veins in his neck prominent, his face a war mask. He met our eyes and his hand shot out again into the window. A couple of people flinched but the window didn't break. His friends laughed but he didn't. His eyes were red, blazing with rage. He hit the window one more time, got a few more flinches, and then his friends pulled him away. He was laughing by the time he reached the corner. Nice world.

I said, "No one knows why Roland has this beef with Socia?"

"Could be anything. You weren't particularly fond of your old man, were you, Kenzie?"

I shook my head.

He pointed at Angie. "You?"

"My father and I got along all right," she said. "When he was home. My mother and I were another story."

"I hated my old man," Devin said. "Turned every waking hour in my house into the Friday night fights. Took so much shit from him growing up, I swore I'd never take it from anyone else for the rest of my life, even if that meant dying young. Maybe Roland's like that. His juvie sheet is one long list of authority problems, going back to the fifth grade when he split open the substitute teacher's head. Bit off some of his ear too."

Fifth grade. Jesus.

Devin said, "Fucked up his share of social workers too, not to mention another teacher. Kicked a cop's head through the windshield of his cruiser when he was taking him to juvie once. Broke the nose of an emergency-room doctor, this while he had a bullet lodged near his spine. Come to think of it—everyone Roland's jammed on has been male. He doesn't respond well to female authority, either, but he doesn't get violent, he just walks away."

"What about Socia?"

"What about him?"

"What's his deal?" I said. "I mean, I know he runs the Saints, but besides that."

"Marion is a true opportunist. Up till about ten years ago, he was just a small-time pimp. A very vicious small-time pimp, but he didn't give the computer an overload when you keyed his name into it."

"And then?"

"Then came crack. Socia knew what it would mean, long before it made the cover of *Newsweek*. He killed the mule of one of the Jamaican syndicates, took over the man's action. We all figured he had about a week to live after that, but he flew to Kingston, showed the Boss the size of his balls, dared him to retaliate." Devin shrugged. "Next thing you know, the man to see for crack in this town was Marion Socia. This was back in the early days, but even now, with all the competition, he's still the top man. He's got an army of kids willing to die for him, no questions asked, and he's got a network that's so detailed, you could bust one of his upper-echelon suppliers and still be four or five buffer people removed from Socia himself."

We sat silent for a while, drinking our coffee.

Angie said, "How's Roland ever hope to beat Socia?"

Devin shrugged. "You got me. I got a hundred bucks on Socia in the pool, myself."

"The pool?" I said.

He nodded. "Of course. The departmental pool, see who wins the gang war. They don't pay me enough to do this job, so I got to take my perks where I find them. Odds on Roland are about sixty to one."

Angie said, "They looked pretty even at the funeral."

"Looks can be deceiving. Roland's tough, he's smart, and he's got a pretty good posse working for him up on Angel Avenue. But he's not his father, not yet. Marion is ruthless and he's got nine lives. There ain't a member of the Saints who isn't convinced he's Satan. You fuck up even slightly in Socia's organization and you die. No outs. No compromises. The Saints think they're in a holy war."

"And the Avengers?"

"Oh, they're dedicated. Don't doubt that. But, push come to shove, enough of them die, they'll back down. Roland's going to lose. Bank on it. Couple years from now, it might be a different story, but he's too green right now." He looked down at his cold coffee and grimaced. "What time is it?"

Angie looked at her watch. "Eleven."

"Hell, it's noon somewhere," he said. "I need alcohol." He stood up, dropped some coins on the table. "Come on, kids."

I stood. "Where?"

"There's a bar around the corner. Lemme buy you a drink before the war."

•

The bar was small, cramped, and the black rubber tile on the floor smelled of stale beer and wet soot and sweat. It was one of those paradoxes that are common in this city— a white Irish bar in a black neighborhood. The men who drank here had been drinking here for decades. They walled themselves up inside with their dollar drafts and their pickled eggs and their frozen attitudes and pretended the world outside hadn't changed. They were construction workers who'd been working within the same five-mile ra- dius since they got their union cards because something's always being built in Boston; they were foremen from the docks, from the General Electric plant, from Sears and Roe- buck. They chased cut-rate whiskey with impossibly cold beer at eleven o'clock in the morning and watched a video- tape of the Notre Dame—Colorado Orange Bowl from last New Year's.

When we entered, they glanced at us long enough to as- sess our color, then resumed their argument. One of them was up on his knees atop the bar, pointing at the screen, counting some of the players. He said, "There, they got eight on the defense alone. Fucking eight. You tell me again about Notre Dame."

The bartender was an old-timer with slightly fewer scars on his face than Devin. He had the bored, opaque face of someone who's definitely heard it all and made up his mind about most of it years ago. He raised a tired eyebrow at Devin. "Hey, Sarge, what can I get you?"

"Bullshit, bullshit, bullshit, bullshit," someone by the TV said. "Count 'em again."

"Fuck you—count 'em again. *You* count 'em."

Devin said, "What's the thrust of the intellectual discourse at the other end of the bar?"

The bartender wiped the bar in front of us as we sat down. "Roy—the guy on the bar—he claims Notre Dame's the better team because they got less niggers. They're counting to decide."

"Hey, Roy," someone yelled, "the fucking quarterback's a nigger. How white can the Fighting Irish be?"

Angie said, "If I wasn't used to this, I'd be embarrassed."

Devin said, "We could shoot 'em all, maybe get a medal for it."

I said, "Why waste the bullets?"

The bartender was waiting. Devin said, "Oh, sorry, Tommy. Three drafts and a shot."

Someone less familiar with him might have assumed he'd ordered for the three of us. I wasn't fooled. "A draft," I said.

Angie said, "Me too."

Devin hammered a box of unopened cigarettes against his wrist, then removed the wrapping. He took one, offered the pack. Angie took another. I resisted. With pain, as always.

At the other end of the bar, Roy—his pale, hairy belly spilling out of a sweaty blue softball shirt—was banging his finger off the TV faster than tapped Morse code on a sinking ship. "One nigger, two, three, four, five…six, another makes seven, eight, nine. Nine and that's just the offense. Buffaloes my ass. Colorado Spearchuckers."

Someone laughed. Someone always does.

I said, "How do these fucks stay alive in this neighbor-hood?"

Devin considered the jar of pickled eggs. "I have a theory about that." Tommy set the three beers in front of him, placed the shot beside them, went back for ours. The shot disappeared down Devin's throat before I saw him pick it up. He wrapped a hand around one of the frosted mugs, downed half a pint before he spoke again. "Cold," he said. "My theory is this—people like that, you got two choices: you either kill 'em or you let 'em be, because you'll never change their minds. I figure the folks in this neighborhood are just too tired to kill 'em." He polished off the rest of his first beer. He still had half a cigarette and two of his drinks were gone.

I always feel like a Chevette with a bad tire chasing a Porsche when I try to keep up with Devin at a bar.

Tommy placed two beers in front of Angie and me, poured another shot into Devin's shot glass.

Angie said, "My father used to come to this bar."

Devin inhaled the second shot sometime while I blinked. "Why'd he stop?"

"He died."

Devin nodded. "That'd do it, sure." He started on his second pint. "Your old man, Kenzie, the hero fireman, he come to places like this?"

I shook my head. "He drank at Vaughn's on Dot Avenue. Only place he went. Used to say, 'A man who ain't faithful to his bar ain't much better than a woman.'"

"A real prince, his father," Angie said.

"Never met the man," Devin said. "Saw that picture though. Two kids from a burning tenth floor." He whistled and drank the rest of his second pint. "Tell you what,

Kenzie—you got half the balls your old man had, you might live through this."

A burst of laughter blew across from the other side of the bar. Roy was pointing at the screen, saying, "Nigger, nigger, nigger, nigger, nigger, nigger, nigger," doing a little drunken dance on his knees. Soon, they'd start telling AIDS jokes, really bust a gut.

I thought about what Devin said. "Your concern is touching," I told him.

He grimaced, his eyebrows furrowed, the third pint washing down his throat. He put it down, wiped his mouth with a cocktail napkin. He said, "Tommy," and waved his arm like a third-base coach sending the runner home. Tommy came down with two more pints and poured him another shot. Devin held up his hand, downed the shot, and Tommy poured another one. Devin nodded, and he left.

Devin turned on the stool, looked at me. "Concern?" he said. He chuckled, a graveyard chuckle. "Tell you what concern changes—nothing. I'm concerned that this city's going to rip itself apart this summer. Won't stop it from happening. I'm concerned too many kids are dying too young over sneakers and hats and five bucks worth of Grade Z cocaine. Guess what though? They're still dying. I'm concerned that shitheads like that"—he jerked a thumb down the bar—"are actually allowed to reproduce and raise new shitheads just as stupid as they are, but it doesn't stop them from mating like rabbits." He threw back the shot, and I had the feeling I'd be driving him home. He was favoring the right elbow on the bar over the left, taking deeper drags on his cigarette. "I'm forty-three years old," he said and Angie sighed quietly. "I'm forty-three," he repeated, "and I got a gun and a badge and I go into gang zones every night and pretend I'm actually doing something, and my *concern* doesn't change the fact that I'm not. I slam sledgehammers into doors in projects that smell of things you couldn't even begin to identify. I go through doors and people shoot at me and children cry and mothers scream and someone gets busted or someone gets killed. And then, then I go home to my shitty little apartment and eat microwave food and sleep until I have to get up and do it again. This," he said, "is my life."

I raised my eyebrows at Angie and she smiled softly, both of us remembering her voice in the chapel the night before. "This is my life?" Lot of people taking stock of their lives these days. Judging by Devin and Angie, I wasn't sure how bright that was.

Somebody down the end of the bar said, "Look at that fucking nigger run, though."

Roy said, "Of course he can run, moron. Been hightailing it from the po-lice since he was two. Probably thinks that's a stolen radio under his arm, 'stead of a football."

Lots of laughter from the group. Wits, one and all.

Devin was watching them now, hollow eyes staring from behind the stream of smoke that flowed from his cigarette. He took a drag from it, the fat forgotten ash tipping forward and dropping to the bar. He didn't seem to notice, even though half of it hit his arm. He downed the rest of his pint and stared at the group and I had the feeling there was going to be some property damage.

He stubbed out his cigarette halfway and stood up. I reached out my hand, stopping three inches from his chest. "Devin."

He pushed it away like it was a subway turnstile and walked down the bar.

Angie turned on her seat, followed him with her eyes. "Eventful morning."

Devin had reached the other end of the bar. One by one,

the men sensed him and turned around. He stood with his legs spread slightly, planted on the rubber tile, his arms hanging loosely by his sides. His hands made small circular motions.

Tommy said, "C'mon, Sarge. Not my place."

Devin said, "C'mere, Roy," very quietly.

Roy climbed off the bar. "Me?"

Devin nodded.

Roy stepped through his friends, pulling the shirt down over his belly. The second he let go of it, it rolled back up like a disobedient shade. Roy said, "Yeah?"

Devin's hand was back down by his side before most of us realized he'd used it. Roy's head snapped back and his legs buckled and he was quite suddenly on the floor with a shattered nose and blood jetting above his face in a small fountain.

Devin looked down at him, kicked his foot lightly. "Roy," he said. He kicked the foot again, a little harder. "Roy, I'm talking to you."

Roy moaned something and tried to raise his head, his hands filling with blood.

Devin said, "A nigger friend of mine asked me to give you that. He said you'd understand."

He walked back down the bar and took his seat again. He made another pint disappear and lit another cigarette. "So, whatta you think?" he said. "Is Roy concerned now?"

NINETEEN

WE LEFT THE BAR ABOUT AN HOUR LATER. ROY'S FRIENDS had already taken him out, presumably to the emergency room at City. They gave Angie and me their hard-guy stares as they dragged Roy past, but they avoided Devin's flat gaze as if he were the Antichrist.

Devin tossed an extra twenty on the bar for Tommy's lost business. Tommy said, "You're a real pisser, Sarge. You gonna come in, put money down for every other fucking day they don't come back?"

Devin grumbled, "Yeah, yeah, yeah," and did a drunken shuffle toward the door.

Angie and I caught up with him on the street. I said, "Let me give you a ride home, Dev."

Devin shuffled his way into the Dunkin' Donuts parking lot. He said, "Thanks anyway, Kenzie, but I got to stay in practice."

I said, "For what?"

"Case I ever drink and drive again. I'll want to remember how I managed this time." He turned, walking backward, and I waited for him to tip.

He reached his rusted Camaro, got his keys out of his pocket.

I said, "Devin," and stepped toward him, reaching for the keys.

His hand closed around my shirt, the knuckles pressing into my Adam's apple, and he walked me back a few feet, his eyes swimming with ghosts. He said, "Kenzie, Kenzie," and pushed me back against a car. He tapped my cheek lightly with his other hand. He's got big hands, Devin. Like steaks with fingers. "Kenzie," he said again and his eyes grew hard. He shook his head from side to side slowly. "I'll drive. OK?" He let go of my collar and brushed at the wrinkles he'd left behind in my shirt. He gave me a smile that had no soul. "You're all right," he said. He turned back to his car and nodded at Angie. "Take care of yourself, Stone Fox." He opened the door and climbed in the car. It took two turns of the ignition for the engine to turn over, then the exhaust pipe banged off the small exit ramp and the car dropped into the street. He weaved into traffic, cut off a Volvo, and turned a corner.

I raised my eyebrows and whistled softly. Angie shrugged.

We drove downtown and got the Vobeast out of the parking lot for a little less than it would have cost me to put a kid through med school. Angie drove it, following me to the garage where I returned the Porsche to its happy home and climbed in with her. She slid across the seat and I chugged the rolling scrap metal onto Cambridge.

We drove through downtown, past where Cambridge becomes Tremont, past the place where Jenna went down like a rag doll in the morning sunlight, past the remains of the old Combat Zone, dying a slow but sure death at the hands of development and the X-rated video boom. Why jack off in a scuzzy movie theater when you can jack off in the comfort of your own scuzzy home?

We drove through South Boston—Southie to everyone who isn't a tourist or a newscaster—past strings of drab three-deckers, packed like a line of Port-o'-Potties at a rock concert. Southie amazes me. A good percentage of it is poor, overcrowded, relentlessly unkempt. The D Street housing projects are as bad as anything you'll find in the Bronx—dirty, poorly lit, teeming with angry, crew-cut punks who roam its streets with bloodlust and baseball bats. During a St. Patrick's Day parade a few years ago, a very Irish kid with a shamrock on his T-shirt wandered in there. He ran into a pack of other Irish kids who also had shamrocks on their T-shirts. Only difference between his T-shirt and theirs was that his said "Dorchester" in green over the shamrock and theirs said "Southie." The D Street kids solved the difference by tossing the kid off a roof.

We were driving up Broadway, past the babies in curlers pushing babies in carriages, past the double- and triple-parked cars and the "Niggers Stay Out" spray-painted on a store grate. Broken glass glittered from the darkness of filthy curbs and trash blew from under cars into the street. I thought of how I could step from this car and poll twenty people here, ask them why they hated "the niggers" so bad, and maybe half would probably tell me, "'Cause they got no fucking pride in their communities, man." So what if Broadway in Southie was identical to Dudley in Roxbury, if slightly lighter?

We crossed into Dorchester, rode up around Columbia Park and down into the neighborhood. I pulled in front of the church and we could hear the phone ringing as we climbed the stairs. Busy day. I caught it on the tenth ring. "Kenzie-Gennaro," I said.

Angie dropped into her seat as the voice on the other end said, "Hold on. Someone here want to talk with you."

I took the receiver with me as I went around the desk and sat down. Angie gave me a "Who is it?" look and I shrugged.

A voice came on the line. "Mr. Kenzie?"

"Last time I checked."

"This Patrick Kenzie?" The voice had an edge to it, someone not used to dealing with smart-asses.

"Depends," I said. "Who's this?"

"You're Kenzie," the voice said. "How's the breathing?"

I inhaled audibly, sucking it way back and expelling it in a long rush. I said, "Much better since I quit smoking, thanks."

"Uh-huh," the voice said, slow like freshly sapped maple. "Well, don't get too used to it. Might be all that more depressing when you can't do it no more." The maple voice was thick but light, a hint of lazy Southern afternoons hidden behind years of Northern living.

I said, "You always talk this way, Socia, or you just in a particularly elliptical mood today?"

Angie sat up and leaned forward.

Socia said, "Only reason you're still walking, Kenzie, is because we got things to talk about. Hell, I might just send someone over anyway, have them take a hammer to your spine. All I need's your mouth as it is."

I sat up and scratched an itch near the small of my back. I said, "Send them by, Socia. I'll do some more amputations. Pretty soon you'll have an army of cripples. The Raven Gimps."

"Easy to talk that way, sitting nice and safe in your office."

"Yeah, well look, *Marion*, I got a business to run."

"You sitting down?" he said.

"Sure am."

"In that chair by the boom box?"

Everything went cold inside of me, a flush of chipped ice spilling through my arteries.

Socia said, "You sitting in that chair, I wouldn't get up anytime soon, less you want to see your ass blow past your head on its way out the window." He chuckled. "Was nice knowing you, Kenzie."

He hung up and I looked at Angie and said, "Don't move," even though her moving wasn't the problem.

"What?" She stood up.

The room didn't explode, but I damn near fainted. At least we knew he didn't put a bomb under her chair too, just for fun. I said, "Socia said there's a bomb under my chair."

She froze, a wax statue in mid-stride. The word "bomb" will do that to people. She took a deep breath. "Call the bomb squad?"

I tried not to breathe. The possibility existed, I told myself, that the weight of the oxygen going into my lungs could put pressure on my lower extremities and detonate the bomb. It also occurred to me how ludicrous that was since the bomb was obviously triggered by a release of pressure, not a gain. So now, I couldn't exhale. Either way I wasn't breathing.

I said, "Yeah, call the bomb squad." It sounded funny, talking while I held my breath, like Donald Duck with a cold. Then I closed my eyes and said, "Wait. Look under the chair first."

It was an old wooden chair, a teacher's chair.

Angie put the phone down. She knelt by the chair. It took a few moments for her to do that. No one wants their eyes an inch from an explosive. She bent her head under the chair and I heard her exhale loudly. She said, "I don't see anything."

I started to breathe again, then stopped. Possibly it was in the wood itself. I said, "Look like someone might have tampered with the wood?"

She said, "What? I can't understand you."

I took a chance and let out my breath and repeated the question.

She was down there for six or seven hours, or so it seemed, before she said, "No." She slid back out from under the chair and sat back on the floor. "There's no bomb under the chair, Patrick."

"Great." I smiled.

"So?"

"So, what?"

"Are you going to stand up?"

I thought of my ass flying over my head. "There's a rush?"

"No rush," she said. "Why don't you stand up?"

"Maybe I like it here."

"Stand up," she said and stood herself. She held her arms out to me.

"I'm working up to it."

"Stand," she said. "Come to me, baby."

I did. I put my arms on the chair and did it. Except, somehow, I was still sitting. My brain had moved, but my body was of another opinion. How professional were Socia's people? Could they fit a bomb seamlessly into a wooden chair? Of course not. I've heard of people dying in a lot of ways, but getting blown up by a completely undetectable bomb in a thin wooden chair isn't one of them. Course, maybe I was being honored by being the first.

"Skid?"

"Yeah?"

"Anytime you're ready."

"OK. Well, see I—"

Her hands grabbed mine and she yanked me up out of the chair. I fell against her and we banged into the desk and didn't blow up. She laughed, an explosion in itself, and I realized she hadn't been entirely sure herself. But she'd pulled me out anyway. She said, "Oh, Jesus!"

I started to laugh too, the laugh of someone who hasn't slept in a week, a laugh along a razor blade. I held on to her, my hands tight around her waist, her breasts rising and falling against my chest. We were both drenched in sweat, but her eyes were pulsing, the dark pupils large and drunk with the taste of a moment that wasn't our last on earth.

I kissed her then and she returned it. For a moment, everything was heightened—the sound of a car horn four stories below, the smell of fresh summer air mingling with spring's dust in the window screen, the salty whiff of fresh perspiration at our hairlines, the slight pain from my still swollen lips, the taste of her lips and tongue still slightly cool from the pale ale we'd drunk an hour before.

Then the phone rang.

She pulled back, her hands on my chest, and slid away from me along the desk. She was smiling, but it was one of disbelief and her eyes were already taking on a spectre of regret and fear. God only knows what mine looked like.

I answered the phone with a hoarse, "Hello."

"You still sitting down?"

"No," I said. "I'm looking out the window for my ass."

"Uh-huh. Well, just remember, Kenzie—anyone can get to anyone, and *anyone* can get to you."

"What can I do for you, Marion?"

"You gone come see me, have a chat with me."

"I am, am I?"

"Bet your ass." He chuckled softly.

"Well, Marion, I'll tell you, I'm booked solid till October. Why don't you try back around Halloween?"

All he said was, "Two-oh-five Howe Street." It was all he had to say. It was Angie's address.

I said, "Where and when?"

He gave it another soft chuckle. He'd read me perfectly and he knew it and knew I knew it too. "We'll meet someplace crowded so you have the illusion of safety."

"Damn white of you."

"Downtown Crossing," he said. "Two hours. In front of Barnes and Noble. And you come alone, or I might just have to pay a visit to that address I mentioned."

"Downtown Crossing," I repeated.

"In two hours."

"So I'll feel safe."

He chuckled again. I figured it was a habit of his. "Yeah," he said, "so you'll feel safe." He hung up.

I did the same and looked at Angie. The room was still overcrowded with the memory of our lips touching, of my hand in her hair and her breasts swelling against my chest.

She was in her seat, looking out the window. She didn't turn her head. She said, "I won't say it wasn't nice, because it was. And I won't try and blame it on you, because I was just as guilty. But I will say, it won't happen again."

Hard to find a loophole in that.

TWENTY

I took the subway to Downtown Crossing, climbed up some steps that hadn't been hosed down since the Nixon years, and stepped onto Washington Street. Downtown Crossing is the old shopping district, before there were malls and shopping plazas, back when stores were stores and not boutiques. It was refurbished in the late seventies and early eighties like most of the city, and after they opened a few boutiques, business came back. Mostly younger business—kids who were bored with the malls, or too cool or too urban to be caught dead in the suburbs.

Washington Street is blocked off to auto traffic for three blocks where most of the shops are, so the sidewalks and streets teem with people—people going to shop, people returning from shopping, and most of all, people hanging out. The sidewalk in front of Filene's was lined with merchant carts and packed with teenage girls and boys, black and white, leaning against display windows, goofing on adult passersby; a few couples French-kissed with the desperation of those who don't share a bed yet. Across the street, in front of The Corner—a minimall with shops like The Limited and Urban Outfitters, plus a large food court where three or four brawls break out a day—a pack of black kids manned a radio. Chuck D and Public Enemy pounded "Fear of a Black Planet" from speakers the size of car tires, and the kids settled back and watched people walk around them. I looked at all the black faces in the massive crowd and tried to guess which ones were Socia's crew, but I couldn't tell. A lot of the black kids were part of the coming-from-shopping or going-to-shop crowd, but just as many were packed together in gangs, and some had that lazy, lethal look of street predators. There were plenty of white kids strewn throughout the crowd who looked similar, but worrying about them wasn't a concern now. I didn't know much about Socia, but I doubted he was an equal opportunity employer.

I saw immediately why Socia had picked this location. A person could be dead ten minutes, lying facedown on the street, before someone paused to wonder what he was stepping on. Crowds are only slightly safer meeting places than abandoned warehouses, and in abandoned warehouses, you sometimes have room to move.

I looked across the street, past The Corner, my eyes bouncing along the heads in the crowd like sheet music, slowing as they reached Barnes and Noble. The crowd thinned somewhat here, a few less teenagers. Guess bookstores aren't ideal places to pick up babes. I was ten minutes early and I figured Socia and his crew had gotten here twenty minutes before me. I didn't see him, but then I didn't expect to. I had the feeling he would suddenly appear an inch away from me, a gun between my shoulder blades.

It didn't come between my shoulder blades. It came between my left hip and the bottom of my rib cage. It was a big .45 and seemed even bigger because of the nasty-looking silencer on the end. Socia wasn't the one holding it either. It was a kid, sixteen or seventeen, but hard to tell with the black leather watch cap pulled down low over a pair of red Vuarnets. He had a lollipop in his mouth that he shifted from one side of his tongue to the other. He was smiling around it, like he'd just lost his virginity, and he said, "Bet you feel seriously fucking retarded about now, don't you?"

I said, "Compared to what?"

Angie stepped out of the crowd with her gun against Lollipop's crotch. She was wearing a cream-colored fedora on her head, and her long black hair was tied in a bun under it. She wore sunglasses that were bigger than Lollipop's and ran the gun muzzle over Lollipop's balls. She said, "Hi."

Lollipop's smile faded, so I replaced it with my own. "Having fun yet?"

The crowd all around us kept moving at their escalator pace, oblivious. Urban myopia. Angie said, "So what's our next move?"

Socia said, "That depends."

He was standing behind Angie and by the way her body tensed, I knew there was another gun back there with him too. I said, "This is getting ridiculous."

Four of us stood in a crowd of thousands, all interconnected like blood cells by fat squat pieces of metal. Someone in the crowd jostled my shoulder, and I hoped like hell no one had a hair trigger.

Socia was watching me, a benign expression on his worn face. He said, "Somebody start shooting, I'll be the one walks away. How 'bout that?"

He almost had a point—he'd shoot Angie, Angie would shoot Lollipop, and Lollipop would definitely shoot me. Almost.

I said, "Well, Marion, seeing how this is already about as crowded as a Japanese camera convention, I don't figure one more body'll hurt. Look at Barnes and Noble."

He turned his head slowly, looked across the street, didn't see anything that alarmed him. "So?"

"The roof, Marion. Look at the roof."

All he could see was a target scope and the muzzle of Bubba's rifle. Big target scope, though. The only way to miss with a scope that big would be in the event of an instant solar eclipse. Even then, you'd have to be lucky.

I said, "We're all in this together, Marion. If I nod, you go first."

Socia said, "I'll take your girlfriend with me. Believe it."

I shrugged. "She ain't my girlfriend."

Socia said, "Like you don't care, Kenzie. Try that shit on someone who—"

I said, "Look, Marion, you're probably not used to this, but what you got here is a no-win situation and not much time to think about it." I looked at Lollipop. I couldn't see his eyes, but drops of sweat were doing relay races down his forehead. Not easy holding a gun steady all this time. I looked back at Socia. "The guy on the roof, he might just get ideas of his own real soon. Figure he can pull the trigger fast, twice"—I glanced at Lollipop—"and take the two of you out before you get a shot off. He might decide to do that on his own, before I nod. Before I do anything. He's been known to...act on his own inner voice before. He's not real stable. You listening, Marion?"

Socia was in his Place—wherever it is people like him go to hide their fear and emotion. He looked around slowly, up and down Washington Street, but never once at the roof. He took his time about it, then looked back at me. "What's my guarantee I put my gun back in my pocket?"

"Nothing," I said. "You want guarantees, go to Sears. I can guarantee you'll be dead if you don't." I looked at Lollipop. "Hell, I'm fixing to use this kid's gun on him as it is."

Lollipop said, "Sure you are, man," but his voice sounded hoarse, an untaken breath sitting atop his esophagus.

Socia looked up and down the street again, then shrugged. His hand came out from behind Angie's back. He held the gun where I could see it—a Bren nine millimeter—then stepped from behind Angie and put it inside his jacket. He said, "Lollipop, put it away."

The kid's name was actually "Lollipop." Patrick Kenzie, Psychic Detective. Lollipop's lip was curled upward toward his nose and his breathing was hard, showing me how tough he was, the gun still in my side, but the hammer down. Stupid. He looked ready to prove his manhood, not because he wasn't terrified, but because he was. Usually the way it works. But he was too busy watching my face, proving how much of a man he was. I pivoted slightly with my hip, no big movement, and the gun was suddenly pointed at air. I took the gun hand in mine, snapped my forehead off the bridge of his nose, cracking the Vuarnets in half, and shoved the gun into his stomach with his own hand. I pulled back the hammer. "You want to die?"

Socia said, "Kenzie, let the boy go."

Lollipop said, "I die if I have to," and bucked against my hand, a line of blood running thickly down his nose. He didn't look pleased at the prospect, but he didn't look unwilling.

I said, "Good. Because next time you pull a gun on me, Lollipop, that's exactly what'll happen." I eased the hammer back down and flicked the safety forward, then ripped the gun from his sweaty hand and put it in my pocket. I raised my hand and Bubba's rifle disappeared.

Lollipop was breathing hard and his eyes never left mine. I'd taken a lot more than his gun. I'd taken his pride, the only commodity worth a damn in his world, and he'd definitely kill me if there was a next time. I was getting real popular these days.

Socia said, "Lollipop, disappear. Tell everyone else to pull back too. I catch up with you later."

Lollipop gave me one last look and entered the stream of people heading down the street toward Jordan Marsh. He wasn't going anywhere. I knew that much. He and the rest of them, whoever and wherever they were, would stay in the crowd, keeping watch on their king. Socia was way too smart to leave himself unprotected. He said, "Come on, let's go sit—"

I said, "Let's sit down right over there."

He said, "I got a better place in mind."

Angie tilted her head in the direction of Barnes and Noble. "You don't have any choice, Socia."

We walked past Filene's and sat on a stone bench in the small cement plaza next door. The scope appeared on the roof again, tilted in our direction. Socia saw it too.

I said, "So, Marion, tell me why I shouldn't do you right here, right now."

He smiled. "Shit. You already in enough trouble with my people as it is. I'm like a god to these boys. You want to fuck with that, be the target of a holy war, go on ahead."

I hate when people are right.

I said, "OK. Why don't you tell me why you're allowing me to live?"

"I'm swell that way sometimes."

"Marion."

"No matter what, though," he said, "I might just kill you for calling me 'Marion' all the time." He sat back on the bench, one leg up there with him, his hands clasped around the knee. A man out for some fresh air.

Angie said, "Well, what do you want from us, Socia?"

"Hell, little girl, you ain't even a part of this. We might let you go on about your life after this is done." He pointed a finger at me. "Him, though, he stick his nose in where it don't belong, shoot one of my best men, fuck with all this shit that ain't his to fuck with."

Angie said, "A common complaint among the married men in our neighborhood." That Angie, what a hoot.

Socia said, "Joke all you want." He looked at me. "But you know this ain't a joke, don't you? This is the end of your life, Kenzie, and it's happening."

I wanted to say something funny, but nothing came to mind. Nothing came even close. It was definitely happening.

Socia smiled. "Uh-huh. You know it. Only reason you're alive right now is because Jenna gave you something, and she told you something else. Now, where's it at?"

I said, "In a safe place."

"In a safe place," he repeated, rolling it off his tongue, slightly nasal inflection. His imitation of Whitespeak. "Yeah, well, whyn't you tell me where this safe place is," he said.

"Don't know it," I said. "Jenna never told me."

"Bullshit," he said and leaned toward me.

"I'm not busting my ass to convince you here, Marion. I'm just telling you so that when you toss my office and apartment and don't find anything, you won't be too surprised."

"Maybe I get some friends, we toss you."

"Your prerogative," I said. "But you and your friends better be real good."

"Why? You think you're real good, Kenzie?"

I nodded. "At this, yeah, I'm real good. And so's Angie, maybe better. And that guy on the roof, he's better than both of us."

"And he's not too fond of black people," Angie said.

"So, you two real proud of yourselves? Got yourselves a three-man KKK to keep the black man from your door?"

I said, "Oh, please, Socia, this ain't color. You're a fucking criminal. You're a douche bag who uses kids to do his dirty work. Black or white, that wouldn't change. And if you try and stop me on this, chances are you'll succeed and I'll die. But you won't stop him." Socia looked up at the roof. "He'll come at you and your whole gang and take you all out and probably half the 'Bury with you. He has about as much conscience as you and even less of a sense of public relations."

Socia laughed. "You trying to scare me?"

I shook my head. "You don't scare, Marion. People like you never do. But you do die. And if I die, so do you. Simple fact."

He sat back on the bench again. Crowds passed us in a steady stream and Bubba's target scope never moved. Socia tilted his head forward again. "All right, Kenzie. We'll give you this round. But, either way, don't matter what, you'll pay up for Curtis."

I shrugged, a heavy weight behind my eyes.

"You got twenty-four hours to find what we're both looking for. If I find it before you, or you find it and don't get it right over to me, your life won't be worth piss."

"Neither will yours."

He stood up. "Lotta people tried to kill me over the years, white boy. No one figured a way to do it right yet. Either way, that's the workings of the world."

He walked off into the crowd, the big scope on the roof following him every inch of the way.

TWENTY-ONE

BUBBA MET US AT THE PARKING GARAGE ON BROMFIELD Street where Angie had parked the Vobeast. He was standing out front as we came up the street, chewing a wad of gum the size of a chicken, blowing bubbles big enough to drive passersby to the curb. He said, "Hey," as we approached, then started on a fresh bubble. A verbal treasure trove, our Bubba.

"Hey," Angie said in a deep baritone that matched his own. She slid her arm around his waist and squeezed. "My God, Bubba, is that a Russian assault rifle under your coat or are you just happy to see me?"

Bubba blushed and his chubby face bloomed for a moment like a cherubic schoolboy. A schoolboy who would put nitro in the toilets, but just the same. He said, "Get her off me, Kenzie."

Angie raised her head and chewed on his earlobe. "Bubba, you're all the man I need."

He giggled. This psychopathic behemoth with a bad attitude and he giggled and pushed her away gently. He looked sort of like the Cowardly Lion when he did it, and I waited for him to say, "Aww g'won." Instead he said, "Cut it out, you tramp," and then checked to see if she was offended.

She caught the look of mortification on his face and it was her turn to giggle, hand over her mouth.

That Bubba. Such a lovable sociopath.

We headed up the garage ramp and I said, "Bubba, you going to be able to stick around for a while, keep a watch on us mere mortals?"

"Course I am, man. I'm there. The whole ride." He reached out and punched my arm playfully. All the feeling drained out of it and it would be a good ten minutes, maybe more, before it came back. Still, it was better than an angry Bubba punch. I'd taken one of those a few years ago—the only time I was ever stupid enough to argue with him—and after I came to, it took a week for my head to stop echoing.

We reached the car and climbed in. As we were leaving the garage, Bubba said, "So, we gonna blow these homeboys back to Africa or what?"

Angie said, "Now, Bubba..."

I knew better than to try and enlighten Bubba on racial matters. I said, "I don't think it'll be necessary."

He said, "Shit," and sat back.

Poor Bubba. All dressed up and no one to shoot.

•

We dropped Bubba off at the playground near his home. He walked up the cement steps and trudged past the jungle gym, kicked a beer bottle out of his way, his shoulders hunched up to his ears. He kicked another bottle and it spun off a picnic table and shattered against the fence. Some of the punks hanging out by the picnic table looked away. No one wanted to catch his eye by mistake. He didn't notice them though. He just kept walking to the fence at the back of the playground, found the jagged hole there and pushed through it. He walked through some weeds and disappeared around the corner of the abandoned factory where he lives.

He has a bare mattress tossed down in the middle of the third floor, a couple of cartons of Jack Daniels, and a stereo that plays nothing but his collection of Aerosmith recordings. The second floor is where he keeps his arsenal and two pit bulls named Belker and Sergeant Esterhaus. A rottweiler named Steve prowls the front yard. If all this *and* Bubba isn't enough to deter trespassers or government officials, almost every other floorboard in the place is booby-trapped. Only Bubba knows the right ones to step on. Some walking suicide once tried to get to Bubba's stash by forcing him to lead him there at gunpoint. Every other month or so, for about a year after that, pieces of the guy were popping up all over the city.

Angie said, "If Bubba could have been born in another time, like say the Bronze Age, he would have been all set."

I looked at the lonely hole in the fence. "Least he would have had someone who shares his sensibilities."

We drove back to the office, and inside, began kicking around Jenna's possible hiding places.

"The room above the bar?"

I shook my head. "If she had, she'd have never left them behind when we came and got her. Place didn't look very burglar proof to me."

She nodded. "OK. Where else?"

"Not the safety-deposit box. Devin wouldn't lie about that. Simone's?"

She shook her head. "You're the first person she showed anything to, right?"

"I think we're working under that assumption, yeah."

"So, that means you're the first person she trusted. She probably figured Simone's view of Socia was too naive. And she was right, I'd say."

I said, "If they were in her apartment in Mattapan,

someone would have them by now and there'd be no reason for any of this."

"So, what's that leave?"

We spent a good ten minutes not coming up with an answer to that one.

"Shit!" Angie said at the end of those ten minutes.

"Apt," I said. "Not too helpful though."

She lit a cigarette, placed her feet up on the desk, and stared at the ceiling. More Sam Spade than I'd ever be. She said, "What do we know about Jenna?"

"She's dead."

She nodded. Softly she said, "Besides that."

"We know she was married to Socia. Common-law or legal, I don't know, but married."

"And had his child. Roland."

"And has three sisters from Alabama."

She sat up in her chair, her feet banging off the floor. "Alabama," she said. "She sent it down to Alabama."

I thought about it. How well did Jenna know these sisters anymore? How much could she trust them? Hell, how much could she trust the mail? This was her chance to be needed, to get a little "justice." To do a little of what people had been doing to her all her life. Would she risk that by putting the major proponent of her vengeance in transit?

"I don't think so," I said.

Angie said, "Why not?" She said it sharply. Her idea—she wasn't going to just let go of it.

I explained my reasoning.

"Maybe," she said, her voice slightly deflated. "Let's keep it on the burner though."

"Agreed." It wasn't a bad idea, and if it came to it, we'd follow it down, but it didn't quite *fit*.

It goes like this a lot. We sit around the office and

bounce ideas off each other and wait for divine interven-
tion. When that doesn't come, we chase down each possibility, and usually—not always, but usually—we end up
tripping over something that should have been obvious
from the beginning.

I said, "We know she had trouble with creditors a few
years back."

Angie said, "Yeah. So?"

"I'm brainstorming here. I never promised pearls of
wisdom."

She frowned. "She has no record, right?"

"Except for a bunch of parking tickets."

Angie flicked her cigarette out the window.

I started thinking about the beers in my apartment.
Heard them calling me, asking for company.

Angie said, "Well, if she had all those parking tickets…"
We looked at each other and said it together: "Where's the
car?"

TWENTY-TWO

WE CALLED GEORGE HIGBY AT THE REGISTRY OF MOTOR Vehicles. It took us fifteen tries to get past the busy signal, and then, once we did, a recorded voice told us that all the lines were busy. Our call would be taken in the order it was received and please stay on the line. I hadn't been planning on doing much till the end of the month anyway, so I cradled the phone against my neck and waited.

The silence ended after about fifteen minutes and the phone rang on the other end—once, twice, three times; four, five, six. A voice said, "Registry of Motor Vehicles."

I said, "George Higby, Vehicle Registration, please."

The voice hadn't heard me. It said, "You have reached the Registry of Motor Vehicles. Our business hours are nine to five P.M., Monday through Friday. If you need further assistance and have a Touch-Tone phone, please press 'one' now." A sonic beep went off in my ear about the same time I realized it was Sunday. If I pressed "one," I'd get another computer that would gladly connect me to another computer and by the time I got pissed off enough to throw my phone through the window, all the Registry computers would be having a good old yuck for themselves.

I just fucking love modern technology.

I hung up and said, "It's Sunday."

Angie looked at me. "Yes, it is. Tell me the date and you'll be my idol."

"Do we have George's home number around here?"

"Possibly. Would you like me to find out?"

"That'd be peachy."

She wheeled her chair over to the PC and entered her password. She waited a moment and her fingers began singing over the keys so fast the computer had a hard time keeping up. Served it right. Probably hung out with the Registry computers on its off days.

Angie said, "Got it."

"Give it to me, baby."

She didn't, but she gave me the number.

George Higby is one of those hapless souls who goes through life expecting the rest of the world to be as nice as he is. Since he gets out of bed each morning with the desire to make the world a better place, a slightly easier place to get along in—he doesn't understand that there are actually people who get up with the desire to make the rest of the world suffer. Even after his daughter eloped with a guitar player twice her age who left her strung out in a Reno motel room; even after she then ran into some especially nasty people and ended up working her sixteen-year-old body on the back streets of Vegas; even after Angie and I flew out there and took her away from these nasty people with the assistance of the Nevada State Police; even after this sweet apple of his eye blamed the mess she'd made completely on him; even after all this—George still meets the world with the nervous smile of someone who only knows how to be open and decent and prays that, maybe just once, the world might reward him. George is the sort of raw material out of which most organized religions create their foundations.

He answered the phone on the first ring. He always does. He said, "This is George Higby," and I half expected him to follow it with, "Want to be friends?"

"Hi, George, it's Patrick Kenzie."

"Patrick!" George said, and I have to admit that the enthusiasm in his voice made me happy to be me all of a sudden. I felt as if I'd been put on this earth for one reason: to call George on July 2 and make his day. He said, "How are you?"

"I'm great, George. How about yourself?"

"Very good, Patrick. Very good. I can't complain."

George was the kind who never could.

I said, "George, I'm afraid this isn't a strictly social call," and realized with more than a small measure of guilt that I'd never made a "strictly social call" to George and probably never would.

"Well, no problem, Patrick," he said, his voice dropping an octave for a moment. "You're a busy man. What can I do for you?"

"How's Cindy?" I asked.

"You know kids today," he said. "At this point in her life, her father is hardly the most important thing to her. That will change, of course."

"Of course," I said.

"Got to let them grow up."

"Sure," I said.

"And then they come back to you."

"They do," I said. Sure they do.

"But enough about me," he said. "I saw you in the papers the other day. Are you all right?"

"Fine, George. The media blew it all out of proportion."

"They'll do that sometimes," he said. "But then, where would we be without them?"

I said, "The reason I called, George, I need a license number and I can't wait until tomorrow."

"You can't get it through the police?"

"No. I need to play this one out by myself for a little while longer before I take it to them."

"OK, Patrick," he said, thinking about it. "OK," he repeated, brightening a bit. "Yeah, we can do that. You'll have to give me ten minutes or so to access the computer down there. Is that all right? Can you wait that long?"

"You're doing me the favor, George. Take all the time you need." I gave him Jenna's name, driver's license number, and address.

"OK. Fifteen minutes at most. I'll call you back."

"You have my number?"

"Of course," he said, as if we all keep the phone numbers of people we met twice two years ago.

"Thanks, George," I said and hung up before he could say, "No, thank *you.*"

We waited. Angie shot a Nerf ball through the hoop above the boom box, and I tossed it back to her each time. She's got a nice arc, but she doesn't use the backboard enough. She leaned back in the chair and sent one up in a high arc. Before the foam ball swished through the hoop she said, "We going to call Devin in on this one?"

I tossed the ball back to her. "Nope."

"Why not, exactly?" She put another one up and missed.

"Because we're not. Use the backboard a little more."

She tossed the ball up above her, bouncing it off the ceiling. "It's not standard procedure," she said in singsong.

"Standard procedure? What, we're the army now?"

"No," she said, the Nerf bouncing off her fingers, down her leg, and across the floor. She turned in her chair. "We're detectives who have a pretty good relationship with the police, and I'm wondering why we're risking that by not letting them in on evidence in a Murder One investigation."

"What evidence?" I leaned out of my chair and scooped up the ball.

"The picture of Socia and Paulson."

"Doesn't prove anything."

"That's for them to decide. Either way, it was the last thing the murder victim gave you before she was killed. That definitely makes it something they'd be interested in."

"So?"

"So, this should be a dual investigation is 'so.' We should be telling them we're going to look at Jenna's car. We should be asking them for the plate number, not having poor George break into the Registry computers."

"And if they were to come across the evidence our clients hired us to find before we do?"

"Then, once they're finished with it, they hand it over to us."

"Just like that?"

"Just like that."

"And if it's incriminating? If it's against our clients' best interests to have the police see it, what then? How good is our business then? If Mulkern wanted to get the police to look for those 'documents' he would have. Instead, he hired us. We're not *law enforcement*, Ange, we're private investigators."

"No shit, Sherlock. But—"

"But what? Where the hell's this coming from? You're talking like a novice."

"I'm no fucking novice, Skid. I just think you should level with your partner about your motives."

"My motives. And what are my motives, Ange?"

"You don't want the police to get their hands on this,

not because you're afraid of what they'll do with it. You're afraid of what they won't do. You're afraid it might just be so bad, as bad as Jenna said, and someone in the State House will make a phone call and the evidence will disappear."

I kneaded the foam ball in my hand. "You're suggesting my motives are contrary to the interests of our clients?"

"You're damn right I am. If these 'documents' are as bad as Jenna said, if they incriminate Paulson or Mulkern, what're you going to do then? Huh?"

"We'll have to see."

"Bullshit we'll have to see. Bullshit. This job should have been over half an hour after we found Jenna in Wickham. But you wanted to play things out, be a goddamn social worker. We're private investigators. Remember? Not moralists. Our job is to turn over what we're hired to find to the people who hired us to find it. And if they cover it up, if they buy off the police, fine. Because we're out of it. We do our job and we get paid. And if—"

"Wait a minute—"

"—you don't do this, if you turn this into some sort of personal crusade to get back at your father through Mulkern, we can kiss this business and this partnership goodbye."

I sat forward, my face two feet from hers. I said, "My father? My fucking father? Where's he come into this?"

"He's been in this. He's Mulkern, he's Paulson, he's every politician you ever met who shakes your hand with one hand and stabs you in the back with the other. He's—"

"Don't you talk about my father, Angie."

"He's dead," she yelled. "Dead. And I'm real sorry to inform you but lung cancer took care of him before you got the chance to do it yourself."

I moved closer. "You my analyst now, Ange?" My face

felt warm and the blood rippled through my forearms, tingling my fingers.

"No, I'm not your fucking analyst, Patrick, and why don't you back the fuck up?"

I didn't move. The trip switch on my temper had been kicked over and I stared into her eyes. They were zipping from side to side with bolts of anger. I said, "No, Ange, you back the fuck up, and take your pop psychology degree and your sentiments about my father with you. And maybe I won't try and analyze your relationship with that Husband of the Year who treats you so well."

The phone rang.

Neither of us moved. Neither of us looked at it. Neither of us softened or backed up.

Two more rings.

"Patrick."

"What?"

Another ring.

"That's probably George."

I felt my jaw unclench a bit, and I turned and picked up the phone. "Patrick Kenzie."

"Hi, Patrick. It's George."

"Georgie," I said, working some false excitement through my vocal cords.

"Do you have a pencil?"

"Detectives always have pencils, George."

"Ha. Of course. Jenna Angeline's car is a nineteen seventy-nine Chevy Malibu. Light blue. License number DRW-four seven nine. There's a boot order in effect on it as of June third."

I felt the rush building from the pit of my stomach, the blood pounding into my heart from open valves. "A boot order?"

"Yes," George said. "The Denver boot. Ms. Angeline didn't like paying her parking tickets it seems."

The Denver boot. The yellow, immovable tire lock. The blue Malibu Jerome's friends had been sitting on when I went to Jenna's place. Parked in front of the house. Not going anywhere anytime soon.

I said, "George, you are the greatest. Swear to God."

"I helped?"

"Damn right you helped."

"Hey, how about having a beer together sometime soon?"

I looked at Angie. She was peering at something on her lap, her hair covering her face, but the anger hung in the room like exhaust fumes. I said, "I'd really like that, George. Give me a call at the end of next week? I should have wrapped this up by then." Or died trying.

"You got it," he said. "You got it."

"Take care, George."

I hung up and looked at my partner. She was doing the pencil against her tooth thing again, looking at me, her eyes flat and impersonal. Her voice was pretty much the same. "I was out of line."

"Maybe not. Maybe I'm just not ready to probe that part of my psyche yet."

"Maybe you'll never be."

"Maybe," I said. "What about you?"

"And the Asshole, as you so kindly refer to him?"

"That guy, yeah."

"Things are coming," she said. "They're coming."

"What do you want to do about the case?"

She shrugged. "You know what I want to do. But, then, I'm not the one who had to watch Jenna die, so I'll let you call it. Just remember, you owe me one."

I nodded. I held out my hand. "Pals?"

She grimaced and reached across and slapped my palm. "When weren't we?"

"About five minutes ago." I laughed.

She chuckled. "Oh, yeah."

•

We parked at the top of the hill, looking down on Jenna's three-decker and the blue Malibu parked out front. The yellow boot was apparent even in the fading light. Bostonians get parking tickets and traffic citations with a consistency most pro sports teams would envy. They also tend to wait until their driver's licenses are about to be renewed before paying attention to them. City officials realized this after a while, took a look at their dwindling coffers, wondered where the graft necessary to put their children through college and their asses on the Vineyard was going to come from, and brought in the Denver boot. It comes, obviously, from Denver, and it clamps around your tire, and that car ain't going anywhere until all those parking fines are paid in full. Tampering with one is a serious offense, punishable by prison and/or a stiff fine. This doesn't deter anyone half as much as the fact that the damn things are almost as hard to remove as an old chastity belt. A friend of mine did it once, with a ballpeen hammer, a chisel, and a whack in just the right place. But the boot must have been defective, because he could never repeat the feat. Depressed the hell out of him too; he could have been set for life—boot destroyer for hire. Making more money than Michael Jackson.

If Jenna had hidden something in that car, it would make a perverse bit of sense. Sure, a car sitting untended in Boston for more than four or five minutes usually loses its stereo and speakers, and more often than not, the rest of it as well. But the chopping block market for fifteen-year-old Chevies ain't what it used to be, and no self-respecting car thief is going to waste precious time screwing around with the boot. So, unless she hid it in her stereo, there was a good chance it was still there. If she'd hidden anything there in the first place. Big if.

We sat and watched the car, waiting for darkness to fall. The sun had set but the sky still held its warmth, a canvas of beige streaked with wisps of orange. Somewhere behind or in front of us—in a tree, on a roof, in a bush, at one with the natural urban world—Bubba lurked in wait, his eyes as constant and emotionless as T. J. Eckleburg's.

We had no music going, because the Vobeast has no radio, and it was damn near killing me. God only knows how people kept their sanity before rock and roll. I considered what Angie had said about my motives, about my father, about taking my anger out on Mulkern and his cronies, anger at a world that had settled the score with my father before I had a chance to. If she was wrong, we'd find out when we finally got our hands on the evidence and I turned it over for another signed check, including the bonus. If she was right, we'd find out about that too. Either way, I didn't like thinking about it.

There was, come to think about it, way too much happening lately that required pauses for introspection. I've never made any bones about it—I love investigating things, as long as I'm not one of them. But suddenly, there were all these hot-blooded confrontations with people in my life— Richie, Mulkern, Angie. All of a sudden I was being asked to reevaluate myself in terms of racism, politics, and the Hero. My three least favorite subjects. Much more introspection and I'd end up growing a long white beard, maybe wearing a white smock, sipping a glass of hemlock while I read *The*

Crito. Maybe I'd move to Tibet, climb a mountain with the Dalai Lama or head to Paris and wear nothing but black, grow myself a keen goatee and talk about jazz all the time.

Or maybe I'd do what I always do—hang out and see what develops. Fatalist to the core.

Angie said, "What do you think?"

The sky was turning to ink, and there wasn't a working streetlight for miles. I said, "Time for a little B and E."

There was no one on the stoops as we came down the hill, but that wouldn't last much longer on a humid Sunday night. This wasn't the type of neighborhood where people took off to the Cape for the Fourth of July. We had to get in, find whatever it was we were looking for, and get out. People who don't have much usually protect what they've got in lethal ways. Whether the trigger's pulled by a Bobby Royce or a little old lady, the damage can often be damn similar.

Angie pulled the slim jim from her jacket as we approached the car, and before you could say "grand theft auto," she'd slid it down beside the window and popped the lock. I had no idea what sort of house Jenna had kept—the only time I'd seen it someone had gone through it like a storm front—but she kept a pristine car. Angie took the backseat, reaching down under the seat and behind it, pulling up the mats, looking for telltale tears in the carpet.

I did pretty much the same in the front seat. I pulled open the ashtray, found it brimming with Marlboro butts, closed it. I took what looked like warranties and repair records and an owner's manual from the glove compartment, but I stuffed it all in the plastic bag I'd brought anyway. Easier to check through it all when we got out of here. I reached under the dashboard, ran my hand around, didn't find anything taped there. I checked the door panels for rips or cuts in the seams. Nada. I took a screwdriver to the running panel on the passenger side; maybe Jenna'd seen *The French Connection.* I opened it: maybe she hadn't.

Angie was doing the same to the panel on the driver's side. When she removed it, she didn't shout "Eureka," so I figured she hadn't found any more than I had. We were steadily getting nowhere when someone said, "Ain't they pretty?"

I sat up in the seat, my hand on my gun, and saw the girl who'd been sitting on the steps the last time I'd been here. Jerome was standing beside her and they were holding hands. Jerome said, "You meet Roland yet?"

I sat up in the seat. "Haven't had the pleasure."

Jerome looked at Angie, kept looking, not wide-eyed, just interested. He said, "The fuck you doing in his mother's car, man?"

"Working."

His girlfriend lit a cigarette. She took a drag, blew the smoke in my direction. A thick ring of red lipstick looped around the white filter. She said, "He's the man was there when Jenna got herself killed by Curtis."

Jerome said, "I know that, Sheila. Damn." He looked at me. "You're a detective, right?"

I looked at Sheila's cigarette again. Something about it annoyed me, but I couldn't figure out what yet. I said, "Yeah, Jerome. Got a badge and everything."

Jerome said, "Beats working for a living."

Sheila took another hit off her cigarette, placed another red ring slightly above the first.

Angie sat up in the seat and lit one too. Carcinogen city. I looked at Sheila, then at Angie. I said, "Ange."

"Yeah?"

"Did Jenna wear lipstick?"

Jerome was watching us with a cocked eyebrow, his

arms folded across his chest. Angie thought about it. She took a few more drags off her cigarette, blew the smoke out in slow streams. She said, "Yeah. Come to think of it. It was subtle, a light pink, but yeah."

I flipped open the car ashtray. "What kind of cigarettes she smoke, you remember?"

"Lights, I think. Or Vantage, maybe. Definitely something with a white filter."

"But she'd just started again," I said, remembering Jenna's claim that she hadn't smoked in ten years until the events of the past few weeks caused her to start back up.

The cigarettes in the ashtray had cork filters and no lipstick rings on them. I yanked the ashtray out, swung my legs out of the car. "Step back for a sec' please, Jerome."

"Yassuh, bawse, whatever you say."

"I said 'please,' Jerome."

Jerome and Sheila took two steps back. I dumped the ashtray on the sidewalk. Jerome said, "Hey, man, some of us got to live here."

Metal gleamed up through the pile of ash. I reached down, scattered the ash, and picked up a key. I said, "We got what we came for."

Angie said, "Neato," and got out of the car.

Jerome said, "Congratulations. Now, pick that shit back up, man."

I held the ashtray by the curb and brushed everything back into it. I put it on the seat and got out of the car. I said, "You're all right, Jerome."

Jerome said, "Thanks. Just knowing I please white folks like yourself makes me a complete man."

I smiled and we walked back up the hill.

•

It was a locker key, number 506. Could have belonged to

a locker at Logan Airport or the Greyhound Station in Park Square or the Amtrak Terminal at South Station. Or any number of bus depots in Springfield or Lowell or New Hampshire or Connecticut or Maine or God knew where else.

Angie said, "So, what do you want to do? Check them all?"

"Don't have much choice."

"That's a lot of places."

"Look on the bright side."

"Which is?"

"Think of all the overtime we can pay ourselves."

She hit me, but not as hard as I thought she would.

TWENTY-THREE

WE DECIDED WE'D START IN THE MORNING. THERE WERE A lot of lockers in the state and we'd need all the energy we had; right now, we were running on fumes. Angie went home and Bubba followed. I slept in the office because it was harder to approach than my apartment; footsteps in the empty church would echo like cannon shots.

While I slept, a knot the size of a seashell worked its way into my neck, and my legs cramped up where they bent on the cot against the wall.

And sometime while I slept, war broke out.

•

Curtis Moore was the first to fall in the line of duty. Shortly after midnight a fire broke out at the nurse's desk in the prison hospital ward. The two cops on duty by Curtis's bed got up to take a look. It wasn't much of a fire—a rag doused in rubbing alcohol tossed in a trash can, a match thrown in for combustion. The two cops and the nurse found a fire extinguisher, doused it, and then it didn't take the cops too long to figure out a possible motive behind it. By the time they burst back in the room, Curtis had a hole the size of a hand in his throat and the initials J. A. carved into his forehead.

Three members of the Raven Saints met their blaze of glory next. Coming back from a late game at Fenway Park and a little subway wilding for a nightcap, they stepped out of Ruggles Station and had a one-sided conversation with an AK-47 pointed from a car. One of them, a sixteen-year-old named Gerard Mullins, took a burst to his upper thighs and abdomen, but didn't die. He played possum in the shadows until the car drove away, and then he started crawling toward Columbus Avenue. He was halfway between the subway station and the corner when they came back and stitched a line from just below his ear to just above his ankle.

Socia was stepping out of a bar on South Huntington, two soldiers a few feet behind him, when James Tyrone, a fifteen-year-old member of the Angel Avengers, stepped from behind a van with a .45 aimed at Socia's nose. He pulled the trigger and the gun jammed, and by the time Socia's bodyguards stopped firing, he was in the middle of South Huntington turning the yellow divider line a dark red.

Three Avengers went down in Franklin Park next. Then, two more Saints caught it while sitting on a stoop in Intervale. Another cycle of retaliation followed that one, and by the time the sun came up, the worst night in Boston gang history leveled out at twenty-six wounded, twelve dead.

•

My phone started ringing at eight. I grabbed it somewhere around the fourth ring. I said, "What?"

Devin said, "You heard?"

I said, "No," and tried to go back to bed.

"Boston's favorite father-and-son team just went to war."

My head dropped off the side of the cot. "Oh, no."

"Oh, yes." He gave me the rundown.

"Twelve dead?" I said. "Jesus." Maybe par for the course in New York, but here it was astronomical.

"Twelve at the moment," he said. "Probably five or six on the critical list who won't make Independence Day. It's a wonderful life, isn't it?"

"Why're you calling me at eight in the morning with this, Dev?"

"Because I want you down here in an hour."

"Me? Why?"

"Because you were the last person to talk to Jenna Angeline, and someone just happened to drill her initials onto Curtis Moore's head. Because you met with Socia yesterday and didn't tell me. Because word around town is you got something both Socia and Roland are willing to kill for, and I'm tired of waiting for you to tell me what that is out of the goodness of your heart. You, Kenzie, because lying is second nature to you, but it's harder to do in an interrogation room. So, get your ass down here and bring your partner with you."

"I think I'll bring Cheswick Hartman with me too."

"Go right ahead, Patrick. And that'll please me so much, I'll press obstruction charges against you and toss you in jail for a night. By the time Cheswick gets you out, all the fuckers we arrested last night from the Saints and Avengers ought to know your ass real intimately."

"I'll be there in an hour," I said.

"Fifty minutes," he said. "The clock started ticking when you picked up the phone." He hung up.

I called Angie, told her I'd be ready in twenty minutes.

I didn't call Cheswick.

I called Richie at home but he was already at work. I tried him there.

"How much you know?" he asked.

"Nothing more than you guys."

"Bullshit. Your name keeps coming up in this one, Patrick. And weird shit's going down at the State House."

I was working my way into a shirt, but I stopped, my right arm sticking out, frozen, like it was in a cast. I said, "What weird shit?"

"The street terrorism bill."

"What about it?"

"It was supposed to go to floor today. Early. So everyone could beat the traffic up to the Cape for the Fourth."

"And?"

"And no one is there. The State House is empty. Twelve kids died last night in gang violence and the next morning, when a bill that's allegedly going to start curbing all that shit is supposed to go to floor, suddenly no one's interested anymore."

"I got to go," I said.

I could have airmailed the phone to Rhode Island and still heard his voice. "What the fuck do you know?"

"Nada. Got to run."

"No more favors, Patrick. No more."

"Love it when you scold me." I hung up.

•

I was waiting in front of the church when Angie pulled up in that brown thing she calls a car. On weekends and holidays, Phil has no need for it; he stocks up on Budweiser and settles into the Barcalounger and watches whatever's on TV. Who needs a car when Gilligan still hasn't gotten off the island? Angie drives it whenever she can so she can listen to *her* tapes; she also claims I'm a lousy driver behind the wheel of the Vobeast because I don't care what happens to it. This isn't entirely true; I would care if something happened to it and I'd like some money from the insurance company if it ever did.

The ride from Angie's to Berkeley Street took less than ten minutes. The city was empty. Those who had gone to the Cape had left Thursday or Friday. Those who were going to the Esplanade for tomorrow's concert and fireworks hadn't started camping out yet. Everyone had taken the day off. During the ride, we saw something few Bostonians ever see—empty parking spaces. I kept asking her to stop at each one and back in and out again, just to see what it felt like.

Upper Berkeley, by Police Headquarters, was different. The block was cordoned off with sawhorses. A beefy patrolman waved us around the block. We could see vans with satellite dishes on top, cables running like overweight pythons across the street, white TV trucks parked on the sidewalk, and the black Crown Victorias of the upper police brass parked three-deep by the curb.

We swung over to St. James and parked easily enough, then walked back to the rear door of the building. A young black cop stood in front of the door, hands crossed behind his back, legs spread in military stance. He glanced at us. "Press goes through the front door."

"We're not press." We identified ourselves. "We have an appointment with Detective Amronklin."

The cop nodded. "Go up these stairs. Fifth floor, take a right. You'll see him."

We did. He was sitting on a table at the end of a long corridor with his partner, Oscar Lee. Oscar is big and black and just as mean as Devin. He talks a little less but drinks just as much. They've been partners so long they even got their respective divorces on the same day. Each has taken a bullet for the other, and penetrating just the surface of their relationship would be as easy as digging through cinder block with a plastic spoon. They noticed us at the same time, looked up, and held their tired eyes on us as we walked down the corridor toward them. They both looked like shit, tired and cranky, ready to stomp on anyone who didn't give them what they wanted. They both had splotches of blood on their shirts and coffee cups in their hands.

We entered the office and I said, "Hey."

They nodded. If they became more similar they'd be joined at the hip.

Oscar said, "Have a seat, folks."

There was a scarred card table in the middle of the room with a telephone and a tape recorder on it. We took seats on the side closest to the wall, and Devin sat down on my right, beside the phone, while Oscar sat to Angie's left, beside the tape recorder. Devin lit a cigarette and Oscar turned on the tape recorder. A voice said: "Recording copied August the sixth, nineteen ninety-three. Listed under bar code number 5756798. Evidence room, Boston police headquarters, precinct nine, 154 Berkeley Street."

Devin said, "Turn it up a bit."

Oscar did, and there were fifteen or twenty seconds of dead air, then the sound of a low rumble and lots of metal on metal sounds, as if a dinner party of ten were all rubbing their knives and forks together. Water dripped somewhere in there too. A voice said, "Cut him again."

Devin looked at me.

The voice sounded like Socia's.

Another voice: "Where?"

Socia: "Fuck do I care? Be inventive. That knee looks sensitive."

There was a moment when the only sound was the dripping water, then someone screamed, long and loud and shrill.

Socia laughed. "I'm doing one of your eyes next, so why don't you tell me, get it over with."

The other voice: "Get it over with. He ain't fucking with you, Anton."

"I ain't fucking with you, Anton. You know that."

A low, wheezing sound. Weeping.

Socia: "Too many tears coming out of that eye. Take it out."

I sat up in my chair.

The other voice said, "What?"

Socia: "I stutter? Take it out."

There was a soft, unpleasant sound, the sound a shoe makes when it steps into slush.

And then the scream. Impossibly high-pitched, a mixture of excruciating pain and horrified disbelief.

Socia: "It's on the floor in front of you, Anton. Give me the name, fuck. Who turned you?"

The screaming hadn't subsided yet. It rang clear and hard and steady.

"Who turned you? Stop screaming." A harsh flesh-on-flesh sound. The screaming blew up to a louder pitch.

"Who fucking turned you?"

The screaming was defiant now, an angry howl.

"Who fu—Fuck it. Rip out the other one. No, not with that. Get a fucking spoon, man."

There was a sound of soft footsteps, squeaking a bit as they walked away from wherever the microphone was.

The screaming turned into a whimper.

Socia, in a soft whisper: "Who turned you, Anton? It'll be over quick, soon as you tell me."

The whimper screeched something unintelligible.

Socia said, "I promise. It'll all be over, soon as you tell me. You'll die quick and painless."

A torn sob, ragged breathing, gasping for air, a steady weeping that lasted for over a minute.

"Come on now. Tell me."

From the sob came: "Na. Na I—"

"Hand me that fucking spoon."

"Devin. The cop! Devin!" It sounded like the words had been pushed out of the body through a torn hole.

Devin reached over and shut off the tape recorder. I realized I was sitting rigid in my chair, half out of it, my spine bowed. I looked at Angie. Her skin was white, her fists tight against the arms of the chair.

Oscar looked bored, staring up at the ceiling. He said, "Anton Meriweather. Sixteen years old. Devin and me turned him in December and he informed on Socia. He was a soldier with the Saints. Oh yeah, he's dead."

I said, "You have this tape. Why's Socia still walking around?"

Devin said, "You ever see a jury try to make a decision on a voice ID? You ever seen how many people a defense attorney will find who sound just like the guy on that tape? Did you hear anyone call Socia by name on that tape?"

I shook my head.

"I just want you to know who you're dealing with here, kids. After Anton gave my name up, they worked on him for another ninety minutes. Ninety minutes. Long time to be alive with your eye ripped out. When we found him, three days later, I didn't recognize him. Neither did his mother. We had to do a dental just to be sure it was Anton."

Angie cleared her throat. "How'd you get that recording?"

Oscar said, "Anton was wearing it. Between his legs. He knew he had the whole thing on tape, all he had to do was say Socia's name, and his brain froze up and he forgot. Pain'll do that." He looked at Devin, then back at me. "Mr. Kenzie, I ain't going to try and turn this into good cop/bad cop, but Devin's a friend of yours, and I'm not. I liked Anton a whole hell of a lot though. So I want to know what you know about the shit going on and I want to know now. You figure a way to do that without compromising your clients, that's OK with me. But if you can't figure a way, you're going to tell me anyway. 'Cause we're tired of picking bodies up off the street."

I believed him. "Ask the questions."

Devin said, "What'd you and Socia talk about yesterday?"

"He thinks I have incriminating evidence on him, things Jenna Angeline gave me. He wants to trade me my life for the evidence. I told him if I died, so did he."

"Compliments of Bubba Rogowski," Oscar said.

I raised my eyebrows slightly, then nodded.

Devin said, "What kind of evidence do you have against Socia?"

"Nothing—"

"Bullshit," Oscar said.

"True shit. I don't have anything that could get Socia convicted of so much as jaywalking."

Angie said, "Jenna Angeline promised us there were things that *she* had access to, but she died before she could tell us what or where they were."

"Word on the street is Jenna gave you something right before Curtis Moore popped her," Oscar said.

I looked at Angie and she nodded. I reached into my pocket, pulled out another Xerox of the photo. I passed it to Devin. "That's what she gave me."

Devin looked at it, looked hard at Paulson, flipped it to Oscar. "Where's the rest of it?"

"That's all there is."

Oscar looked at it, looked at Devin. He nodded, looked at me. "You're fucking with the wrong people," he said. "We will throw your tight ass in jail."

"That's all I got."

He slammed a bear's hand down on the table. "Where's the original? Where are the others?"

"I don't know where the others are, and I have the original," I said. "And I'm not giving it up. Throw me in jail. Toss me in a cell with a couple of Saints. Whatever. I don't care. Because I got a lot better chance staying alive in that hole with that picture hidden somewhere than I do out on the street without it."

"You don't think we can protect you?" Devin said.

"No, guys, I don't think you can protect me. I don't have anything on Socia, but he thinks I do. As long as he thinks that, I breathe. Soon as he realizes I'm bluffing, he plays catch-up for Curtis Moore and I end up like Anton." I thought of Anton and felt nauseous.

Oscar said, "Socia's got too much on his slate right now to worry about you."

"That's supposed to make me feel better? What, I got a week or so of happiness before he cleans his slate and remembers me? No way. You want to hear what I think about this, or you want to keep chasing your tails around this point?"

They looked at each other, communicating the way only guys like them can. Devin said, "All right. Tell us what you think's going on."

"Between Socia and Roland—I don't have a clue. Honestly." I picked the photocopy off the table, held it up so they could see it. I said, "But I do know the street terrorism bill was supposed to go before the state senate this morning."

"So?"

"So it didn't. Today of all days, and they're all acting like suddenly the problem's disappeared."

Devin looked at the photocopy, raised an eyebrow. He picked up the phone in front of him, punched a few numbers, waited. "Patch me through to Commander Willis, State House Police." He drummed his fingers on the table, looked at the photocopy. He reached out, took it out of my hands, placed it in front of him, looked at it some more. The rest of us had nothing better to do, so we watched him. "John? This is Devin Amronklin.... Yeah, I got my hands full.... Huh?... Yeah, I think there'll be more. Plenty more.... Look, John...I need to ask you something. Any pols come in today?" He listened. "Well, the Guv, of course. What else is he going to do? And...yeah, yeah. But what about that bill they were sup—Uh-huh...And who was that?...Sure, take your time." He let the phone drop to his neck and drummed his fingers some more. He brought it up to his ear. "Yeah, I'm here....OK, John. Thanks a lot....No, nothing, really. Just curious. Thanks again." He looked at the three of us. "On Friday, someone moved that they all enjoy the long weekend like everyone else."

"Who was that someone?" Angie asked.

Devin tapped the photocopy. "A Senator Brian Paulson," he said. "Mean anything to you?"

I stared back at him.

"No cameras or tape recorders in the walls," he said.

I glanced at the photocopy. "I can't reveal the names of my clients."

Devin nodded. Oscar smiled. They liked that. I'd just told them exactly what they wanted to know. Devin said, "This is big, isn't it?"

I shrugged. Another confirmation.

Devin looked at Oscar. "You got anything else?"

Oscar shook his head. His eyes were bright.

Devin said, "Let's walk them down. Sound good to you, Detective Lee?"

When we stepped out the back door, Oscar told the young cop to go get a cup of coffee. He shook Angie's hand, then mine. He said, "Depending how far this goes, we could lose our badges on this one."

I said, "I know."

Devin looked around the back of the building. "Bucking city hall's one thing, the State House is something else entirely."

I nodded.

Oscar said, "Vine," and looked at Devin.

Devin sighed. "No shit."

Angie said, "Vine?"

Oscar said, "Chris Vine. Vice cop a few years back. Swore he had evidence on a senator, hinted about it going higher than that."

I said, "What happened?"

Devin said, "Someone found two kilos of heroin in his locker."

"Box of hypodermics too," Oscar said.

Devin nodded. "Couple weeks later, Vine ate his gun."

Oscar gave Devin another look. There was something alien in both their eyes. It might have been fear. Oscar said, "You be careful, the both of you. We'll contact you."

"Agreed."

Devin said, "If you're still tight with Richie Colgan, I'd say now might be a good time to use him."

"Not quite yet."

Oscar and Devin looked at each other again, let out big bursts of breath. Oscar looked up at the sky. "Going to be a serious shitstorm any day now."

Angie said, "And the four of us without umbrellas."

We all got a chuckle out of that. A short one though. Laughter at a wake.

TWENTY-FOUR

WE TOOK BOYLSTON DOWN TO ARLINGTON AND CAME BACK around the block to the Greyhound Station. We waded through a listless sea of hookers, pimps, grifters, and assorted terminal cases before we found the dark green metal checkerboard of lockers. Number 506 was at the top of its row and I had to reach up a bit to try the key.

It didn't fit. One down.

We tried a couple of smaller places. Nothing.

We drove out to the airport. Logan Airport has five terminals, lettered *A* through *E. A* had no 506. B terminal had no lockers. C had no 506 in Arrivals. We walked down to Departures. Like the rest of the city, it was a ghost town, the waxed floor still slick and unscuffed, reflecting the bright fluorescents overhead. We found 506, took a deep breath, let it out when the key didn't fit.

Same thing in *D* and *E*.

We tried some places in East Boston, Chelsea, Revere— nada.

We stopped at a sandwich shop in Everett and took a seat by the window. The morning had died and the sky had hardened to a damp newspaper gray. It didn't seem particularly cloudy, just resolutely sunless. A red Mustang pulled in across the street and the driver looked in the record store in front of him, probably waiting on a friend.

Angie said, "You think he's the only one?"

I shook my head, swallowed a bite of roast beef. "He's the point man."

We both looked across at him. He was parked a good forty yards back, a thin black head shaven till it gleamed. No sunglasses this time. Probably didn't want anything obstructing his vision when he took a shot at me.

"Where do you think Bubba is?" I said.

"If we could see him, he wouldn't be doing his job."

I nodded. "Still, be nice if he fired a flare every now and then, if only for my peace of mind."

"He is your peace of mind, Skid."

Hard to argue with the truth.

·

We led the Mustang back with us through Somerville and up onto 93, heading into the city. We got off at South Station and parked on Summer Street. The Mustang cruised past, following the traffic past the post office. He turned right, and we got out and walked up to the main entrance.

South Station used to look like a great location for a gangster movie. It's huge, with enormous cathedral ceilings and parquet marble floors that seem to run on into infinity. Used to be all this space was interrupted only by a wooden newsstand, a shoeshine booth, and a few dark mahogany circular benches, expansive and double-tiered like human water fountains. It was the perfect place to wear powder-blue wool suits and matching fedoras, sit and watch people from behind a newspaper. Then came hard times, forgotten times, and the marble grew brown and scuffed, the newsstand needed a paint job or a wrecking ball, and the shoeshine stand disappeared entirely. Then, a few years ago, refurbishment. Now there's a hot dog/pizza place with a yellow neon sign, an Au Bon Pain with Cinzano umbrellas over black wrought-iron tables, and a new newsstand that looks like a cross between a fern bar and a bookstore. The whole place looks smaller, the moody dark hues that pooled in shadows around shafts of faded sunlight have been replaced with glaring bright lights and an ambience of faked happiness. Spend all the money you want on ambience, it still won't change the fact that a train station is a place where people wait, usually without much glee, for a train to come take them away.

The lockers are in the back near the rest rooms. As we headed toward them, an old guy with stiff white hair and a PA system for vocal cords announced: "The Ambassador bound for Providence, Hartford, New Haven, and New York City, now boarding on track thirty-two." If the little dink had had a megaphone I would have lost an ear.

We walked down a dark corridor and stepped into yesterday. No glaring fluorescents, no ferns, just marble and dim yellow lamps that were one step removed from candles. We searched the rows of lockers in the semidarkness, trying to make out the faded, stenciled brass numbers, until Angie said, "Here."

I patted my pockets. "You got the key, right?"

She looked at me. "Patrick."

"Where's the last place we used it?"

"Patrick," she said again, only this time her teeth were gritted.

I held it up. "God, you can't take a joke anymore."

She snatched the key from my hand, slipped it into the lock, and turned it.

I think she was more surprised than I was.

The bag inside was blue plastic. The word "Gap" was

stenciled in white letters across the middle. Angie handed it to me. Light. We looked back in, felt around. Nothing more. Angie let the door clang behind us and I carried the bag in my left hand as we walked back down the corridor. A veritable spring to our steps. Payday.

Or Payback Day, depending on your perspective.

The bald kid who'd been driving the Mustang was coming across the terminal toward us fast. He saw us, surprised, and started to turn away. Then he noticed the bag. Real bright fucking move on my part, not putting it under my coat. Baldie raised his right hand over his head and his left dug under his warm-up jacket.

Two kids disengaged themselves from the corner of the Au Bon Pain counter, and another one—a guy, older than the three of them—sauntered toward us from the left, near the entrance.

Baldie had his gun clear now, holding it down by his leg, walking casually, his eyes never leaving us. The terminal was packed, the oblivious crowd between us and Baldie scooping up their coffee cups and newspapers and luggage and heading out toward the track. Baldie was starting to smile, the crowd and twenty yards all that remained between us. My gun was in my hand now, the bag in front of it. Angie had her hand stuffed in her pocket, both of us taking tender steps forward as the crowd streamed past us, jostling us every now and then. Baldie was moving just as slowly, but with confidence, as if all his movements had been choreographed. His smile was huge, an adrenaline junkie's smile, sucking its fuel from the tension. Fifteen yards between us now, and Baldie starting to rock forward just a bit as he walked, getting high off it.

Then Bubba stepped out of the crowd and blew off the back of his head with a shotgun.

The kid vaulted up in the air, arms spread wide, chest out in a swan dive, and hit the ground on his face. The crowd erupted, scattering across the marble, crashing into one another, no real sense of direction except to get as far away from the corpse as possible, like pigeons without wings, tripping and sliding, trying to scramble back up off the marble before they got trampled. The guy on our left aimed an Uzi, one-handed, straight across the terminal at us and we dropped to our knees as it let loose, the ricochets chucking out pieces of the wall behind us. Bubba's shotgun went off again, and the guy jerked up in the air like he'd just pulled the rip cord on a parachute. He flew back through a window but only half the glass shattered. He hung there, half in, half out, in a glass web.

I took aim at the other two kids as Bubba jacked the shells out of the shotgun and slammed two more home. I squeezed off three shots and the kids dove into a fray of black iron tables. It was impossible to get a clear shot with the crowd in the way, so Angie and I fired at the tables, the bullets popping off the black iron legs. One of the kids rolled onto his back as Bubba turned in his direction. He fired a .357 and the round hit Bubba high in the chest. The shotgun shattered the glass six feet above their heads, and Bubba went down.

A police unit came off Atlantic, bounced straight up onto the curb, and stopped just short of the glass doors. What remained of the crowd seemed to have all come to its senses at once; everyone lay flat on their bellies on the marble, hands protecting heads, luggage providing extra cover like leather retaining walls. The two kids stumbled over the tables and headed toward the tracks, firing in at us from the other side of the windows.

I started toward the middle of the terminal, toward

Bubba, but a second police unit jumped the curb, skidding to a stop. The first two cops were already inside, pumping rounds at the two kids near the tracks. Angie grabbed my arm and we ran toward the corridor. The window to my left shattered, dropping out of the pane in a white cascade. The cops were coming closer, firing with accuracy now as the two kids stumbled into each other, trying to get a clear shot at us. Just before we made the corridor, one of them suddenly spun around like a top and sat down. He looked confused, glass falling around him like snow.

Angie kicked the alarm bar on the back door and the siren blast filled the terminal, bleating its call onto the street as we ran behind a row of trucks toward the corner. We cut out into traffic and went around the block, charging back up to Atlantic. We stopped on the corner, took a couple of deep breaths, held them as two more cruisers blew past us. We waited for the light, sweat pouring off our faces. When it turned red, we trotted across Atlantic, through the red dragon's arch and down into Chinatown. We walked up Beach Street, past some men icing down their fish, past a woman tossing a barrel of fetid water off the back of a tiny loading dock, past an old Vietnamese couple, still dressed in the garb they'd worn during the French occupation. A small guy in a white shirt argued with a beefy Italian truck driver. The truck driver kept saying, "We go through this every day. Speak fucking English, goddamnit," and the small guy said, "No speak English. You charge too fucky much, goddamnit." As we passed, the truck driver said, "Now 'too fucky much' that I can understand." The small guy looked fit to shoot him.

We caught a cab at the corner of Beach and Harrison, told the Iranian driver where we wanted to go. He looked at us in the rearview. "Tough day?"

No matter where you are, "tough day" and "too fucky much" seem to be part of the universal language. I looked at him and nodded. "Tough day," I said.

He shrugged. "Me too," he said and pulled onto the expressway.

Angie leaned her head against my shoulder. "What about Bubba?" Her voice was hoarse and thick.

"I don't know," I said and looked at the Gap bag in my lap.

She took my hand and I held on tight.

TWENTY-FIVE

I SAT IN THE FRONT PEW OF ST. BART'S AND WATCHED ANGIE light a candle for Bubba. She stood over it for a moment, her hand cupped around it until the yellow flame grew fat with oxygen. Then she knelt and bowed her head.

I started to bow mine, then stopped halfway, caught in the middle as always.

I believe in God. Maybe not the Catholic God or even the Christian one because I have a hard time seeing any God as elitist. I also have a hard time believing that anything that created rain forests and oceans and an infinite universe would, in the same process, create something as unnatural as humanity in its own image. I believe in God, but not as a he or a she or an it, but as something that defies my ability to conceptualize within the rather paltry frames of reference I have on hand.

I stopped praying—or bowing, for that matter—a long time ago, around the time my prayers became whispered chants pleading for the Hero's demise and the courage necessary to have a hand in it. I never did get the courage, and the demise happened slowly, witnessed by my impotent stew of leftover emotions. Afterward, the world went on and any contract between God and myself had severed, interred in the hole with my father.

Angie stood up, blessed herself, and walked down off the carpeted altar to the pew. She stood there, looking down at the Gap bag beside me, and waited.

Bubba was dead, dying, or severely wounded because of this innocuous-looking bag. Jenna was dead too. So were Curtis Moore and two or three guys in the Amtrak station and twelve anonymous street kids who'd probably felt dead for a long time. By the time this was all over, Socia or I would join those statistics too. Maybe both of us. Maybe Angie. Maybe Roland.

A lot of pain in such a simple plastic bag.

"They'll get here soon," Angie said. "Open it."

"They" were the police. It wouldn't take Devin and Oscar long to identify the Unidentified White Male and the Unidentified White Female who shot it out at the train station with gang members, aided by a known gunrunner named Bubba Rogowski.

I loosened the string at the top of the bag, reached in, and my hand closed around a file folder, maybe a quarter-inch thick. I pulled it out and opened it. More photographs.

I stood and laid them out on the pew. There were twenty-one in all, their surfaces splintered by the triangles of shadow and light cast by the stained-glass windows. Not one of them contained anything I'd want to look at; all of them contained things I had to.

They were from the same camera and location that produced the photograph Jenna had given me. Paulson was in most of these, Socia in a few. The same scuzzy motel room, the same grainy texture to the film, the same high camera angle, leading me to assume they were stills from a videotape, the camera probably positioned eight or ten feet up, possibly behind a double mirror.

In most of the photos, Paulson had removed his underwear but retained his black socks. He seemed to be enjoying himself on the small twin bed with torn, stained sheets.

The same couldn't be said for the other person on the bed. The object of Paulson's affection—if you could call it that—was a child. A young, extremely skinny black boy who couldn't have been any older than ten or eleven. He wasn't wearing any socks. He wasn't wearing anything at all. He didn't seem to be having as much fun as Paulson.

He did seem to be in a lot of pain.

Sixteen of the twenty-one photographs captured the sex act itself. In some of these, Socia appeared, leaning into the frame to give Paulson what appeared to be directions. In one, Socia's hand gripped the back of the child's head, yanking it back toward Paulson's chest, like a rider reining in a horse. Paulson didn't seem to mind or even notice, his eyes glazed, his lips pursed in pleasure.

The child seemed to mind.

Of the five remaining photographs, four were of Paulson and Socia as they drank dark liquid from bathroom glasses, chatting it up, leaning against the dresser, having a swell old time. In one of those, the boy's slim leg was apparent, just out of focus, tangled in the filthy bedsheets.

Angie said, "Oh, my God," in a cracked, high-pitched voice that sounded like it came from someone else. The knuckles of her right hand were in her mouth, and her whitening skin rippled. Tears welled in her sockets. The warm, stilted air in the church closed in on me for a moment, a weight against my chest that left me slightly lightheaded. I looked down at the photographs again, and nausea eddied against the walls of my stomach.

I forced myself to look down at the photos, to hold my eyes there, and soon, my eyes were drawn to the twenty-first the way they would drift toward and fasten onto a single flame in the corner of a dark screen. This was the photograph, I knew, that had already burned its way into my dreams and my shadows, into that part of my mind that I have no control over. Its image would reappear in all its wanton cruelty for the rest of my life, particularly when I was least prepared for it. It was not taken during the act, but afterward. The boy sat on the bed, uncovered and oblivious, his eyes taking on the ghostly image of what he'd already ceased being. In those eyes was the shriveled cast of dead hope and a closed door. They were the eyes of a brain and a soul that had collapsed under the weight of sensory overload. The eyes of the walking dead, their owner oblivious to his loss, his nakedness.

I shuffled the photographs back into a pile and closed the file. Numbness was already settling in, clotting the flow of horror and bewilderment. I looked at Angie, saw the same process taking place in her. The shakes had stopped and she stood very still. It wasn't a sweet feeling, possibly it was harmful in the long run, but at the moment, it was absolutely necessary.

Angie looked up, her eyes red but dry. She pointed at the file. "No matter what, we take them down."

I nodded. "Going to have to take it to them."

She shrugged and leaned back against the baptismal font. "Oh well."

I took one photo from the folder—one that showed the act—the boy, Socia, and Paulson's body but not his head. Socia was Devin's, maybe, but Paulson was mine. I took the rest of the folder to one of the rear confessionals, stepped through the heavy burgundy partition, and bent by the floor. I used my penknife on a square of marble that's been loose since I was an altar boy. I lifted it out and placed the folder down in the two-foot hole. Angie was behind me now, and I held out my hand. She placed her .38 in it and I added the nine millimeter, then closed the hole back up again. The square fit neatly, without any noticeable gaps, and I realized then that I'd co-opted one of the great Catholic traditions: concealment.

I stepped back out of the confessional and we walked down the center aisle. At the door, Angie dipped her fingers into the holy water and blessed herself. I thought about it, figuring I'd need all the help I could get on this one, but there's one thing I hate more than a hypocrite: a pious one. We pushed open the heavy oak doors and stepped into the late afternoon sunlight.

Devin and Oscar were parked out front, leaning over the hood of Devin's Camaro, a spread of McDonald's food in front of them. They didn't so much as look up at us before Devin said, around a mouthful of Big Mac, "You have the right to remain silent. Anything you say can and will be used against you in a court of law. Hand me those fries, partner. You have a right to an attorney...."

•

It was well into the next morning before they finished with us.

Devin and Oscar were obviously taking a lot of heat. Gangland shootouts in Roxbury or Mattapan are one thing, but when it rises from the ghettos and rears its ugly head in the heart of the city, when Joe and Suzy Citizen have to stumble over their Louis Vuitton luggage to duck out of the way of gunfire, then there's a problem. We were cuffed. We were booked. Devin took the photo from me without a word before we got to the station, and they took everything else shortly after.

I stood in a lineup with four cops who didn't look remotely like me, and stared into a white light. Beyond it, I heard a cop saying, "Take your time. Look closely," followed by a woman's voice: "I didn't really get a good look. I only saw the big black guy."

Lucky me. If there's gunfire, people usually see the black guy.

Angie and I met up again later when they sat us down on a bench beside a mangy wino named Terrance. Terrance smelled like a banana stew, but he didn't seem to mind. He gladly explained to me, while brushing his teeth with his index finger, why the world was so out of control. Uranus. The good green folks who inhabit this planet don't have the technology to build modern cities; Terrance told us they can build farmhouses that would make your mouth water, but skyscrapers are beyond them. "But they want 'em bad, you see?" Now that we'd built all those skyscrapers, the Urani were ready to take over. They pissed through the rain, filling our water supply with a violence-inducing drug. Within ten years, Terrance confided in us, we'd have all killed each other off and the cities would be theirs. A big green party in the Sears Tower.

I asked Terrance where he'd be then, and Angie elbowed me in the ribs for encouraging him.

Terrance stopped brushing his teeth for a moment and looked at me. "Back on Uranus, of course." He leaned in close and I almost passed out from the smell. "I'm one of them."

I said, "Of course you are."

They came and got Terrance a few minutes later, took him off to his spaceship or a secret meeting with the government. They left us where we were. Devin and Oscar walked by a few times without glancing our way. A lot of other cops did the same, not to mention some hookers, an army of bail bondsmen, a bunch of PDs with awkward briefcases and the lean faces of those who don't have time to eat. As darkness fell, then deepened, a lot of hard-looking guys, built like Devin—powerful and low to the ground—headed toward the elevators, bulky Teflon vests under dark blue windbreakers, M-16s in their hands. The Anti-Gang Task Force. They held the elevators until Devin and Oscar joined them, then they all went down in two cars.

They never offered us a phone call. They'd do that just before or within the first few minutes of our interrogation. Someone would say, "What, nobody told you you could make a phone call? Jeeze. All our lines must have been busy."

A kid in patrolman's blues brought us some lukewarm coffee from a machine. The old cop who'd taken our prints stood across from us behind a desk. He stamped a stack of papers, answered the phone a lot, and if he remembered us at all, he was doing a good job of hiding it. At one point, when I stood up stretch, he half-glanced my way and out of the corner of my eye I saw a cop appear in the hallway on my left. I got a drink from the water fountain—not an easy thing to manage with your hands cuffed—and sat back down.

Angie said, "They won't tell us about Bubba will they?"

I shook my head. "If we ask about him, it puts us at the crime scene. If they tell us before we ask, they lose everything, gain nothing."

"Pretty much what I figured."

She slept for a while, her head on my shoulder, her

knees close to her chest. The weight of her body probably would have cramped a muscle after a while if there'd been any left to cramp; after nine or ten hours on this bench, a simple stretching exercise would have been orgasmic.

They'd taken my watch, but the darkest blue of night had already begun to give way to the first false light of early morning by the time Devin and Oscar returned. I guessed it was around five. Devin said, "Follow us, Kenzie," as he passed.

We peeled ourselves off the bench and staggered down the hallway after them. My legs refused to straighten completely and my lower back felt like I'd swallowed a hammer. They led us into the same interrogation room where'd we'd met about twenty hours before, let the door swing back into my face as I approached. I pushed it open with my cuffed hands and we did our Quasimodo imitations through the doorway.

I said, "You ever hear of the ACLU?"

Devin tossed a walkie-talkie down on the table in front of him. He followed with a huge ring of keys, then sat back in a chair and watched us. His eyes were ragged and red, but darkly vibrant, an amphetamine vibrancy. Oscar's looked the same. They'd probably been up forty-eight hours straight. Someday, when all this was over and they were both spending Sundays in their La-Z-Boys watching football games, their hearts would finally play catch up, do what no bullet had ever managed. Knowing them, they'd probably go the same day too.

I held out my hands. "You going to take these things off?"

Devin looked at my wrists, then at my face. He shook his head.

Angie sat down. "You're an asshole."

"I am," Devin said.

I took a seat.

Oscar said, "Case you two are interested, they upped the ante in the war tonight. Someone fired a grenade through the window of a Saints' crack house. Took out damn near everyone inside, including two babies, couldn't have been more than nine months, the oldest. We're not positive yet, but we think two of the dead might have been white college kids, there on a buy. Probably the best thing could have happened. Maybe somebody'll care now."

I said, "What'd you do with that photograph?"

"Filed it," Devin said. "Socia's already wanted for questioning on seven deaths in the last two nights. If he ever comes to ground, that photo will be one more thing to nail him with. The white guy in the photo, the one on top of the little kid—somebody tells me who he is, maybe we can do something about it."

"Maybe if I was allowed back out on the street, I could do something in ways you couldn't."

Devin said, "Like shoot up another train station?"

Oscar said, "You wouldn't last five minutes on the street anymore, Kenzie."

Angie said, "Why's that?"

"Because Socia knows you have incriminating evidence on him. Hard evidence. Because your main protection, Patrick, ain't in the game anymore and everyone knows it. Because your life ain't worth a nickel bag as long as Socia's still walking around."

"So what's the charge?" I asked.

"Charge?"

"What're you charging us with, Devin?"

Oscar said, "Charging?" Couple of parrots, these two.

"Devin."

"Mr. Kenzie, I have nothing to hold you on. My partner

and I *were* under the impression that you might have been involved in some nasty business down at South Station early yesterday afternoon. But, since no witnesses can place you there, what can I say? We fucked up. And we're too sorry about it, believe me."

Angie said, "Take the cuffs off."

"Would that we could find the key," Devin said.

"Take the fucking cuffs off, Devin," she said again.

"Oscar?"

Oscar pulled out all his pockets.

"Oscar doesn't have them either. We'll have to call around."

Oscar stood up. "Maybe I take a look around, see if I can scare them up."

He left and we sat there, Devin watching us. We watched him back. He said, "Think about protective custody."

I shook my head.

"Patrick," he said in a tone my mother used to use, "it's a rolling battleground out there. You won't make it until sunrise. Angie, neither will you if you're with him."

She tilted her chair back, turned her beautiful, weary face toward me. She said, "'Nobody hands me my guns and says run. Nobody.'" Just like James Coburn in *The Magnificent Seven*. Her full mouth burst wide, the smile that blew into my chest was devastating. At that moment, I think I knew what love was.

We looked at Devin.

He sighed. "I saw the movie too. Coburn died in the end."

"There's always reruns," I said.

"Not out there, there isn't."

Oscar came back through the door. He said, "Well, lookee here," and held up a small key ring.

"Where'd you find 'em?" Devin asked.

Oscar tossed them onto the table in front of me. "Right where I left them. Funny how that works sometimes, huh."

Devin pointed at us. "They think they're cowboys."

Oscar pulled back his chair and settled heavily into it. "Then we'll bury them with their boots on."

TWENTY-SIX

WE COULDN'T GO HOME. DEVIN WAS RIGHT. I HAD NO MORE cards to play, and Socia had nothing to gain as long as I continued breathing.

We sat around for another two hours while they finished up some paperwork and then they took us out a side door and drove us a few blocks away to the Lenox Hotel.

As we got out of the car, Oscar looked over at Devin. "Have a heart. Tell 'em."

We stood on the curb, waited.

Devin said, "Rogowski's got a broken collarbone and he lost a shitload of blood, but he's stable."

Angie sagged against me for a moment.

Devin said, "Been swell knowing you," and drove off.

The folks at the Lenox didn't seem too pleased we'd chosen their hotel at eight in the morning, sans luggage. Our clothes, appropriately, looked as if we'd sat on a bench all night, and my hair was still speckled with chips of marble from the shoot-out at South Station. I gave them my Visa Gold Card and they asked for more ID. While the concierge copied the numbers of my driver's license onto a pad of paper, the reservations clerk called in my Visa number for authorization. Some people you can never please.

After they ascertained that I was who I said I was and that we probably wouldn't make off with much more than a bath towel and some sheets, they gave us a room key. I signed my name and looked up at the reservations clerk. "Is the TV in our room bolted to the wall or could it just roll on out of there?"

She gave me a very tight smile but didn't answer.

The room was on the ninth floor, overlooking Boylston Street. Not a bad view. Directly below us wasn't much—a Store 24, a Dunkin' Donuts—but beyond, a nice stretch of brownstones, some with mint-green roof gardens, and beyond them, the dark, rolling Charles striped against a pale, gray sky.

The sun was rising steadily. I was dead tired, but more than sleep, I needed a shower. Too bad Angie's quicker than I am. I sat in a chair and flicked on the TV. Bolted to the wall, of course. The early news was running a commentary about yesterday's gang violence in South Station. The commentator, broad-shouldered with bangs that looked as if they'd been sharpened to points with a razor, was damn near quivering with righteous anger. Gang violence, he said, had finally reached our front doors and something had to be done about it, no matter what.

It's always when it reaches our "front doors" that we finally consider it a problem. When it's confined to our backyards for decades, no one even notices it.

I turned off the TV, switched places with Angie when she came out of the bathroom.

By the time I'd finished, she was asleep, lying on her stomach, one hand still on the phone where she'd hung it up, the other still closed around the top of the towel. Beads of water glistened on her bare back above the towel line, her slim shoulder blades rising and falling with each breath.

I dried off and went to the bed. I pulled the covers out from under her and she groaned softly, raising her left leg closer to her chest. I placed the sheet over her and shut off the light.

I lay down on the right side of the bed, a few feet away from her on top of the sheet, and prayed she didn't roll over in her sleep. If her body touched mine, I was afraid I'd dissolve into it. And probably not mind.

That being the major problem, right there, I turned onto my side, facing the wall, and waited for sleep.

•

Some time shortly before I woke up, I saw the boy in the photos. The Hero was carrying him down a dank hallway, both of them enshrouded in shower steam. Water dripped steadily from the ceiling. I yelled something to the boy, because I knew him. I knew him in that dank hallway as his legs kicked out from under my father's arm. He seemed small in my father's arm, smaller still because he was naked. I called to him and my father turned back toward me; Sterling Mulkern's face was under the dark fireman's helmet. He said, "If you had half the balls your old man had..." in Devin's voice. The boy turned too, the face craning around my father's elbow bored and disinterested, even as his bare legs flailed. His eyes were empty, like a doll's, and I felt my legs buckle when I realized nothing would ever shock or scare him again.

I woke up to Angie kneeling over me, her hands on my shoulders. She said, "It's OK, it's OK," in a soft whisper.

I was very aware of her bare legs against mine as I said, "What?"

"It's OK," she said. "Just a dream."

The room was pitch dark but light exploded behind the heavy curtains. I said, "What time is it?"

She stood up, still wearing the towel, and walked to the window. "Eight o'clock," she said. "P.M." She opened the curtain. "On the Fourth of July."

The sky was a canvas of explosive colors. Whites, reds, blues, even some orange and yellow. A clap of thunder rocked the room and a starburst of blue and white ignited the sky. A shooting star of red rocketed through the middle and set off a smaller starburst that bled all over the blue and white. The whole display hit its peak then collapsed at once, the colors arcing downward and sputtering out in a cascade of dying embers. Angie opened the windows and the Boston Pops boomed Beethoven's Fifth as if they had a wall of speakers wrapped around the Hub.

I said, "We slept fourteen hours?"

She nodded. "Shoot-outs and interrogations will do that to you, I guess."

"I guess so."

She came back to the bed, sat on the corner. "Boy, Skid, when you have a nightmare, you have a *nightmare*."

I rubbed my face. "Sorry I woke you."

"Had to get up some time. Speaking of which, do we have a plan of any sort?"

"We have to find Paulson and Socia."

"That's an objective, not a plan."

"We need our guns."

"Definitely."

"Probably not going to be easy getting to them with Socia's people all over the place."

"We're the inventive type."

•

We took a cab back to the neighborhood, gave the driver an address about a half-mile past the church. I didn't see anyone lurking in the shadows as we passed, but you're not supposed to: that's why there are shadows; that's why they lurk. Some kids—ten or twelve years old at most—were shooting bottle rockets at the passing cars, tossing packs of firecrackers out into the middle of the avenue. The car directly behind us took a direct hit to its windshield and screeched to a halt. The guy jumped out running, but the kids were gone before he'd even reached the curb, hopping fences like hurdlers, disappearing into their own backyard jungle.

Angie and I paid the cabbie and walked through the backyard of the public grammar school—the "project" school we called it when we were kids, because only the kids from the housing projects went there. In the back of the schoolyard, hanging in a loose pack around the fire escape, twenty or so of the older neighborhood kids pounded back some beers, a boom box tuned to WBCN, a few passing around a joint. When they saw us, one of them turned the boom box up louder. J. Geils Band's "Whammer Jammer." Fine with me. They had already decided we weren't cops and now they were deliberating how bad they were going to scare us for being stupid enough to walk through their hangout.

Then a few of them recognized us as we passed under a streetlight and seemed pretty depressed—can't scare people who know your parents. I recognized their leader, Colin, right off. Bobby Shefton's kid; good-looking, even if he was as obviously Irish as a potato famine—tall, well-built, a short-cropped head of dirty blond hair around a chiseled face. He was wearing a white and green BNBL tank top and a pair of pleated walking shorts. He said, "'S up, Mr. Kenzie?"

They nodded to Angie. No one wants to get too well acquainted with a woman whose husband's jealous streak is legend.

I said, "Colin, how'd you guys like to make fifty bucks before the liquor store closes?"

His eyes lit up for a moment before he remembered how cool he was. He said, "You go in and buy the shit for us?"

"Of course."

They kicked the idea around for a second and a half or so. "You got it. What do you need?"

I said, "It involves screwing with people who might be packing."

Colin shrugged. "Niggers ain't the only ones with guns anymore, Mr. Kenzie." He pulled his own from under his tank top. A couple of other kids did too. "Since they tried to take over the Ryan playground a couple months back, we stocked up a bit." For a moment I thought back to my days on this fire escape—the good old days of tire irons and baseball bats. When a switchblade was rare. But the ante kept getting upped, and obviously, everyone was willing to meet it.

My plan had been to get them to pack around us as we walked back up to the church. With hats, in the darkness, we could probably pass as kids, and by the time Socia's people figured it out, we'd be in the church with our guns. It had never been much of a plan. And I realized now that I'd missed the obvious because of my own racism. If the black kids had guns, only went to figure, the white kids would have them too.

I said, "Tell you what. I changed my mind. I'll give you a hundred bucks *and* the booze for three things."

Colin said, "Name 'em."

"Let us rent two of your guns." I tossed him my car keys. "And go boost my car from in front of my house."

"That's two things."

"Three," I said. "Two guns and one car. What're they teaching you kids these days?"

One of the kids laughed. "Helps if you go to school."

Colin said, "You just want to rent the guns? You'll definitely bring them back?"

"Probably. If not, we'll kick in enough to buy you two more."

Colin stood, handed me his gun, butt first. A .357, scratched along the barrel, but well oiled. He slapped a buddy's shoulder and the buddy handed his gun to Angie. A .38. Her favorite. He looked at his buddy. "Let's go get Mr. Kenzie's car."

While they were gone, we walked across the street to the liquor store and filled their order—five cases of Bud, two liters of vodka, some OJ, some gin. We carried it back across the street and had just given it to the kids when the Vobeast came hurtling down the avenue and smoked rubber the last quarter block to the curb. Colin and his pal were out of it before it stopped rolling. "Get going, Mr. Kenzie. They're coming."

We scrambled into the car and pulled off the curb as the headlights loomed large and malevolent in back of us. There were two sets of headlights and they were right behind us, three silhouettes in each car. They started firing half a block past the school, the bullets ripping into the Vobeast. I cut across the wrong lane of traffic and jumped the divider strip as we entered Edward Everett Square. I banged a right past a tavern, punched the pedal as we lit down the small, densely packed street, the cars fat on both sides. In my rearview, I saw the first car spin around the corner and straighten out cleanly. The second car, though, didn't make the turn. It bounced off a Dodge and the front axle snapped in two. Its fender plowed into asphalt and it flipped up onto its grill.

The first car was still firing away, and Angie and I kept ducking our heads, not sure which explosions came from a gun muzzle and which came from the barrage of fireworks in the sky overhead. Straight out, like this, there was no way we'd last. A Yugo could outrun the Vobeast, and the streets were growing tighter and tighter with less cover and more parked cars.

We crossed over into Roxbury and my back window imploded. I took enough shards of glass in my neck to think I'd been shot for a moment, and Angie had a cut on her forehead that was bleeding a thick river down her left cheekbone. I said, "You OK?"

She nodded, scared but pissed off too. She said, "Goddamn them," and swiveled on the seat, pointing the .38 at the space where the window used to be. My ear exploded as she squeezed off two shots, her arm steady.

Angie's one hell of a shot. The windshield of the car splattered into two big spiderwebs. The driver spun the wheel and they rammed a white panel truck, bounced back into the street sideways.

I didn't stop to check their condition. The Vobeast careened onto a badly paved stretch of road that rocked our heads off the ceiling. I spun the wheel to the right and turned onto a street that was only marginally better. Someone screamed something at us as we went past, and a bottle shattered against the trunk.

The left side of the street was one big abandoned lot, scorched overgrown weeds pouring up out of piles of gravel, crumbled cinder block and brick. To our right, houses that should have been condemned a half-century ago sagged toward the earth, carrying the weight of poverty and neglect with them until the day they'd spill into one another like dominoes. Then the right side of the street would look identical to the left. The porches were crowded and no one seemed too pleased with the whiteys in the rolling piece of shit tearing down their street. A few more bottles hit the car, a cherry bomb blew up in front of us.

I reached the end of the street, and just as I saw the other car appear a block back, I took a left. The street I turned onto was even worse, a bleak, forgotten path through brown weeds and the skeletal remains of abandoned tenements. A few kids stood by a burning trash can tossing firecrackers inside, and behind them two winos tackled one another for the rights to that last sip of T-bird. Beyond them, the condemned tenements rose in crumbling brick, the black windows empty of glass, singed in places by some forgotten fire.

Angie said, "Oh, Christ, Patrick."

The street dead-ended, no outlet, twenty yards away. A heavy cement divider and years of weeds and rubble stood in our way. I looked behind me as I began to apply the brakes, and saw the car turning the corner toward us. The kids were walking away from the barrel, smelling the battle and getting out of the line of fire. I stood on the brakes and the Vobeast gave me a belligerent "fuck you" in reply. Metal clacked against metal, and I might as well have been in a Flintstone car. It seemed to almost pick up a last burst of speed just before we hit the divider.

My head popped off the dashboard and a rush of metal taste fragmented within my mouth as the impact shook me. Angie had been a little more prepared. She snapped forward, but her seatbelt held her in place.

We barely looked at one another before we jumped out of the car. I scrambled across the hood as the brakes behind us squealed on the torn cement. Angie was sprinting like an Olympian across the lot of weeds and cinder block and broken glass, her chest out, her head thrown back. She was a good ten yards ahead of me by the time I got going. They fired from the car, the bullets chunking into the ground beside me, what remained of natural soil spitting up between the garbage.

Angie had reached the first tenement. She was looking at me, waving me to go faster, her gun pointed in my general direction, craning her head for a clear shot. I didn't like the look in her eyes at all. Then I noticed the shafts of light jerking up and down in front of me, shining off the tenement, jagged where my body blocked them. They'd driven in after us. Exactly what I'd been afraid of. Somewhere in all these weeds and gravel, roads had existed before this area was condemned. And they'd found one.

A burst of gunfire stitched a pile of torn brick as I jumped over it and reached the first tenement. Angie turned as I came through the doorway and we ran inside, ran without thinking, without looking, because we were running into a building that had no back wall. It had crumbled some time ago, and we were just as out in the open as we'd been before.

The car came across the middle of the building, rocketing over an old metal door ahead of us. I took aim because there was nothing to hide behind. The front passenger and the guy in the backseat were sticking black weapons out the windows. I got off two shots that punched the front door before they let loose, tongues of fire bursting from their muzzles. Angie dove to her left, landing behind an overturned bathtub. I went up in the air, nothing to cover me, and I was halfway down when a bullet burned across my left bicep and snapped me around in midair. I hit the ground and fired again, but the car had gone out the other side and was circling for another pass.

Angie said, "Come on."

I got up and saw what she was running for. Twenty yards ahead of us were two more tenement towers, intact it seemed, and packed close together. Between them was a dark blue alley. A hazy yellow streetlight shone at the end of it, and it was much too thin for a car to work its way into. Silhouettes of misshapen hulks of metal stood out in dark shadows between the two towers.

I ran across the open lot, hearing the engine coming off to my left, blood pouring down my arm like warm soup. I'd been shot. Shot. I saw their faces again as they fired, and I heard a voice that I soon realized was mine saying the same thing, over and over again: "Fucking niggers, fucking niggers."

We reached the alley. I looked behind me. The car was stalled by something in the gravel, but the way they were rocking it from the inside, I didn't think they'd stay that way long. I said, "Keep going."

Angie said, "Why? We can pick them off as they come in."

"How many bullets you got left?"

"I don't know."

"Exactly," I said. "We could run out trying to pick them off." I worked my way over an upturned dumpster. "Trust me."

Once we made it to the end of the alley, I looked back and saw the headlights arcing to the left, moving again, coming around to meet us. The road at the end of the alley was a faded yellow cobblestone. We stepped out onto it, hearing the big engine roaring closer. The yellow streetlight we'd seen was the only one for two blocks. Angie checked her gun. "I have four bullets."

I had three. She was the better shot. I said, "The streetlight."

She fired once and stepped back as the glass fell in a

small shower to the street. I jogged across the street into a mass of brown weeds. Angie climbed down behind a torched car directly across from me. Her eyes peered over the blackened hood, looking at me, both of our heads nodding forward, the adrenaline rippling through us like fission.

The car fishtailed around the corner, hurtling over the torn cobblestone toward us, the driver craning his head out the window, looking for us. The car began to slow as it got closer, trying to figure out where we could have gone. The shotgun passenger turned his head to his right, looked at the scorched car, didn't see anything. He turned back, and started to say something to the driver.

Angie stood up, took aim over the blackened hood, and fired two shots into his face. His head snapped to the side, bounced off his shoulder, and the driver looked at him for one moment. When he looked back, I was running up to the window, gun extended. He said, "Wait!" through the open window and his eyes loomed large and white just before I pulled the trigger and blew them out through the back of his head.

The car went left, hit an old shopping cart on its way to the curb, bouncing up and over it before ramming a wooden telephone pole and cracking the wood at a point about six feet off the ground. The guy in the backseat shattered the window with his head. The telephone pole wavered in the fragrant summer breeze for a moment, then dropped forward and crushed the driver's side of the car.

We approached slowly, guns pointed at the hole in the back window. We were about three feet away, side by side, when the door creaked open, the lower corner hitting the sidewalk. I took a deep breath and waited for a head to show.

It did, followed by a body that dropped to the pavement, covered in glass and blood.

He was alive. His left arm was twisted out behind him at an impossible angle and a large flap of skin was missing from his forehead, but he was trying to crawl anyway. He got two or three feet before he collapsed, rolling over onto his back, breathing hard.

Roland.

He spit some blood onto the sidewalk and opened one eye to look at me. The other eye was already beginning to swell under the mask of blood. He said, "I'll kill you."

I shook my head.

He managed to sit up a bit, resting on his good arm. He said, "I'll kill you. The bitch too."

Angie kicked him in the ribs.

All the pain he was in and he rolled his head at her and smiled. " 'Scuse me."

I said, "Roland, you got this all backward. We're not your problem. Socia's your problem."

"Socia dead," he said, and I could tell a few of his teeth were broken. "He just don't know it yet. Most of the Saints coming over with me. I get Socia any day now. He lost the war. Just a matter of picking his coffin."

He managed to open both eyes then, for just a moment, and I knew why he wanted me dead.

He was the kid in the photographs.

"You're the—"

He howled at me, a stream of blood jetting from his mouth, trying to lunge for me when he couldn't even get off the ground. He kicked at me and banged his fist off the ground, probably driving shards of glass all that much farther into the skin and bone. His howl grew louder. "I fucking kill you," he screamed. "I fucking kill you."

Angie looked at me. "We let him live, we're both dead."

I considered it. One shot is all it would take. Out here on the cusp of the urban wasteland with no one around to question. One shot and no more Roland to worry about. Once we settled with Socia, back to our regular life. I looked down at Roland as he arched his back and jerked up, trying to stand, like a bloody fish on newspaper. His sheer effort scared the shit out of me. Roland didn't seem to know pain or fear any longer, just *drive*. I looked at him steadily, considering it, and somewhere in that raging, hulking mass of hatred, I saw the naked child with the dying eyes. I said, "He's already dead."

Angie stood over him, gun pointed down, hammer pulled back. Roland watched her and she stared back at him flatly. But she couldn't do it either, and she knew no amount of standing there would change that. She shrugged and said, "Have a nice day," and we walked toward the Melnea Cass Boulevard, four blocks west, shining like civilization itself.

TWENTY-SEVEN

WE FLAGGED DOWN A BUS AND CLIMBED ON. EVERYONE ON it was black and when they saw us—bloody, torn clothes—most of them found some sort of excuse to move to the back. The bus driver closed the door with a soft *whoosh* and pulled off down the highway.

We took seats near the front, and I looked at the people on the bus. Most of them were older; two looked like students, one young couple held a small child between them. They were looking at us with fear and disgust and some hatred. I had an idea what it must be like to be a couple of young black guys in street clothes boarding a subway car in Southie or White Dorchester. Not a nice feeling.

I sat back and looked out the window at the fireworks in the black sky. They were smaller now, less colorful. I heard an echo of my voice as a carload of murderers chased me across an open lot firing bullets at my body, and my hatred and fear distilled into color. "Fucking niggers," I'd said, over and over. I closed my eyes, and in the darkness, they still took note of the light bursting above me in the sky.

Independence Day.

The bus dropped us at the corner of Mass. Ave. and Columbia. I walked Angie back to her house and when we reached it, she touched my shoulder. "You going to get that looked at?"

For all the pain, when I looked at it on the bus, I realized it had only grazed me, cutting the skin like the slash of a good knife—hardly lethal. It needed cleaning and it hurt like hell, but it wasn't worth a cosmetic job in an over-crowded emergency room at the moment. "Tomorrow," I said.

Her living-room curtain parted slightly: Phil, thinking he was the detective. I said, "You better go in."

The prospect didn't seem to appeal to her all that much. She said, "Yeah, I guess I better."

I looked at the blood on her face, the cut on her fore-head. "Better clean that up too," I said. "You're looking like an extra in *Dawn of the Dead*."

"You always know the right thing to say," she said and started toward the house. She saw the parted curtain and turned back toward me, a frown on her face. She looked at me for almost a full minute, her eyes large and a little sad. "He used to be a nice guy. Remember?"

I nodded, because I did. Phil had been a great guy once. Before bills came and jobs went and the future became a vi-cious joke of a word, something to describe what he'd never have. Phil hadn't always been the Asshole. He'd grown into it.

"Good night," I said.

She crossed the porch and went inside.

I walked up onto the avenue, headed toward the church. I stopped in the liquor store and bought myself a six-pack. The guy behind the counter looked at me like he figured I'd die soon; a little over an hour ago—one that seemed like a lifetime now—I'd bought enough liquor to start my own company, and now I was back for more. "You know how it is," I said. "Fourth of July."

The guy looked at me, at my bloody arm and dirty face. "Yeah," he said, "tell that to your liver."

I drank a beer as I walked up the avenue, thinking about Roland and Socia, Angie and Phil, the Hero and me. Dances of pain. Relationships from hell. I'd been a punching bag for my father for eighteen years, and I'd never hit back. I kept believing, kept telling myself, It'll change; he'll get better. It's hard to close the door on optimistic expectations when you love someone.

Angie and Phil were the same way. She'd known him when he was the best-looking guy in the neighborhood, a charmer and natural leader who told the funniest jokes, the warmest stories. He was everyone's idol. A great guy. She still saw that, prayed for it, hoped against hope—no matter how cynically she viewed the rest of the world—that people change for the better sometimes. Phil had to be one of those people, or what gave anything purpose?

And then there was Roland—taking all that hate and ugliness and depravity that had been shoved into him since childhood at every turn, and spinning around and spewing it back at the world. Waging war against his father and telling himself that once it was done, he'd be at peace. But he wouldn't. It never works that way. Once that ugliness has been forced into you, it becomes part of your blood, dilutes it, races through your heart and back out again, staining everything as it goes. The ugliness never goes away, never comes out, no matter what you do. Anyone who thinks otherwise is naive. All you can hope to do is control it, to force it all into one tight ball in one tight place and keep it there, a constant weight.

I reached the belfry—still less risky than my apartment—and went inside. I sat at my desk, drank my beer. The sky was empty now, the celebration ended. The fourth would be the fifth soon and the migration back from the Cape and the Vineyard had probably already begun. The day after a holiday is like the day after your birthday—everything seems old, like tarnished copper.

I placed my feet up on the desk and leaned back in the chair. My arm still burned and I straightened it out in front of me and poured half a beer on it. Homemade anesthesia. The cut was wide but shallow. In a few months the scar tissue would pale from a dull red to a duller white. It would barely be noticeable.

I raised my shirt, looked at the jellyfish on my abdomen, the scar that would never fade, never be mistaken for anything innocuous, for anything but what it was: a mark of violence and depraved indifference, a cattle brand. The Hero's legacy, his stamp on this world, his attempt at immortality. As long as I was alive, carrying this jellyfish on my stomach, then so was he.

When I was growing up, my father's fear of flame burgeoned in direct proportion to his success in fighting it. By the time he reached the rank of lieutenant, he'd turned our apartment into a battle zone against fire. Our refrigerator contained not one, but three boxes of baking soda. Two more in the cupboard below the sink, one above the oven. There were no electric blankets in my father's home, no faulty appliances. The toaster was serviced twice a year. Every clock was mechanical. Electrical cords were checked twice a month for cracks in the rubber; sockets were investigated every six weeks. By the time I was ten, my father pulled all plugs from the sockets nightly to minimize any stray currents of malevolent electricity.

When I was eleven, I found my father sitting at the kitchen table late one night, staring at a candle he'd placed before him. He was holding his hand over the flame, patting it occasionally, his dark eyes fixed on the ropes of blue and yellow as if they could tell him something. When he saw me, his eyes widened, his face flushed, and he said, "It can be contained. It can," and I was stunned to hear the thinnest chords of uncertainty in the deep timbre of his voice.

Because my father's shift began at three in the afternoon and my mother worked nights as a cashier at Stop and Shop, my sister, Erin, and I were latchkey kids long before the term became fashionable. One night, we tried to cook blackened redfish, something we'd had during a trip to Cape Cod the previous summer.

We poured every spice we could find into the skillet, and within minutes, the kitchen had filled with smoke. I opened the windows while my sister unlatched the front and back doors. By the time we remembered what caused the smoke in the first place, the pan had caught fire.

I reached the oven just as the first fat parachute of blue flame floated into a white curtain. I remembered the fear in my father's voice. "It can be contained." Erin picked the pan up off the burner and brown grease splattered her arm. She dropped the pan, and the contents spread across the top of the oven like napalm.

I thought of my father's reaction when he discovered we'd allowed it into his home, the embarrassment he'd feel, the rage that his embarrassment would turn into, thickening the blood in his hands until they turned to fists and came looking for me.

I panicked.

With six cartons of baking soda in reach, I grabbed the first liquid I saw off the top of the fridge and poured a half-pint of eighty proof vodka into the middle of a grease fire.

A tenth of a second after, I realized what was going to happen and I tackled my sister just before the top half of the room exploded. We lay on the floor and watched in awe as the wallpaper above the oven stripped away from the wall, as a cloud of blue, yellow, black, and red mushroomed across the ceiling, as a hundred fireflies erupted into the side of the fridge.

My sister rolled away and grabbed the fire extinguisher from the hall. I got one from the pantry, and as if the last five minutes hadn't happened, as if we were truly the children of an illustrious firefighter, we stood in the center of the kitchen and doused the oven, the wall, the ceiling, the fridge, and the curtain. Within a minute, black-and-white foam covered our bodies like birdshit.

Once our adrenal glands had closed their floodgates and our shakes had stopped, we sat down in the center of our ruined kitchen, and stared at the front door where my father entered every night at eleven-thirty. We stared at it until we both wept, kept staring long after we'd run out of tears.

By the time my mother returned from work, we'd fanned all the smoke out of the apartment, wiped all scorch marks off the fridge and oven, and thrown away the charred strips of wallpaper and what remained of the curtain. My mother looked at the black cloud burned into her ceiling, at the scorched wall, and sat down at the kitchen table and stared blankly at something in the pantry for a full five minutes.

Erin said, "Mum?"

My mother blinked. She looked at my sister, then at me, then at the vodka bottle on the counter. She tilted her head toward it and looked at us. "Which of you...?"

I couldn't speak, pointed a finger at my chest.

My mother walked into the pantry. For a small, thin woman, she moved as if she were overweight, with slow lumbering steps. She returned with the iron and ironing board, placed them in the center of the kitchen. In times of crisis, my mother always clung to routine, and it was time to iron my father's uniforms. She opened the window and began pulling them from the clothesline. With her back to us, she said, "Go to your rooms. I'll see if I can talk to your father."

I sat on the corner of my bed, hands in my lap, facing the door. I left the lights off, closed my eyes in the darkness, my hands clasped tight.

When my father came home, his usual thumping about the kitchen—tossing his lunch box on the table, rattling ice cubes in a glass, falling heavily into a chair before pouring his drink—was mute. The silence in the apartment that night was longer and thicker and more pregnant with dread than I have ever experienced since.

My mother said, "A mistake, that's all."

"A mistake," my father said.

"Edgar," my mother said.

"A mistake," my father said again.

"He's eleven. He panicked."

"Uh-huh," my father said.

Everything else that happened seemed to unfold in that weird compression of time that people experience just before they get in a car wreck or fall down a flight of stairs— everything speeds up and everything slows down. A lifetime passes, in all its minute detail, in the space of a second.

My mother screamed, "No!" and I heard the ironing board topple to the kitchen linoleum, and my father's footsteps hammered the floorboards toward my room. I tried to keep my eyes closed, but when he kicked the door in, a splinter grazed my cheekbone, and the first thing I saw was the iron in my father's hand, the electrical cord and plug missing. His knee hit my shoulder and knocked me back on the bed and he said, "You're so desperate to find out what it feels like, boy?"

I looked in his eyes because I didn't want to look at the iron, and what I saw in those dark pupils was an unnerving mixture of anger and fear and hatred and savagery and yes, love, some bastardized version of that too.

And that's what I fixated on, clung to, prayed to, as my father ripped my shirt up to my sternum and pressed the iron against my stomach.

•

Angie once said, "Maybe that's what love is—counting the bandages until someone says, 'Enough.'"

Maybe so.

Sitting at my desk, I closed my eyes, knowing I'd never sleep with the adrenaline doing its stock-car derby in my blood, and when I woke up an hour later, my phone was ringing.

I managed to say, "Patr—" before Angie's voice tumbled over the line. "Patrick, come over here. Please."

I reached for my gun. "What's the matter?"

"I think I just got divorced."

TWENTY-EIGHT

WHEN I GOT THERE, THERE WAS A SQUAD CAR DOUBLE-parked in front of the house. Directly behind it was Devin's Camaro. He was standing on the porch with Oscar, talking to another cop, a kid. Too many cops were starting to look like kids to me, I thought, as I climbed the steps.

They were standing over a huddled lump of flesh by the railing, the young cop giving it smelling salts. It was Phil, and my first thought was, Jesus Christ, she killed him.

Devin looked at me and raised his eyebrows, a smile the size of Kansas on his face. He said, "We answered the call because we asked that anything at her or your address be rerouted to us." He looked down at Phil, at the contusions that covered his face like lesions. He looked back at me. "Oh happy day, huh?"

She was wearing a white shirt over a pair of faded cobalt shorts. There was a red bubble on her lower lip and mascara ran down her face. Her hair was in her eyes as she stepped gingerly out onto the porch in bare feet. She saw me then and came toward me in a rush. I held her and her teeth dug into my shoulder. She was crying softly.

I said, "What did you do?" trying to keep the happy surprise out of my voice, but probably not succeeding.

She shook her head and held on tightly.

Devin was leaning against Oscar, the two of them happier than I'd seen them since they both stopped paying alimony on the same day. Devin said, "Wanna know what she did?"

Oscar said, "Make him beg."

Devin reached into his pocket, giggling. He held a Taser gun up in front of my face. "This is what she did."

"Twice," Oscar said.

"Twice!" Devin repeated gleefully. "Damn lucky he didn't have a friggin' coronary."

"Then," Oscar said, "she laid a beating on him."

"Went nuts!" Devin said. "Nuts! Booted him in the head, the ribs, punched the fuck out of him. I mean, look at him!"

I'd never seen Devin so thrilled.

I looked. Phil was coming to now, but once he felt all that pain, I'm quite sure he would've preferred sleep. Both eyes were almost completely swollen. His lips were black. He had dark bruises over seventy-five percent of his face at least. If what Curtis Moore had done to me had made me look like I'd been in a car accident, Phil looked like he'd been in a plane crash.

The first thing he said when he came to was, "You're arresting her, right?"

Devin said, "Of course, sir. Of course."

Angie stepped out of my arms, looked at him.

Oscar said, "You're pressing charges, sir?"

Phil used the railing to get to his feet. He held onto it like it might just up and run away any second. He started to say something, then leaned over the railing and threw up into the yard.

"Pretty," Devin said.

Oscar walked over to Phil, put a hand on his back as he retched some more. Oscar talked to him in a low soft voice, as if there was nothing out of the ordinary going on, as if he was used to carrying on conversations with people who vomited all over their lawns. "See, sir, the reason I ask if you're going to press charges is 'cause some people don't like to do that in this sort of situation."

Phil spit a few times into the yard, wiped his mouth with his shirt. Always the gentleman. He said, "What do you mean—'this sort of situation'?"

"Well," Oscar said, "this sort of situation."

Devin said, "Sort of situation where a tough guy like yourself gets his ass handed to him by a woman couldn't weigh more than a hundred fifteen pounds soaking wet. Sort of situation that can become real popular conversation in neighborhood bars. You know," he said, "sort of situation that makes a guy look like a serious pussy."

I coughed into my hand.

Oscar said, "Won't be so bad, sir. You just go on into court, tell the judge your wife likes to beat you up every now and then, keep you in line. That sort of thing. Ain't like the judge'll check to see if you're wearing a dress or anything." He patted him on the back again. Not hard enough to send him down the block, but close. He said, "You feeling better now?"

Phil turned his head, looked at Angie. "Cunt," he said.

No one held her back because no one wanted to. She came across the porch in two strides as Oscar stepped out of the way and Phil barely got an arm up before she clocked him in the temple. Then Oscar stepped forward again, pulled her back. She said, "Phillip, I'll kill you if you *ever* come near me again."

Phil put a hand to his temple and looked on the verge of tears. He said, "You guys saw that."

Oscar said, "Saw what?"

Devin said, "I'd take the lady at her word, Phillip. She has a gun and a permit to use it from what I understand. It's a miracle you're still breathing as it is."

Oscar let Angie go and she walked back to Devin and me. I thought I saw smoke coming out of her ears for a moment. Oscar said, "You going to press charges or not, Phillip?"

Phil took a moment to consider it. Thought about the bars he'd be unable to show his face in. Every one in this neighborhood for sure. Thought of the whistles and homosexual jokes that would follow him to the grave, the bras and panties that would show up in his mailbox on a regular basis. He said, "No, I'm not pressing charges."

Oscar tapped his cheek with his hand. "That's real manly of you, Phillip."

The young cop came out of the house carrying Angie's suitcase and set it in front of her.

"Thank you," she said.

We heard a sound like a cat lapping at wet food, and when we looked over, we saw that Phil was weeping into his hands.

Angie gave him a glare of such withering and final scorn that the temperature on the porch must have dropped by ten degrees. She picked up her suitcase and walked to Devin's car.

Oscar slapped Phil's hip and Phil's face came out of his hands. He looked up into Oscar's huge face and Oscar said, "Anything happens to her while me and him"—he pointed at Devin—"are alive, I mean anything, like she gets hit by some lightning or her plane crashes or she breaks a nail, *anything*—and we're going to come play with you, Phillip. Know what I mean?"

Phil nodded and then the convulsions returned and he began sobbing again. He hit his fist against the railing and got them under control and his eyes fell on mine.

I said, "Bubba really misses you, Phil."

He began to shake.

I turned and as I walked down the steps, Devin said, "Hey, Phil, is payback a bitch, or what?"

Phil turned around and got sick again. We walked down to Devin's car and I sat in the backseat with Angie. Camaros have just enough legroom in their backseats to make a dwarf comfortable, but tonight I wasn't complaining. Devin pulled down the street, looked in his rearview at Angie a few times. "No accounting for taste, is there?"

Oscar looked back at Angie. "Boggles the mind. Absolutely boggles the mind."

TWENTY-NINE

DEVIN SAID, "SOCIA'S DEFINITELY LOST THE WAR. HE'S BEEN underground for two days, and half his guys have gone over to the Avengers. No one counted on Roland being such a tactician." He looked back at us. "Marion won't last the week. Lucky for you, huh?"

"Yeah," I said, thinking, that still leaves Roland.

"Not for me," he said. "I lost a hundred bucks in the fucking pool."

Oscar said, "Should have bet on Roland."

"Now you tell me."

They dropped us off at my apartment. Oscar said, "We'll have a unit roll the block every fifteen minutes. You'll be fine."

We said good night, walked up to the apartment. There were eight messages on my answering machine but I ignored it. I said, "Coffee or beer?"

"Coffee," Angie said.

I put some in the filter, turned on the Mr. Coffee. I took a beer from the fridge, came back into the living room. She was curled in the corner of the couch, looking smaller than I'd ever seen her. I sat across from her in an armchair and waited. She placed an ashtray on her thigh, lit a cigarette, her hand trembling. She said, "Hell of a Fourth, huh?"

"Hell of a Fourth," I agreed.

She said, "I came home and I was not in good shape."

"I know."

"I mean, I just killed someone for God's sake." Her hand trembled so badly the ash dropped off the cigarette onto the couch. She brushed it into the tray. "So, I came in and there he is, bitching at me about the car still being parked down at South Station, about me not coming home last night, asking me—no, telling me—that I was fucking you. And I think to myself, I just got in the door, damn lucky to be alive, blood all over my face, and he can't think of anything more original to say than 'You're fucking Pat Kenzie'? Christ." She ran a hand up her forehead, pulled the hair back off her face, held it there. "So, I said, 'Get a life, Phillip,' or something to that effect and I start walking by him and he goes, 'Only thing you'll be able to fuck once I get finished with you, babe, is yourself.'" She took a drag on the cigarette. "Nice, huh? So, he grabs my arm and I get my free hand in my purse and I shoot him with the stun gun. He hits the floor, then he half gets up and I kick him. He's off balance, goes tumbling back out the door onto the porch. And I hit him with the stun gun again. And I'm staring down at him, and it all went away. I mean everything—every feeling I ever had for him just sort of flushed out of my system and all I saw was this piece of shit who had *abused* me for twelve years, and I...went a little hoopy."

I doubted that part about the feelings. They'd come back. They always did, usually when you were least prepared for them. I knew she'd probably never love him again, but the emotion would never leave, the reds, the blues, the blacks of all the different things she had felt during that marriage, they'd reverberate time and again. You could leave a bedroom, but the bed stayed with you. I didn't tell her this, though; she'd learn it soon enough on her own.

I said, "Judging by what I saw, you went a lot hoopy."

She smiled slightly, let her hair fall back in front of her eyes. "Yeah. I suppose so. Long time coming though."

"No argument," I said.

"Pat?" She's the only person who can call me that without setting my teeth on edge. On those rare times she does, it sounds OK, it feels kinda warm.

"Yeah?"

"When I was looking down at him, afterward, I kept thinking about the two of us in that alley with the car heading around the block toward us. And I was terrified then, don't get me wrong, but I wasn't half as terrified as I could have been, because I was with you. And we always seem to make it through things if we're together. I don't doubt things as much when I'm with you. You know?"

"I know exactly," I said.

She smiled. Her bangs covered her eyes and she kept her head down for a moment. She started to say something.

Then the phone rang. I damn near shot it.

I got up, grabbed it. "Hello."

"Kenzie, it's Socia."

"Congratulations," I said.

"Kenzie, you have to meet me."

"No, I don't."

"Jesus, Kenzie, I'm a dead man you don't help me."

"Listen to what you just said, Marion, and think."

Angie looked up and I nodded. The softness in her face receded like surf from a reef.

"All right, Kenzie, I know what you're thinking, sitting there all safe, saying, 'Socia done now.' But I ain't done. Not yet. And I have to, I'll come looking for you and make sure I take you with me on the way to the grave. You got what I need to stay alive and you gone give it to me."

I thought about it. "Try and take me out, Socia."

"I'm a half mile from your house."

That stopped me, but I said, "Come on over. We'll have a beer together before I shoot you."

"Kenzie," he said, suddenly sounding weary, "I can get to you and I can get to your partner, that one you look at like she hold all the mysteries to life. You ain't got that psycho with the hardware to protect you no more. Don't make me come for you."

Anyone can get to anyone. If Socia made it his sole objective to make sure my funeral preceded his by a few days or a few hours, he could do it. I said, "What do you want?"

"The fucking pictures, man. Save both our lives. I'll tell Roland if he kill me or you, those pictures definitely see the light. That's exactly what he don't want, people saying Roland take it up the bunghole."

What a prince. Father of the Year.

I said, "Where and when?"

"Know the expressway on-ramp, beside Columbia Station?"

It was two blocks away. "Yeah."

"Half an hour. Underneath."

"And this'll get you both off my back?"

"Fucking right. Keep me and you breathing for some time."

"Half an hour."

•

We got the photographs and guns from the confessional. We xeroxed the photos on the machine Pastor Drummond uses for his Bingo sheets in the basement, put the originals back in their place, and went back to my apartment.

Angie drank a tall cup of black coffee and I checked our weapons supply. We had the .357 with two bullets left, the .38 Colin had given us and the .38 Bubba had acquired for us, the nine millimeter, and the .45 I'd taken off Lollipop, silencer attached. We also had four grenades in the fridge, and the Ithaca twelve-gauge.

I put on my trench coat and Angie put on her leather jacket and we took everything but the grenades. Can't be too safe with people like Socia. I said, "Hell of a Fourth," and we left the apartment.

Part of I-93 stretches over the neighborhood. Underneath it, the city leaves three deposits—sand, salt, and gravel—for emergencies. These three cones rise up twenty feet, the bases about fifteen feet wide. It was summer, so they weren't in all that much use. In Boston though, you have to be prepared. Sometimes Mother Nature plays a joke or two on us, drops a snowstorm on us in early October just to show what a card she is.

You can enter the area from the avenue or from the back entrance of the Columbia/JFK subway station or from Mosley Street if you don't mind climbing over some shrubs and walking down an incline.

We climbed some shrubs and walked down the incline, kicking clouds of brown dirt in front of us until we reached bottom. We stepped around a green support beam and came out between the three cones.

Socia was standing in the middle, where the bottoms converged into a ragged triangle. A small kid stood beside him. Unformed cheekbones and baby fat betrayed his age, even if he thought the wraparounds and the hat on his head made him look old enough to buy a pint of scotch. If he was any older than fourteen, he aged well.

Socia's hands hung empty by his sides, but the kid's were

dug into the pockets of a team jacket, and he flapped them back and forth against knobby hips. I said, "Take your hands out of your pockets."

The kid looked at Socia, and I pointed the .45 at him. "Which word didn't you understand?"

Socia nodded. "Take 'em out, Eugene."

Eugene's hands came out of the jacket slowly, the left empty, the right holding a .38 that looked twice as big as his hand. He tossed it into the salt pile without my asking, then started to place his hands back in his pockets. He changed his mind and held them out in front of him as if he'd never noticed them before. He folded them across his chest eventually and shifted his feet. He didn't seem to know exactly what to do with his head either. In quick, rodent's motions, he looked at me, then at Angie, over at Socia, back at the place where he'd tossed the gun, then up at the dark green underside of the expressway.

All the salt and exhaust fumes and cheap wine aromas down here, and the stench of the kid's fear hung in the air like a fat cloud.

Angie looked at me and I nodded. She disappeared around the cone on our left while I watched Socia and Eugene. We knew no one was hanging around on the expressway above, because we'd checked as we came down Mosley. No one was on the roof of the subway station; we'd scoped it out coming down the hill.

Socia said, "Just me and Eugene. No one else."

I didn't see much reason to doubt him. Three days had aged Socia faster than four years in the White House had aged Carter. His hair was mangy. His clothes hung on him like they'd hang on a wire hanger, and there were beige food stains on the fine linen. His eyes were pink, a crack head's eyes, all burning adrenaline and shadow seeking. His thin wrists trembled and his skin had the pallor of a mortician's handiwork. He was on borrowed time, and even he knew he was way past due.

Looking at him, for a twentieth of a second or so, I felt something akin to pity. Then I remembered the photos in my jacket, the skinny boy he'd killed, a hardened robot rising up from the ashes who looked like the boy, talked like the boy, but had left his soul back in a motel room with stained sheets. I heard the tape of him popping Anton's eye from the socket. I saw his wife going down in a hail of bullets on a soft summer morning, eyes glazed with eternal resignation. I thought of his army of Eugenes, who closed their glass eyes and hurtled forward to die for him, inhaled his "product," and exhaled their souls, I looked at Marion Socia and it wasn't about black or white, it was about hate. Just knowing he existed made me hate the nature of the world.

He nodded toward Eugene. "Like my bodyguard, Kenzie? Am I scraping the bottom of the barrel, or what?"

I looked at the boy, could only imagine what those words did to the eyes behind those glasses.

I said, "Socia, you're a fucking pig."

"Yeah, yeah, yeah." He reached into his pocket and I placed the .45 against his throat.

He looked down at the silencer nestled against his Adam's apple. "Think I'm foolish?" He pulled a small pipe from his pocket. "Just grabbing some lightning." I took a step back as he extracted a thick rock from his other pocket and placed it in the pipe. He lit it and sucked back hard, closing his eyes. In a frog's voice he said, "You bring what I need?" He opened the lids again and the whites of his eyes fluttered like a bad TV.

Angie came up beside me, and we stared at him.

He chucked the smoke from his lungs in a blast and

smiled. He handed the pipe to Eugene. "Aaah. What you two looking at? Little repressed white children appalled by the big black demon?" He chuckled.

"Don't flatter yourself, Socia," Angie said. "You're no demon. You're a garden snake. Hell, you aren't even black."

"Then what am I, missy thing?"

"An aberration," she said and flicked her cigarette off his chest.

He shrugged, brushed at the ash on his jacket.

Eugene was sucking the small pipe as if it were a reed poking above a waterline. He handed it back to Socia and tilted his head back.

Socia reached out and slapped my shoulder. "Hey, boy, give me what I come for. Save us both from that crazy dog."

"'That crazy dog'? Socia, you created him. You stripped him bare and left him with nothing but hate by the time he was ten."

Eugene shifted on his feet, looked at Socia.

Socia snorted, toked from the pipe. The smoke flowed slowly out of the corners of his mouth. "What do you know about anything, white boy? Huh? Seven years back, that bitch took my boy away from me, tried to teach him all about Jesus and how to behave for the white man, like he had a chance in the first place. Little nigger boy from the ghetto. She try and slap a restraining order on me. On me. Keep me away from my own child so she could fill his head with a lot a shit about the American Dream. Shit. American Dream to a nigger is like a centerfold hanging in a prison cell. Black man in this world ain't nothing unless he can sing or dance, throw a football, make you whiteys happy." He took another hit off the pipe. "Only time you like looking at a nigger is when you in the audience. And Jenna, bitch tries to pass all that Tom bullshit onto my boy, tell him God will provide. Fuck that. Man does what he does in this world and that's it. Ain't no accountant up above taking notes, no matter what the preachers say." He tapped the pipe hard against his leg, dumping the ash and resin, his face flushed. "Come on now, Kenzie, give me that shit and Roland leave you alone. Me too."

I doubted that. Socia would leave me alone until he was secure again, if that ever happened. Then he'd start worrying about all the people who had something on him, who'd seen him beg. And he'd wipe us all out to preserve his illusion of himself.

I looked at him, still scrambling to decide if I had any options other than the one he offered. He stared back. Eugene took a step away from him, a small one, and his right hand scratched his back.

"Come on. Give it here."

I didn't have much choice. Roland would definitely get to me if I didn't. I reached into my pocket with my free hand and extracted the manila envelope.

Socia leaned forward slightly. Eugene's right hand was still scratching at his back and his left foot tapped up and down on the cement. I handed the envelope to Socia, and Eugene's foot picked up speed.

Socia opened the clasp and stepped back under the streetlight to survey his handiwork. "Copies," he said.

"Very good. I keep the originals."

He looked at me, saw it wasn't negotiable, and shrugged. He looked at them one by one, taking his time, as if they were old postcards. A couple of times, he chuckled softly.

I said, "Socia, there's something I don't get."

He smiled, a ghostly one. "Lot you don't get, white boy."

"Well, at this particular moment in time, then."

"What is it?"

"Did you transfer the original photos from videocassette?"

He shook his head. "Eight millimeter home movie camera."

"So, if you have the original film, why are all these people dying?"

He smiled. "Don't have the original." He shrugged. "First house Roland's boys hit was a place I keep on Warren. Firebombed it, hoping I was in it. I wasn't."

"But the film is?"

He nodded, then looked back down at the Xeroxed photos.

Eugene was leaning forward, craning his head to get a look over Socia's shoulder. His right hand was buried behind his back now and his left scratched furiously along his hip. His small body rippled, and I could hear a hum coming from his mouth, a low buzzing sound I doubt he knew he was making. Whatever it was that he was getting ready to do, it was coming soon.

I took a step forward, my breathing shallow.

Socia said, "Well, how about all this? Boy could have been a movie star. Eh, Eugene?"

Eugene made his move. He bounced forward, a stumble almost, and his hand cleared his back with a pistol in it. He jerked his arm up but it glanced off Socia's elbow. Socia was turning away as I stepped forward, pivoting as I grasped Eugene's wrist, turning my back in toward his chest. Socia's ankle turned against the pavement. He tipped toward the ground and the gun boomed twice in the still humid air. I snapped my elbow back into Eugene's face and heard bone crack.

Socia bounced off the pavement and rolled into the salt cone, the photocopies exploding in a flurry. Eugene dropped the gun. I let go of his slick wrist and he fell straight back to the pavement, a soft pop as his head hit cement.

I picked up the gun and looked at Angie. She stood in a target shooter's stance, her arm steady as it swung the .38 back and forth between Socia and Eugene.

Eugene sat up, hands on his legs, blood flowing from a broken nose.

Socia lay against the salt pile, his body slack in the dark shadow of the expressway. I waited, but he didn't move.

Angie stepped over to him and looked down. She reached out for his wrist and he rolled over on his back. He looked at us and laughed, a rich, explosive bellow. We watched as he tried to get control of it, but it was beyond him. He tried to sit up straight against the cone, but the movement loosened the salt above him and it cascaded down inside his shirt. This made him laugh even harder. He slid back down into the salt like a drunk on a waterbed, slapping it with his hand, the laughter rippling into the atmosphere and momentarily overpowering the din of cars passing overhead.

Eventually he sat forward, holding his stomach. "Hoo boy. Ain't there no one to trust in this world no more?" He giggled and looked at the boy. "Hey, Eugene, how much Roland pay you to Judas me?"

Eugene didn't seem to hear him. The color of his skin had taken on the unhealthy hue of someone fighting back nausea. He took deep breaths and held a hand to his heart. He seemed oblivious to the broken nose, but his eyes were wide with the enormity of what he'd just attempted and what it had gotten him. Unfathomable terror swam in his irises, and I could tell his brain was scrambling to get past it, searching his soul for the courage necessary to achieve resignation.

Socia stood and brushed some salt from his suit. He shook his head slowly, then bent to pick up the scattered photocopies. "My, my. Ain't going to be a hole deep enough or a country wide enough to hide your ass in, child. Roland or no Roland, you dead."

Eugene looked at his shattered sunglasses lying on the ground beside him and threw up on his lap.

Socia said, "Do that all you want. Won't help you none."

The back of my neck and the lower half of my ears felt sickly warm, the blood boiling in a whirlpool just below the skin. Above us, the metal expressway extension rattled as a convoy of semis roared over in a screaming cacophony.

I looked down at the boy and I felt tired—horrendously tired—of all the death and petty hate and ignorance and complete and utter carelessness that had assaulted me in a maelstrom this last week. I was tired of all the brick-wall debating—the black versus white, the rich versus poor, the mean versus innocent. Tired of spite and senselessness and Marion Socia and his offhand cruelty. Too tired to care about moral implications or politics or anything except the glass eyes of this boy on the ground who didn't seem to know how to cry anymore. I was exhausted by the Socias and the Paulsons, the Rolands and the Mulkerns of this world, the ghosts of all their victims whispering a growling wind of pleas into my ear to make someone accountable. To end it.

Socia was searching the shadows between the cones. "Kenzie, how many of these pictures were there?"

I pulled back the hammer on the .45 as the truck tires overhead slapped the heavy metal with relentless fury, roaring onward to a destination that could have been a thousand miles away or right next door.

I looked at the nose I'd broken. When did he forget how to cry?

"Kenzie. How many fucking pictures you give me?"

Angie was staring at me, and I knew the sounds that howled from above raged in her head too.

Socia scooped up another photocopy. "Fuck, man, this better be all of it."

The last of the trucks rattled past, but the wail continued, pounding at a fever pitch against my eardrums.

Eugene groaned and touched his nose.

Angie looked over at Socia as he searched the ground in a crablike walk. She looked back at me and nodded.

Socia straightened and stepped under the light, holding the photocopies in his hand.

I said, "How many more will it take, Socia?"

He said, "What?" shuffling the edges of the photocopies into a neat stack.

"How many more people are you going to chew up before it's finally enough? Before even *you* get sick of it?"

Angie said, "Do it, Patrick. Now."

Socia glanced at her, then over to me, his eyes a blank. I don't think he understood the concept of my question. He stared at me, waiting for me to elaborate. After a minute or so, he held up the photocopies. His thumb rose up the front one, pressing between Roland's bare thighs. He said, "Kenzie, is this all of it or not?"

"Yeah, Socia," I said, "this is all of it." I raised the gun and shot him in the chest.

He dropped the photocopies and raised a hand to the hole, stumbling back but staying on his feet. He looked at the hole, at the blood on his hand. He seemed surprised, and for a brief moment, terribly afraid. "The fuck you do that for?" He coughed.

I pulled back on the hammer again.

He stared at me, and the fear left his eyes. The irises

peppered over with a cold satisfaction, a dark knowledge. He smiled.

I shot him in the head and Angie's gun went off at the same time. The bullets hammered him back into the salt pile, and he rolled onto his back and slid to the cement.

Angie's body was shaking a bit, but her voice was steady. "Guess Devin was right."

I looked down at Socia. "How's that?"

"Some people, you either kill them or leave them be, because you'll never change their minds."

I bent down and began picking up the photocopies. Angie knelt by Eugene and cleaned his nose and face with a handkerchief. He didn't seem surprised or elated or disturbed by what had happened. His eyes were glazed, somewhat off-center. Angie said, "Can you walk?"

"Yes." He stood up unsteadily, closed his eyes for a few seconds, then exhaled slowly.

I found the photocopy I was looking for, wiped it off with some gravel, and placed it in Socia's jacket. Eugene stood firmly now. I looked at him. "Go home," I said.

He nodded and walked off without a word. He climbed the incline and disappeared on the other side of the shrubs.

Angie and I took the same route a minute later, and as we walked toward my apartment, I slipped my arm around her waist and tried not to think about it.

THIRTY

His last week alive, my father's six-foot two-inch frame weighed 112 pounds.

In his hospital room at three in the morning, I listened to his chest rattle like shards of broken glass boiling in a pot. His exhalations sounded as if they were forcing their way out through layers of gauze. Dried spittle whitened the corners of his mouth.

When he opened his eyes, the green irises seemed to swim, anchorless amid the white. He turned his head in my direction. "Patrick."

I leaned in toward the bed, the child in me still cautious, still watching his hands, ready to bolt if they moved too suddenly.

He smiled. "Your mother loves me."

I nodded.

"That's something to—" He coughed and the force of it bowed his chest, brought his head off the pillow. He grimaced, swallowed. "That's something to take with me. Over there," he said and rolled his eyes back into his head as if they could catch a glimpse of where he was going.

I said, "That's nice, Edgar."

His feeble hand slapped my arm. "You still hate me, do you?"

I looked in those unhinged irises and nodded.

"What about all that shit the nuns taught you? What about forgiveness?" He raised a tired, amused eyebrow.

"You used it all up, Edgar. A long time ago."

The feeble hand reached out again, grazed my abdomen. "Still mad about that little scar?"

I stared at him, giving him nothing, telling him there was nothing left to take anymore, even if he were strong enough.

He waved the hand in a dismissive gesture. "Fuck ya, then." He closed his eyes. "What'd you come for?"

I sat back, looked at the wasted body, waiting for it to stop having an effect on me, for that poisonous sludge of love and hate to quit sluicing through my body. "To watch you die," I said.

He smiled, eyes still closed. "Ah," he said, "a vulture. So you are your father's son, after all."

He slept for a while after that, and I watched him, listening to the broken glass rattling through his chest. I knew then that whatever explanation I'd been waiting for my whole life was sealed in that wasted frame, in that rotted brain, and it was never coming out. It was going to ride with my father on his black journey to that place he saw when he rolled his eyes back into his skull. All that dark knowledge was his alone, and he was taking it with him so he'd have something to chuckle about during the trip.

At five-thirty, my father opened his eyes and pointed at me. He said, "Something's burning. Something's burning." His eyes widened and his mouth opened as if he were about to howl.

And he died.

And I watched him, still waiting.

THIRTY-ONE

IT WAS ONE-THIRTY IN THE MORNING ON THE FIFTH OF JULY when we met Sterling Mulkern and Jim Vurnan at the Hyatt Regency bar in Cambridge. The bar is one of those revolving lounges, and as we flowed around in a slow circle, the city glittered and the red stone footbridges on the Charles seemed old and good and even the ivy-covered brick of Harvard didn't annoy me.

Mulkern was wearing a gray suit over a white shirt, no tie. Jim was wearing an angora crew-neck sweater and tan cotton pants. Neither of them looked pleased.

Angie and I wore the usual and neither of us cared.

Mulkern said, "I hope you have a good reason for calling us out at this hour, lad."

I said, "Of course. If you wouldn't mind, please tell me what our deal was."

Mulkern said, "Come now. What's this?"

I said, "Repeat the terms of the contract we made."

Mulkern looked at Jim and shrugged. Jim said, "Patrick, you know damn well we agreed to your daily fee plus expenses."

"Plus?"

"Plus a seven thousand dollar bonus if you produced the documents that Jenna Angeline stole." Jim was irritable; maybe his blond Vassar wife with the Dorothy Hamill do was making him sleep on the couch again. Or maybe I'd interrupted their bimonthly tryst.

I said, "You advanced me two thousand dollars. I've worked on this for seven days. Actually, if I wanted to be technical, this is the morning of the eighth, but I'll give you a break. Here's the bill." I handed it to Mulkern.

He barely glanced at it. "Ludicrously exorbitant, but we hired you because you allegedly justify your fees."

I sat back. "Who put Curtis Moore on to me? You or Paulson?"

Jim said, "What in the hell are you talking about? Curtis Moore worked for Socia."

"But he managed to begin tailing me about five minutes after our first meeting." I looked at Mulkern. "How convenient."

Mulkern's eyes showed nothing, a man who could withstand a thousand suppositions, no matter how logical, as long as there was no proof to back them up. And if there was proof, he could just say, "I don't recall."

I sipped my beer. "How well did you know my father?"

"I knew your father well, lad, now get on with it." He looked at his watch.

"You knew he beat his wife, abused his children."

Mulkern shrugged. "Not my concern."

"Patrick," Jim said, "your personal life is irrelevant here."

"Somebody has to have a concern here," I said. I looked at Mulkern. "If you knew about my father, Senator, as a public servant, why didn't you do something about it?"

"I just told you, lad—not my concern."

"What is your *concern*, Senator?"

"The documents, Pat."

"What is your concern, Senator?" I asked again.

"The Commonwealth of course." He chuckled. "I'd love to sit here and explain the utilitarian concept to you, Pat, but I haven't the time. A few cuffs on the side of the head from your old man is not a call for action, boy."

A few cuffs. Two hospital stays in the first twelve years of my life.

I said, "Did you know about Paulson? I mean, everything?"

"Come now, boy. Complete your contract and let's go about our separate ways." His upper lip was slick with perspiration.

"How much did you know? Did you know he was fucking little boys?"

"There's no need for that sort of language here," Mulkern said and smiled, looking around the room.

Angie said, "Tell us what sort of language fits your sense of propriety and we'll see if it applies to child molestation and prostitution and extortion and murder."

"What're you talking about now?" Mulkern said. "Crazy talk is what I'm hearing. Crazy talk. Give me the documents, Pat."

"Senator?"

"Yes, Pat?"

"Don't call me 'Pat.' It's something you do to a dog, not something you call a person."

Mulkern sat back and rolled his eyes. I obviously had no grip on this edge of the planet. He said, "Lad, you—"

"How much did you know, Senator? How much? Your aide-de-camp is doing little kids and people end up dying all over the place because he and Socia took a couple of home movies for themselves and things got out of hand. Didn't they? What'd Socia blackmail Paulson so he'd change the nature of his pressure on the street terrorism bill? And

Paulson, what'd he have a few too many drinks mourning his lost innocence, and Jenna found them? Found photos of her son being molested by the man she worked for? Maybe even voted for? How much did you know, Senator?"

He stared at me.

"And I was the magnet," I said. "Wasn't I?" I looked at Jim and he stared back, blank-faced. "I was supposed to lead Socia and Paulson to Jenna, help them clean up the mess. Is that it, Senator?"

He met my anger and indignation, and he smiled. He knew I had nothing on him, just questions and suppositions. He knew that's all anyone ever had, and his eyes hardened in victory. The more I asked, the less I'd get. The way of things.

He said, "Give me the documents, Pat."

I said, "Let me see the check, Sterl."

He held out his hand and Jim put a check in it. Jim was looking at me as if we'd been playing the same game together for years, yet only now was he realizing that I had no grasp of the rules. He shook his head slowly, a den mother's motion. Jim would've made some fine convent a good nun.

Mulkern filled in the "pay to the order of" part of the check but left the amount blank. He said, "The documents, Pat."

I reached down to the seat and handed him the manila envelope. He opened it, took the photos out, held them on his lap. He said, "No copies this time? I'm proud of you, Pat."

I said, "Sign the check, Senator."

He leafed through the rest of the photos, smiled sadly at one, put them back in the envelope. He picked up the pen again, tapped it against the tabletop lightly. He said, "Pat, I think you need an attitude adjustment. Yes. So I'm going to cut your bonus in half. How about that?"

"I made copies."

"Copies don't mean a thing in court."

"They can make a hell of a stink though."

He looked at me, sized me up in a second, and shook his head. He bent toward the check.

I said, "Call Paulson. Ask him which one's missing."

The pen stopped. He said, "Missing?"

Jim said, "Missing?"

Angie said, "Missing?" just to be a smart-ass.

I nodded. "Missing. Paulson can tell you there were twenty-two in all. You got twenty-one in that envelope."

"And where would it be?" Mulkern asked.

"Sign the check and find out, dickhead."

I don't think Mulkern had ever been called a "dickhead" in his life. He didn't seem too fond of it either, but maybe it would grow on him. He said, "Give it to me."

I said, "Sign that check, no 'attitude adjustments,' and I'll tell you where it is."

Jim said, "Don't sign it, Senator."

Mulkern said, "Shut up, Jim."

I said, "Yeah, shut up, Jim. Go fetch the Senator a bone or something."

Mulkern stared at me. It seemed to be his main method of intimidation and it was lost on someone who'd just spent the past few days getting shot at. It took him a few minutes, but I think he got it. He said, "Whatever happens, I'll ruin you." He signed the check with the proper amount and handed it over.

"Shucks," I said.

"Hand over the photograph."

"I told you I'd tell you where it was, Senator. I never said I'd hand it over to you."

Mulkern closed his eyes for a moment and breathed heavily through his nostrils. "Fine. Where is it?"

"Right over there," Angie said and pointed across the bar.

Richie Colgan stuck his head out from behind a fern. He waved to us, then looked at Mulkern and smiled. A big smile. The corners of his mouth damn near reached his eyelids.

Mulkern said, "No."

Angie said, "Yes," and patted his arm.

I said, "Look on the bright side, Sterl—you didn't have to write Richie a check. He fucked you over for free." We stood up from the table.

Mulkern said, "You're done in this town. You won't even be able to get welfare."

I said, "No kidding? Hell then, I might as well just go over to Richie and tell him you gave me this check for my help in covering up your involvement in this whole affair."

Mulkern said, "And what would you have then?"

"I'd have you in the same position you're ready to put me in. And hell if it wouldn't make my day." I reached down, picked up my beer, finished it. "Still want to wreck my name, Sterl?"

Mulkern held the envelope in his hand. He said, "Brian Paulson's a good man. A good politician. And these photos are almost seven years old. Why bring this to the surface now? It's old news."

I smiled and quoted him: "'Everything but yesterday seems young,' Senator." I nudged Jim with my elbow. "Ain't that always the way?"

THIRTY-TWO

We tried to have a conversation with Richie in the parking lot but it was like trying to talk to someone as he passed by on a jet. He was rocking forward on his feet and he kept interrupting to say, "Hold that thought, would you?" Then he'd whisper something into his handheld tape recorder. Probably wrote most of his column standing in the parking lot of the Hyatt Regency.

We said our good-nights and he bounced on the balls of his feet all the way to his car. We might have killed Socia, but Richie was going to bury Paulson.

We took a cab home; the still streets were littered with the residue of fireworks; the wind carried a bitter tang of gunpowder. The rush of burying Mulkern's whipping boy in front of him was already beginning to dissipate, leaking out of the cab onto those desolate streets, drifting off somewhere into the shadows that swept over us between the streetlights.

When we reached my place, Angie went straight to the fridge, took a bottle of zinfandel from the door. She took a glass too, though after watching her drink it, there didn't seem much point; the only way she could have gone through it any faster would have been intravenously. I took a couple of beers and we sat in the living room with the windows open, listening to the breeze blow a beer can down the avenue, tipping it against the asphalt, rolling it steadily toward the corner.

I knew that in a week or so, I'd look back on this with pleasure, savor the look on Mulkern's face as he realized he'd just paid me a large sum of money to blow a hole in his life. Somehow I'd managed to pull off the rarest of feats—I'd made someone in the State House accountable. In a week or so, that would feel good. Not now though. Now we were facing something else entirely, the air heavy with the impending weight of our own consciences.

Angie was halfway through the bottle when she said, "What's going on?"

She stood up, the wine bottle hanging loosely between her index and middle fingers, tapping against her thigh.

I got up, not sure I was ready to face this yet. I got two more beers, came back. I said, "We killed someone." It sounded simple.

"In cold blood."

"In cold blood." I opened one beer, placed the other on the floor beside the chair.

She drained her glass, poured some more. "He wasn't dangerous to us."

"Not at that moment, no."

"But we killed him anyway," I said. It was numbing and repetitive, this conversation, but I had the feeling we were each trying to say exactly what we'd done, no bullshit, no lies to come back and haunt us later.

"Why?" she asked.

"Because he repulsed us. Morally." I drank some beer. It could have been water for all I tasted it.

"A lot of people morally repulse us," she said. "We going to kill them too?"

"I don't think so."

"Why not?"

"Not enough bullets."

She said, "I don't want to joke about this. Not now."

She was right. I said, "Sorry."

She said, "In the exact same situation, we'd do it again."

I thought of Socia holding up the photograph, running his finger between his son's legs. I said, "Yes, we would."

"He was a predator," she said.

I nodded.

"He allowed his child to be molested for money, so we killed him." She drank some more wine, not quite inhaling it anymore. She was standing in the middle of the floor, pivoting slowly on her left foot every now and then, the bottle swinging like a pendulum between her fingers.

I said, "That's about the size of it."

She said, "Paulson did similar things. He molested that child, probably hundreds of others. We knew that. We didn't kill him."

I said, "Killing Socia was an impulse. We didn't know we were going to do it when we met him."

She laughed, a short harsh sound. "We didn't, huh? Why'd we take a silencer with us?"

I let the question fall between us, tried not to answer it Eventually I said, "Maybe we did go there knowing we'd kill him given half an excuse. He deserved it."

"So did Paulson. He's alive."

"We'd go to jail if we killed Paulson. Nobody cared about Socia. They'll chalk it up to the gang war, be happy he's gone."

"How convenient for us."

I stood up, came across to her. I put my hands on her shoulders, stopped her lazy pivot. I said, "We killed Socia on impulse." If I said it enough, maybe it'd become true. "We couldn't get to Paulson. He's too well insulated. But we took care of him."

"In very civilized fashion." She said "civilized" the way some people say "taxes."

"Yes," I said.

"So we took care of Socia according to the laws of the jungle, and we dispatched Paulson in accordance with the laws of civilization."

"Exactly."

She looked into my eyes and hers were swimming with alcohol and exhaustion and ghosts. She said, "Civilization seems to be something we choose when it fits our purpose."

Not much I could argue with there. A black pimp was dead and a white child molester was preparing a press release over a bottle of Chivas somewhere, each one as guilty as the other.

People like Paulson would always be able to hide behind power. They might face disgrace, they might even do six months in a federal country club and face public castigation, but they'd breathe. Paulson might actually come out of this OK. A few years back, a congressman who'd admitted to having sex with a fifteen-year-old boy was reelected. I guess, to some people, even statutory rape is relative.

And people like Socia could slip through for a while, maybe a long while. They'd kill and maim and make the lives of everyone around them ugly and bleak, but sooner or later, they usually ended up like Socia himself—brain leaking out under an expressway. They ended up on page thirteen of the Metro section and the cops shrugged and didn't work too hard to find their killers

One disgraced, one dead. One breathing, one dead. One white, one dead.

I ran my hands through my hair, felt the grit and oil from the last day, smelled the trash and waste on my fingers. At that moment, I truly hated the world and everything in it.

L.A. burns, and so many other cities smolder, waiting for the hose that will flood gasoline over the coals, and we listen to politicians who fuel our hate and our narrow views and tell us it's simply a matter of getting back to basics while they sit in their beachfront properties and listen to the surf so they won't have to hear the screams of the drowning.

They tell us it's about race, and we believe them. And they call it a "democracy," and we nod our heads, so pleased with ourselves. We blame the Socias, we occasionally sneer at the Paulsons, but we always vote for the Sterling Mulkerns. And in occasional moments of quasi-lucidity, we wonder why the Mulkerns of this world don't respect us.

They don't respect us because we are their molested children. They fuck us morning, noon, and night, but as long as they tuck us in with a kiss, as long as they whisper into our ears, "Daddy loves you, Daddy will take care of you," we close our eyes and go to sleep, trading our bodies, our souls, for the comforting veneers of "civilization" and "security," the false idols of our twentieth-century wet dream.

And it's our reliance on that dream that the Mulkerns, the Paulsons, the Socias, the Phils, the Heroes of this world depend upon. That's their dark knowledge. That's how they win.

I gave Angie a weak smile. "I'm tired," I said.

"Me too." She gave me her own weak smile. "Exhausted." She walked to the couch, spread the sheet I'd left across it. She said, "We'll figure it out someday. Right?"

"Yeah. Someday," I said, walking toward my bedroom. "Sure."

THIRTY-THREE

THE PHOTOGRAPH WE'D GIVEN RICHIE SHOWED SENATOR Paulson in all his glory. It showed very specifically what he got his sense of glory from. Roland's body took up a third of the frame and you got a good sense of his age, of the youth in the body under Paulson. No doubt about his sex. But unlike most of the other photographs, you couldn't see Roland's face, just his small ears and head. Socia was standing in the bedroom, watching with a bored expression on his face, smoking a cigarette.

The *Trib* ran the photo with appropriate softening and black bars over the places you'd imagine. Beside the photograph was another—one of Socia lying on his back in the gravel, his body looking like an inflatable doll someone had forgotten to inflate. His head was thrown back, the small pipe still in his hand. Over the photo it said: MAN IN PAULSON PIC KILLED GANG-LAND-STYLE.

In addition to his column, Richie's byline ran over the Socia murder story too. He said the police had no suspects as of yet, that any fingerprints could have been obscured if the killer had had the sense to rub his hands in the gravel before he touched anything. The killer had. He mentioned that the Xerox of the Paulson photo had been discovered in

Socia's bloody linen jacket. He mentioned Socia's common-law marriage to Jenna Angeline, the same Jenna Angeline who'd been a cleaning woman for, among others, Senators Paulson and Mulkern. They reran her death photograph too, the State House looming up behind her.

It was the biggest local scandal since the DA bungled the Charles Stuart case. Maybe bigger. We'd have to wait until it all came out in the wash.

One thing that wouldn't come out in the wash was Roland. I doubt Paulson knew the identity of the child he'd been with that day; over the ensuing years, I'm sure there were so many more. And if he did know, I doubted he'd be shouting it from the rooftops. Socia wasn't up to much public speaking these days, and Angie and I were unequivocally not involved.

Richie was one hell of a reporter. He tied Paulson to Socia and Socia to Jenna by the third paragraph, then noted that Paulson had gone on record in Friday's legislative session motioning for an extra day off, the precise day the street terrorism bill was scheduled to come to the floor. Richie never insinuated, he never accused. He just laid fact after fact down on everyone's breakfast table and let them draw their own conclusions.

I had my doubts about how many of them would get it, but I figured enough would figure it out.

Paulson was reportedly on vacation at the family home in Marblehead, but by the time I caught the morning news on TV, there were Devin and Oscar in front of the cameras in Marblehead. Oscar said, "Senator Paulson has one hour to turn himself in to the Marblehead Police Department or we're going in after him."

Devin didn't say anything. He stood beside his partner, beaming, a cigar the size of a Boeing in his mouth.

The reporter said to Oscar, "Sergeant Lee, your partner looks rather pleased about this."

Oscar said, "He's so happy he don't know whether to shit or—" and they cut to a commercial.

I flipped around, saw Sterling Mulkern on Channel Seven. He was coming up the State House steps, an army of people trotting beside him, Jim Vurnan trying to keep pace a few steps back. He sliced through the mass of microphones like an oar through a dead sea, a chant of "No comment," coming from his lips all the way through the front doors. I was kind of hoping he'd keep things lively, throw in a few "I don't recalls" to break up the monotony, but I guess pleasing me wasn't at the top of his "to do" list this morning.

Angie had been awake for a few minutes by this time, her face propped up on the arm of the couch where she'd slept, her eyes puffed with sleep, but alert. She said, "Sometimes, Skid, this job ain't half bad."

I was sitting on the floor at the foot of the couch. I looked at her. "Does your hair always stand on end first thing in the morning?"

Not a smart thing to say when you're sitting near someone's foot. The next thing I said was, "Ouch."

She got up, tossed the sheet over my head, and said, "Coffee?"

"I'd love some." I pulled the sheet off my face.

"Make enough for the both of us then, would you?" She stumbled into the bathroom and turned the shower on.

On Channel Five, the two anchors were in early, promising to stay with me until all the facts were in. I wanted to tell them they'd be having pizzas delivered to the station for the next ten years if that's what they were waiting for, but I let it slide. They'd figure it out.

Ken Mitchum, on Channel Seven, said it was possibly the biggest scandal since the Curly years.

Channel Six was doing the Charles Stuart comparison by the time I caught up with them, paralleling the racial overtones that had tinged both cases. Ward was smiling as he reported this, but Ward always smiles. Laura, on the other hand, looked pissed off. Laura is black; I didn't blame her.

Angie came back out of the shower, newly dressed in a pair of my gray shorts and a white Polo sweatshirt. The sweatshirt was mine too, but damn if she didn't look better than me in it. She said, "Where's my coffee?"

"Same place as the bell. Let me know when you find the both of them."

She frowned, brushing out her hair, head tilted to one side.

The photograph of Socia's corpse flashed on the screen. She stopped brushing for a moment. I said, "How do you feel?"

She nodded toward the TV. "Fine, as long as I don't think about it. Come on, let's get out of here."

"And go where?"

"Well, I don't know about you, babe, but I want to spend some of that bonus money. And," she said, straightening up, tossing her long hair behind her, "we have to visit Bubba."

"Have you considered that he may be angry with us?"

She shrugged. "You got to die some time, right?"

I picked up a Nintendo Gameboy for Bubba, bought a bunch of Kill-the-Commie-Terrorist games to go with it. Angie bought him a Freddy Krueger doll and five issues of *Jugs* magazine.

There was a police guard at his door, but after making a

few phone calls, he allowed us to go in. Bubba was reading a worn copy of *The Anarchist's Cookbook* when we entered, learning all sorts of new and nifty ways to build a hydrogen bomb in his backyard. He looked up at us, and for the single longest second of my life, I couldn't tell if he was angry or not.

He said, "'Bout time someone I liked showed up."

I learned how to breathe again.

He was paler than I'd ever seen him and the whole left side of his chest and arm was in a cast, but take away the cast and I've seen people with a bad cold who looked less healthy. Angie bent over and kissed his forehead, then suddenly pulled his head to her chest and held it there for a moment, her eyes closed. "I was worried about you, you maniac."

"What don't kill me only makes me bloody."

Bubba. Deep as always.

He said, "A Freddy Krueger doll! Hot shit!" He looked at me. "What'd you bring me, homeboy?"

•

We left after a half hour or so. The doctors had initially thought he'd be in ICU for at least a week, but now they were saying he could be released in another two days. He'd face an indictment, of course, but he assured us, "What's a witness? Really. I never met one. They those people who always seem to get amnesia just before I'm supposed to go to trial?"

We walked down Charles Street into the Back Bay, Angie's credit card burning a hole in her pocket. Bonwit Teller never stood a chance. She hit the place like a cyclone and by the time we left, we were carrying half the first floor in paper bags.

I did a half hour's shopping at Eddie Bauer, another

twenty minutes at the Banana Republic in Copley Place, my stomach beginning to churn in the atmosphere of four-story marble waterfalls and solid gold window frames and Neiman-Marcus displays of eighty-five-dollar argyle socks. If Donald Trump puked, Copley Place is probably what would hit the toilet.

We took the back entrance out of there, the best place to find a cab in the city in midafternoon. We were trying to figure out where we were going to eat lunch, when I saw Roland standing at the bottom of the escalator, his huge frame spread lazily across the exit way, one arm in a cast, one eye closed shut, the other looking steadily at us.

I reached under my untucked shirt, got a firm grip on the nine millimeter, cold against my stomach but warm in my hand.

Roland stepped back. "I want to talk."

I kept my hand on my gun.

Angie said, "So talk."

"Take a walk with me." He turned and walked out through the revolving door.

I'm not quite sure why we followed him, but we did. The sun was strong, the air warm but not too humid as we walked up Dartmouth, away from the staid hotels and the quaint shops, the yuppies sipping cappucino amidst the illusion of civilization. We crossed Columbus Avenue and went down through the South End, the restored brown-stones eventually giving way to the sorrier-looking ones, those that hadn't been touched by the frontier mentality of the fern-and-Perrier crowd yet. We kept going, none of us saying a word, farther down into Roxbury. As soon as we crossed over the border, Roland said, "Just want to speak to you a minute."

I looked around me, saw nothing that gave me comfort,

but somehow, I trusted him. Having checked inside the hollows of the sling that supported his arm and seeing no gun there, I had one concrete reason to feel this way. But that wasn't all of it. What I knew of Roland, he wasn't like his father. He didn't lull you into death with a few words and a hypnotist's inflection. He just came straight at you and sent you to your coffin.

Another thing I was realizing, for sure—the kid was huge. I'd never been this close to him when he'd been on his feet, and it was damn near awe-inspiring. He was closing in on six foot four or so and every inch of skin that covered his body was bunched tight with coiled muscle. I'm six feet even and I felt like a dwarf.

He stopped in a wornout field, a construction site waiting to happen, the next place big business would go to encroach and keep encroaching, pushing Roxbury west or east until it became another South End, another place to have a good drink and hear underground music. And its people would roll east or west too, while politicians cut ribbons and shook the hands of entrepreneurs and talked of progress, pointed to declining crime statistics in the area with pride, while ignoring the rising crime statistics in the areas where the displaced had settled. Roxbury would become a nice word again, Dedham or Randolph a bad one. And another neighborhood would dissolve.

Roland said, "You two killed Marion."

We didn't say anything.

"You think it would...please me? That it? Keep me from your door?"

I said, "No. Didn't have much to do with you at the time, Roland. He pissed us off. Simple as that."

He looked at me, then off beyond the lot. We weren't too far from the decrepit tenements where he'd chased us the night before. All around us were worn buildings and sparse fields of city growth. Not much more than a stone's throw from Beacon Hill.

He seemed to read my thoughts. He said, "That's right. We're sitting on your doorstep."

I looked back, saw the skyline glittering above us in the midafternoon sun, close enough to kiss. I wondered what it must be like, living here, this close, knowing you'd never get to taste it. Not for free. A couple of miles and a world away.

I said, "Oh well."

Roland said, "You can't keep doing this to us forever. Can't hold us back."

I said, "Roland, 'we' didn't create you. Don't try and put that off on the white man too. Your father and you made you what you are."

"And what am I?" he said.

I shrugged. "A sixteen-year-old killing machine."

"Damn right," he said. "Damn right." He spit on the ground to the left of my foot. He said, "But I wasn't always."

I thought of the skinny boy in the photographs, tried to imagine what benevolent, possibly hopeful thoughts had run through his brain before someone had burned it out of him, overloaded the circuits until the good had to go just to make way for all the bad. I looked at the sixteen-year-old man in front of me, the massive, bulked-up stone with the bad eye and the arm in the cast. I couldn't, for the life of me, connect the two.

I said, "Yeah, well, we were all little boys once, Roland." I looked at Angie. "Little girls too."

Roland said, "The white man—"

Angie dropped her shopping bag and said, "Roland, we're not going to listen to this 'white man' shit. We know all about the white man. We know he has the power and we know the black man doesn't. We know the way the world works and we know that way sucks. We know all that. We're not too pleased with ourselves either, but there you are. And maybe if you had some suggestions on how to change things for the better, we'd have something to talk about. But you kill people, Roland, and you sell crack. Don't expect violins."

He smiled at her. It wasn't the warmest smile I'd ever seen—Roland has about as much warmth in him as a polar cap—but it wasn't completely cold either. He said, "Maybe. Maybe." He scratched at the skin just above his cast with his free hand. "You kept…that thing out of the papers, so maybe you think I owe you." He looked at us. "I don't. Don't owe nobody nothing, because I don't ask for nothing." He rubbed the skin beside his bad eye. "But, then, I don't see much point in killing you no more either."

I had to remind myself he was sixteen years old.

I said, "Roland, let me ask you something."

He frowned, seemed bored suddenly. "Go ahead."

"All this hate, all this anger in you—any of it go away when you found out your father was dead?"

He turned a cube of cinder block over with his foot and shrugged. "No. Maybe if I'd been able to pull the trigger myself, maybe then."

I shook my head. "Doesn't work that way."

He kicked at another hunk of cinder block. "No," he said, "I suppose it don't." He looked off beyond the weeds and the tenements on the other side of the lot, past the torn brick blocks with coils of soldered metal sticking out of them like flags.

His empire.

He said, "You two go on home. We forget about each other."

I said, "Deal," but I had a feeling I'd never forget Roland, even after I read his obituary.

He nodded, more to himself than us, and started to walk off. He'd crested a small slope of industrial waste, when he stopped, his back to us. Somewhere, not far away, a siren rang hollowly. He said, "My mother, she was all right. Decent."

I took Angie's hand in mine. "She was," I said. "But she was never needed."

His shoulders moved slightly, possibly a shrug, possibly something else. "Can't say that she was," he said and started walking again. He crossed the lot as we watched him, shrinking slowly as he neared the tenements. A lone prince on his way to the throne, wondering why it didn't feel as sweet as it should.

We watched him disappear through a dark doorway as a breeze—cool for this time of summer—came off the ocean and swept north past the tenement, past us with chilled fingers that mussed our hair and widened our eyes, moving on into the heart of the city. Angie's warm hand tightened around mine as we turned and sidestepped the rubble, following the breeze back to our part of town.